Dear Reader,

This month we are proud to [bring you] books with very different themes and setti[ng]. Australian author Tegan James's debut *Scarlet* novel is a mixture of mystery and passion with a glorious outback setting; Vickie Moore offers us mystery, too, but her romance is set in a thrilling Gothic castle. From Jan McDaniel we have a story which will tug at your heartstrings . . . and we think you'll find the ending thought-provoking and a little surprising. And last, but by no means least, Maxine Barry, one of our most prolific and popular authors, has created a pair of lovers who strike sparks off each other against a beautiful English countryside backdrop.

You'll have noticed that our back covers have changed slightly and for three of our authors this month we're delighted to share with you some of the praise for their previous *Scarlet* romances. We hope you find these review quotes interesting. Let us know if any of them agree with your opinion of a particular *Scarlet* title, won't you?

Till next month,

Sally Cooper

SALLY COOPER,
Editor-in-Chief – *Scarlet*

P.S. UK readers will notice another change this month – a slight price increase. But we're sure you'll agree that *Scarlet* romances are still great value for money.

About the Author

Jan McDaniel is the author of over 20 published romance novels. A native of Detroit, Michigan, she now makes her home in Chattanooga, Tennessee, with her husband, Bruce, their two teenagers and an assortment of dogs and cats.

Before turning to full-time fiction writing, Jan worked as a newspaper reporter and technical editor.

If you would like to write to Jan (c/o *Scarlet*) she'll be delighted to hear from you.

Other *Scarlet* titles available this month

IN SEARCH OF A HUSBAND – Tegan James
SHADOWED PROMISES – Vickie Moore
DEAR ENEMY – Maxine Barry

JAN McDANIEL

KEEPSAKES

Enquiries to:
Robinson Publishing Ltd
7 Kensington Church Court
London W8 4SP

First published in the UK by Scarlet, 1997

Copyright © Jan McDaniel 1997
Cover photography by J. Cat

The right of Jan McDaniel to be identified as author
of this work has been asserted by her in accordance
with the Copyright, Designs and Patents Act 1988.

All rights reserved. No part of this publication
may be reproduced in any form or by any means
without the prior written permission of the publisher.

This book is sold subject to the condition that it shall
not, by way of trade or otherwise, be lent, re-sold,
hired out or otherwise circulated in any form of binding
or cover other than that in which it is published and
without a similar condition including this condition being
imposed on the subsequent purchaser.

A copy of the British Library Cataloguing in
Publication data is available from the British Library

ISBN 1-85487-967-7

Printed and bound in the EC

10 9 8 7 6 5 4 3 2 1

To my husband, Bruce

With deepest gratitude for technical information on manufacturing ceramic figurines to: David A. Harris of Mountain View Ceramic Center, Inc., Chattanooga, Tennessee, U.S.A. and Ben Hubbard of the Glendale Mold Shop, Los Angeles, California, U.S.A. Also to my many generous friends and fellow writers on the RW-L e-mail loop and here in East Tennessee for their invaluable assistance. Special thanks to Roberta Calhoun and her society.

CHAPTER 1

A movement in the dark shadows at the far end of the grounds below captured Simon Blye's attention as he was following Kay Harmon down the steep stone walkway leading from his hilltop house to the driveway.

'Come to Philadelphia with me?' Kay invited over her shoulder.

'Hmm? Watch your step, Kay,' he cautioned, his own attention directed more to the activity in the bushes than the treacherous stairs.

He gazed back towards the section of chain-link fence he'd been eyeing and now saw only leaves scattering in the breeze, branches swaying and casting dappled patterns beneath the white light of a full moon. Well, he'd been staring at a computer screen for hours now; was it any wonder his eyes were playing tricks on him? Still, he wanted a closer look to make sure.

'You need to get away for a while, Simon,' Kay coaxed, as she reached the drive at the end of the stairs and turned to face him.

Distracted and still feeling oddly uneasy, he ran his glance over Kay's red silk dress. He hadn't touched anything soft enough to satisfy him in a very long while, but he was only fleetingly tempted.

Not now. Not Kay.

His marketing manager's smile conveyed she'd noticed his lingering gaze along with his indecision.

'Cut loose some time, Simon,' she challenged. 'I never could understand why you decided to move from New York back to this rural watering hole.' Standing close enough for him to smell her perfume, she patted her chestnut-brown waves.

One side of his mouth curled in a hint of a smile, then suddenly he was all business again. 'No place like home. Just go wrap up the deal with Henderson's. Get us in their department stores before the holidays. With the peasant girl.' He reached a long, muscle-roped arm to open the driver's door of his silver Jaguar. 'You're not about to jump ship, are you, Kay?'

Kay batted her eyes and rolled them. 'Now? With the uproar you're about to cause? Are you kidding?' she relented with a long-suffering sigh. 'I plan to be right up there with you.'

Simon watched her climb into the car and wished she'd hurry and go.

He leaned over the still open door. 'Good. And no drag racing,' he chided.

Kay grinned, letting him know she forgave him for resisting her yet again. She groped for the seat-belt. 'This deal's really got to be important for you to be lending me your car while mine's in the shop.'

Hands in the pockets of his loose cotton trousers, Simon straightened and shrugged. He wanted to go and seal this agreement himself, but he had work here that only he could do. 'She's insured.' He gave the fender a pat. 'And I have the truck here.'

Exhaling quickly, Kay started the engine. 'I'll call you tomorrow after I check in.'

Simon gave a nod of agreement. 'Goodnight, Kay. And thanks.'

'Get some rest,' she ordered. 'You work too hard.' Kay shifted and painstakingly turned the car around, leaving him standing alone in the driveway.

He stood watching but did not wave as she finally remembered the headlights and the car inched down the long, winding drive. It disappeared briefly under the wooden covered bridge he'd had constructed over the narrow brook just inside the gate.

Within moments, the Jag re-emerged, crawled the remaining twenty feet or so to the road, then turned right on to the country highway. He cringed at the roar of her revving the engine, watching his car spew gravel and shoot into the night like a space shuttle off a launching pad. Shaking his head, Simon raked a hand through his hair and laughed softly. Poor Kay drove like a stunt pilot. Her car was in the garage now because she'd wrecked it yesterday. No casualties, thank God.

A swift gust of wind ruffled his hair and swept a blizzard of dried leaves off the tree branches. The air carried the mild chill of a Pennsylvania autumn and smelled of apples. But in short sleeves, he remained comfortable. The coolness felt good to him after being confined in his upstairs office since early this afternoon.

He itched to get back to work after being interrupted by his meeting with Kay, who'd had a friend drop her off about an hour ago. He'd stopped then to drill her on the Henderson pitch.

But the stirring he'd seen by the fence still bothered him. These days he watched his back constantly, trusting no one completely. Paranoia? No one had warned him success came with certain drawbacks.

His cramped legs needed stretching anyway. He wanted to satisfy himself that he'd seen nothing more than a deer or a shadow before he turned in for the night. The house and garden were equipped with a state-of-the-art security system, but he normally never activated it this early. He'd grown up in a house where the doors were seldom locked, and he detested the hassle of alarms and codes. Something deep inside him longed to believe he didn't really need these damn contraptions, although he was less hopeful of that every day. Wasn't much left to trust in.

He headed around the hill towards the back of the house, where steam rose from the surface of a heated pool sunk into a plateau of level ground at the foot of the hill. The rectangle of blue water glistened under the vapor lights.

Just as he was about to round the corner, he noticed more movement at the back of the fence and, tensing like a bird dog, he halted in his path. His muscles coiled, he held his breath and watched. His eyes widened with mounting alarm.

Hot damn, it was a human being. The dark hairs on his arms stood on end as he prepared to round the hillside for a confrontation.

A body clad in army green slithered across the small strip of grass between the woods and his fence, then hunkered against the wire. Simon mentally cursed himself for not having activated the security system.

With a quick turn, wide, dark eyes set in a small, round face panned the area. *What the hell . . .?* Instinctively, he braced himself to dash into the house and report the intruder to the authorities. He just hoped this creep wasn't armed. A gun would turn this into a whole new ballgame. Simon didn't know who might want to kill him, but he didn't doubt for an instant that he had enemies.

As the intruder raised two arms to grasp the top of the fence and stuck the toe of a tennis shoe in the mesh, a platinum-blonde ponytail swung out of the back of a baseball cap, glowing near-white in the moonlight. A woman? Simon halted.

I'll be damned. Relief filtered through him, and he relaxed his tightened muscles. The situation was less serious than he'd imagined.

He stepped to one side, out of sight behind the slope. He knew of only one woman in this town

6

who had white-blonde hair. Jarred's grand-daughter? Here? His first impulse was to jump out, yell, 'Boo!' and scare the kid back home. His second was to wait. If he chased her off, he might never learn what business she believed she had on his property.

Folding his thick arms across his chest, he sidestepped closer to the hillside, leaning against the damp earth so she wouldn't accidentally spot him.

Amusement, curiosity and irritation mingled as he watched her struggle to hurdle the six-foot fence. He tried to determine whether it was her audacity or her stupidity that most astonished him.

Her midnight-blue eyes, wide as those of a hunted doe, were riveted straight ahead, the visor of the brown plaid cap pulled low over her forehead. Her delicate face resembled a doll's, her lips pouty and insolent. Simon noticed she was no kid any more, nor was she the aloof business executive she'd been parading around town disguised as these past few weeks. A little girl playing dress-up in her tailored linen suits and stern upswept hairstyle. In different circumstances, he might enjoy the challenge of slackening those lips into a quite different expression.

7

Startled by a stabbing in his loins, he immediately dismissed that notion. Yardley Kittridge had always been off-limits to him, and the thought of kissing her was as dangerous as the idea of drinking bleach. She was poison. But, staring into his swimming pool, Simon slowly contemplated how everything had changed now. Maybe even that?

Her grandfather was dead, and Simon was more powerful than the lofty Kittridges. Simon just needed to make them understand that.

So what was prissy Miss Yardley doing climbing into his garden dressed like a commando headed to the platoon softball game?

Her dark, baggy pants and jacket camouflaged her trim, lean figure. Despite her slender, athletic build and usual grace, she climbed the fence with clumsy, halting movements. Obviously, Yardley Kittridge was untrained in rappeling. Or maybe she was just too scared to move easily. She damn well should be.

With increasing interest and curiosity, he watched her struggles. He knew he should stop her before she fell and bruised her tender little tush. But her expression of grim determination forced him to hold back. At the moment she reminded Simon too much of Jarred to merit his sympathy. All his life, Simon had watched

Jarred Kittridge reign over this town like a dictator. Jarred had uncaringly destroyed lives while his family enjoyed and flaunted luxuries. Even in the sad decline of his final days, the old man had remained mean-spirited enough to try to block the building permit for Simon's factory, knowing Simon had gone into debt buying his land and hiring contractors.

Simon saw no reason to show the old codger's granddaughter mercy. Especially now that she'd turned to crime. Did that family's nerve have any bounds? They all thought the name Kittridge gave them license to do anything. Fleetingly, he wondered what she wanted, then suddenly, in a revelation that flashed in his head bright as lightning, he knew.

And his anger flared. He was going to have to teach these Kittridges that he held the power now. Starting with this one.

She was poised atop the fence.

Silently, he watched, leaning back, crossing his arms, then grinning. *Come on, babe. Let's break into the big, bad man's house. Come and get your surprise.*

He gleaned an odd satisfaction from watching her as she swung her legs over the top rail. But instead of sliding down, she awkwardly turned herself around and perched there like a canary.

As she sat suspended atop the metal pole, Simon grew impatient. An average ten-year-old could have scaled that fence in ten seconds.

Get it over with, kid. Don't spoil my evening now.

Still she hesitated, her features knotted with confusion and panic. She swept a tentative glance across the yard, tottering on the narrow rail. He flattened his back against the grassy mound.

For a split-second, he feared she was about to retreat. A part of him almost wanted her to. What a shame a woman this pretty had to be a Kittridge. Well, she was or she wouldn't be here. If only he had a big, hungry dog to turn loose.

Victory. She bent her arms and legs to leap off the fence. He almost wanted to tell her sliding down would make for an easier landing than the flying leap she was preparing for.

Welcome to my parlor.

Simon decided to allow her to reach the house before he brought the game to an end. He was curious to see how she intended to get in. And he had no doubt that was where she was headed. He'd always prided himself on his patience. Let her incriminate herself completely.

Unexpectedly, a soft, decisive curse sliced the night's silence.

Returning his attention to her, he saw she was still on the fence. Hanging on the fence. By the seat of her pants.

He muffled a laugh. This was too rich to be true. She was dangling on the wire like a lovely Christmas tree ornament Santa Claus had left behind. For him. *And I haven't even been very good this year*. He stepped forward.

Only for you, Mimi, Yardley thought, her insides a-tremble as she scaled Simon Blye's fence. She couldn't believe her luck tonight. After watching the house only a few minutes, she'd seen Simon's silver Jag roll out of the driveway then speed towards town. He really should drive more carefully.

Only after she was sure he was gone had she attempted to get over his fence. It shouldn't have been this hard. Why was she so clumsy lately? She told herself she could have gotten better purchase if her palms weren't slippery with sweat and her legs shaking like cranberry sauce on Thanksgiving.

'He has an alarm system but he never uses it,' Mimi had assured her earlier. 'Wait until he leaves.'

'How do you know so much about him?' Yardley had marveled. Even a charlatan like Simon Blye was entitled to his privacy.

Mimi had dismissed her granddaughter's concerns with a flick of one long, slender hand. 'He and the Higginses use the same cleaning service. You know how those domestics love to gossip.'

For three nights now, Yardley had crouched in the woods, waiting for him to leave, hoping he wouldn't. Didn't the man ever venture out from his little fortress?

Then, tonight, she'd watched the Jag disappear towards town. She couldn't believe she was actually robbing him. Her deeply ingrained moral fabric rebelled against this. Yet she must get it over with.

In this case, it's not really stealing, dear. At the moment, Mimi's assurance rang hollow. Breaking into a house – even to retrieve your own property – smacked of thievery.

Yardley made a good accountant, a lousy criminal. Her dinner was threatening to come up as she scaled the top of the fence. She took slow, deep breaths, hoping to calm herself.

Her jacket pocket held a copy of Mr Blye's house key. She knew exactly where to find what she was after. Upstairs in his bedroom. Top shelf of the closet.

In and out in five minutes flat if she quit stalling. She heard her own heart galloping against the gentle cacophony of night noises.

She just wanted to get this over with and be at home taking a long, hot bubble bath.

Closing her eyes, she pushed off towards the ground, bewildered as her own trousers tethered her to the fence.

'Society ball canceled tonight?' The deep, mocking voice floated out of the shadows.

Yardley's heart stopped.

Simon Blye strolled forward, hands in his pockets, coal-black hair blowing in a breeze suddenly arctic against her damp skin. His dark eyes blazed, and she dreaded the implications of his smile, accented by the small, round birthmark over the left corner of his mouth. The skin at the corners of his eyes crinkled devilishly.

He strode closer, looming like a dark giant against the backdrop of moonlight with his tall physique and muscled chest bulging beneath his jersey polo-shirt, purposely taking his time.

Panicked, Yardley burst into action, squirming to untangle herself. She felt like a fly caught in the spider's web.

'Hey, take it easy, babe,' he warned. 'You'll hurt yourself.'

Even ripping her trousers off completely would be a small concession to escaping, she realized. Frantically, she jerked her hip away from the fence.

Simon rushed forward and caught her, pinning her back against the wire mesh. 'Allow me, Ms Kittridge,' he insisted. The intensity in his eyes curdled her blood. Her stomach roiled. He leaned forward, smashing his chest against hers. 'You'll tear your pants.'

He wasn't rough enough to hurt her, but she was smothering – afraid to breathe and involuntarily press her breasts closer against him. He smelled spicy and exotic like sandalwood incense. Despite her panic, a primal heat spread through her middle at the contact. Simon Blye had a raw male appeal – pleasant to admire from afar, and she often had. And even in this situation her body was responding to his bold grasp as though it were an embrace.

'P-p-please,' she sputtered.

His body was muscular but trim and well-proportioned. His skin burned hers against the cool autumn air. He exuded an aura raw and sensual as a lion's. Raising his head, he pressed his chest harder against her.

His mouth hovered an inch from hers.

'Be still,' he ordered. His breath grazed her cheek in a long stream of heated air.

His dark, calculating eyes frightened her. She clung to the fence, paralysed and struggling to control her ragged breathing. As he bowed his head to look down, she stared into his mass of shining coal-black hair and wanted to spit in it. The heat of his face radiated through her chest. Anger welled inside her at his exaggerated enjoyment of toying with her. Okay, this looked bad, but he didn't have to be so mean.

Why was he still here anyway? She had seen the Jag pull away! Had he known she was coming and set her up somehow? But only Mimi knew where she was tonight. And Mimi would never have warned him. This was her idea to begin with.

And a very bad one, Yardley conceded now, her face burning with humiliation as Simon leaned around her to thoroughly inspect her trousers where they were hung. Damn bully. He could at least give her a chance to explain.

Somehow, she had to get away from him.

'Hmm,' he mused, inspecting the point where a sharp wire end had jabbed up inside her trousers. 'Tsk, tsk. I'll have to talk to that contractor about this dangerous wire. If I'd wanted barbed wire, I would have ordered it.'

'You've made your point, Mr Blye. Just please let me down,' she implored. Now, she felt the wire stabbing her. She could free herself if he'd move away.

He looked wounded. 'Leave you up here and let the sheriff find you like this? That's damn uncharitable. Hell of a way to treat a burglar. Especially with your being a Kittridge.'

'I swear, I'll never bother you again – ' she began, cut short by his laughter.

'Save it. You can explain yourself to the law. Trespassing is trespassing. Probably a light sentence unless you're charged with breaking and entering. Depends on your previous record. I don't know if that will stick, since you didn't make it all the way inside. We can sort out the details later. You're anxious to get down. Maybe if we slip your pants off – '

'No!'

He shrugged. Planting one splayed hand solidly under her rump, he deliberately threaded his other, not around her hip, but between her legs. Indignation seethed through her. She hated Simon Blye.

Nonchalantly, he reached upward for the fence. She froze, knowing that if she moved a hair'sbreadth, if his arm slipped, he'd be touching her even more insultingly. She blinked back tears of humiliation.

Even though he held back by inches, the heat of his arm seared through the crotch of her dungarees. She clamped her muscles to fend off the reflexive fire shooting through her. How dared he? If he so much as brushed her trouser leg, she would kick him, no matter that she was half his size.

'There!' he proclaimed as he disengaged the fabric. Slowly, he retraced his arm. He stared defiantly into her eyes as he was doing it. Yardley glared back, blinking back her rising tears and refusing to show any reaction. He must have a sad, empty life if he was liking this.

Helplessly, she dropped against him. Circling her waist with his big, steady hands, he eased her down, planting her on the grass.

Her knees were wobbling, legs shaking, and her head spinning.

As he slackened his grasp, she bolted drunkenly.

Shaking his head, he caught her waist with little effort. 'Not so fast, babe. Let's go inside and wait for the sheriff.' He nudged her towards the back door. 'You were planning to come in anyway, weren't you?'

Yardley glowered at him.

He glowered back. Then a shadow crossed his eyes, and he quickly looked away. 'Hurry up. I haven't got all night,' he grated. 'You must have an angel watching over you tonight. If I hadn't seen you and had gone inside, I'd have flipped a couple of switches and you'd be fried like a Sunday chicken by now. You did realize you were climbing an electric fence?'

Yardley blanched, increasingly light-headed and dizzy. She tried to focus on him, but he had four eyes now.

'Hey. Are you all right?' His voice echoed through a long tunnel.

She swung her hand out to grab on to anything stable and solid, but came up with only empty air. She felt as though her head was being wrapped in plastic. Her knees buckled, she couldn't breathe, and the world grew fuzzy.

Simon Blye and everything else around her faded. She crumpled into a heap on the damp grass.

'Yardley?'

Something inside her face popped.

Yardley opened her eyes. She groaned when she saw Simon Blye leaning over her solicitously. At least he'd finally acknowledged he knew her name wasn't 'Babe'.

With one flattened hand, she pushed weakly at his chest. 'Get away from me. I'd hoped I was having a nightmare.'

'One of your own making, sweetheart. I don't remember inviting you here.'

Yardley's eyelids fluttered shut, and she turned her head away from him. She wished he'd go away.

Simon leaned closer. 'You really did pass out. Who's your doctor? I'll call him.'

She turned back to face him. 'No doctor.'

He nodded gravely. 'It's starting to make sense now. How long have you been an addict?'

Offended despite her wooziness, Yardley shook her head. 'I'm not into drugs, Mr Blye. Although after tonight I may consider taking up the habit.'

'I hear the stuff is easy to get in jail.'

Groggily, she raised a hand to her smarting jaw. 'I don't need a doctor, and I'm in no mood to visit the emergency room simply because I fainted. You didn't have to slap me.'

His dark eyebrows knit together and he craned to examine the pink spot on her cheek. 'You wouldn't wake up. Or did you have your heart set on spending the night?'

She paled.

He set a hand on her shoulder, but for once his touch was light and reserved. 'You are sick,' he observed. 'Look, kid, if you are on drugs – '

She shook her head. 'I'm fine. I just got down off the fence too fast.'

'So you're an old hand at breaking into houses?'

'Certainly not!'

Simon stood, bending over her and adding to her discomfiture by reaching out and grasping her under the arms.

'Let's sit up, now, eh?' he suggested as he boosted her. His arms were incredibly strong, and she slipped easily into a sitting position. He leaned her forward like a rag doll as he reached behind her with one hand and propped pillows against the headboard of the bed.

Bed? Sweet Jesus! She swept a worried glance around the room and realized she was indeed in what appeared to be his bed. The red plaid quilt was turned back only enough to free the pillows, and she was situated atop it. She looked around the room, a neat square lair of deep blues and pine, a stone hearth centering the opposite side of the room. The scent of him wafted from the pillowcases, and her eyes drifted to the slightly ajar closet door.

He sat on the edge of the mattress and stuck a glass under her face.

'Drink,' he ordered.

Hesitantly, she accepted the glass, careful to avoid contact with his fingers. Staring down into clear liquid and ice, she sniffed the contents.

Watching her, Simon laughed.

Her gaze shot up to meet his amused one. His roguish black hair dipped insolently across his forehead.

'Mineral water,' he assured her mockingly. 'Why would I poison you, sweetheart? Drink up, now.'

Slowly, she sipped the cool liquid, grudgingly savoring the relief it brought to her dry mouth.

She was aware of his steady surveillance as she drank. He waited patiently until she was through, then relieved her of the glass and set it on the nightstand, which also held a clock radio, some loose change and a paperback edition of a best-selling legal thriller.

'Feel better?' The note of genuine concern in his voice surprised her. She realized she must have scared the hell out of him by fainting. Despite his smug demeanor, he'd be hard-pressed to explain an unconscious Kittridge in his back yard. Small payback, but she embraced even that meager victory.

Resting her head against the pillows, she closed her eyes briefly, then opened them. 'Yes, thank you. I wouldn't have fainted if you hadn't jumped out of the bushes and startled me.'

'And just let you break into my house? Get real, babe. The name Kittridge impresses me less than anyone else around here.'

She swung questioning eyes up to him. 'After everything my grandfather did for you? I remember watching you in his workshop.'

'He never meant to really help me. Just fuel for his ego. He worked pretty damn hard to keep me out of business, though. How come you never came inside the workshop, always just hung back by the door?'

Yardley rocked her forehead in her palm. She wasn't going to argue with Simon about Granddad. And neither was she going to listen to this ape berate the old man. Her grief was too strong and fresh to express it. Especially under these circumstances.

And she certainly wasn't going to admit she'd enjoyed watching Simon because she'd found him the most magnificent looking male she'd ever set eyes on. And that Granddad would have sent her far away if he'd ever caught her flirting with someone like Simon

Blye. But she attributed her adolescent fascination with him to the raging hormones of puberty. At the moment, she hated the sight of him. Still, she hadn't believed Simon had ever noticed her watching him.

Now, Simon shook his head. 'Apparently you've overcome your shyness.'

'Did you call the sheriff yet?' she asked.

Simon swung his locked hands between his knees, on which his elbows were propped. Then he turned his head sharply to meet her gaze. 'Maybe I won't have to,' he suggested. 'It all depends on you.'

Yardley raised rounded eyes to meet his cool gaze. She didn't dare imagine what price he might ask to spare her from the law.

CHAPTER 2

Simon studied Yardley as she glanced down at her disheveled appearance, brushing at the dry leaves sticking to her jacket. Refusing to look at him, she removed the baseball cap, setting it beside her, then reached both hands behind her head to unfasten the ponytail. A veil of yellow silk tumbled down her back, shimmering in the light as she shook her hair loose.

God, she's beautiful, Simon marveled. Impulsively carrying her to his bed had been a poor choice born of panic. While bed seemed the appropriate place to set an unconscious person, now that she was awake her presence was triggering the wrong kinds of internal responses. He'd moved into the house months ago and had yet to bring a woman into this room. Until now.

Didn't the Kittridges have enough working in their favor without nature producing one so adorable?

Without pausing to look up at him, she pulled her arms out of the sleeves of the canvas jacket, revealing a white sweater that hugged her well-rounded but modestly sized breasts. Simon's chest tightened, and he felt a sharp pull in his loins.

She turned her face to him unexpectedly and caught him staring. For a moment, Simon felt as though he were the guilty party here. He reminded himself that this beauty was a thief. He couldn't let his guard down, no matter how fetching she looked.

He had begun to regret bullying her outside, especially when she'd passed out at his feet and he'd carried her limp body inside the house. He knew she hadn't been faking; she'd felt so small and still in his arms. As he'd raced inside with her, he'd kept looking down to make sure she was still breathing.

Okay, so maybe he'd given her too good a scare. She was awake and alert now, and he couldn't afford to feel sorry for her. He was used to fighting his battles with other men, not against females who looked and smelled and most likely tasted good.

'So, you're going to let me go?' she asked finally.

Simon chuckled softly. 'And ruin the strip show?'

To her credit, she didn't blush. 'What's off is all that's coming off. Maybe you'd better call the sheriff, Mr Blye. I'm not stuck on the fence now.'

He crimped one narrow, dark eyebrow. 'Your call. Either I turn you in and you and Granny can buy your way out of it, as I have no doubt you will, or you do something for me and we call it even.'

'I have no intention of sleeping with you.' She raised her chin up high, blue eyes blazing.

'A damn shame. But unfortunately irrelevant.'

She glared at him through lowered eyelids. Simon imagined he saw smoke spewing from her ears. Figured she'd assume that was what he wanted. Probably the first thing most men wanted from her, but Simon had other priorities. He wouldn't exactly have minded getting her between his sheets, and at the moment he was trying hard not to dwell on the fact that she was sitting on them. Jarred wasn't likely to come after him from out of his cold grave. But Simon couldn't fathom imposing himself on a woman who didn't like him nor enjoy what she was doing.

Anyway, Yardley didn't seem the kind who could be pressed that far, even if his inclinations had been running in that direction. Women seldom turned out to be as they seemed. She didn't look like a damn cat-burglar either.

He rubbed his jaw. 'First off, I want to know why you dropped by.'

She studied the pattern in his dark blue carpet. Then she raised her eyes. 'You already know, don't you?'

He nodded grimly. 'The mold for the peasant girl.'

'The one you stole from my grandfather.'

Simon reeled back in startled indignation. 'Jarred told you that?' The old man had been many things, but this was the first Simon had known him to lie. Nothing Jarred had done should have surprised him. Still, the knife dug deeper into the old wounds.

'How else would you have gotten it?'

Simon gave a low, caustic chuckle. 'Of course. How else?'

He watched the muscles in her slender neck contract.

She spoke with slow deliberation. 'I know you have it. I know you're planning to put the figurine into production.'

27

'How in the hell . . .?' Caught off-guard, he stopped himself, realizing what he'd inadvertently confirmed.

He studied her smug expression. She might look small and harmless, but she was every bit as dangerous and crafty as the old man himself. Maybe more so. He'd never been distracted by thoughts of kissing Jarred!

'How were you going to get into the house?' he asked, refusing to let her hold the upper hand for long.

She drew in a quick breath and looked down at her hands. 'Break a window,' she blurted.

Simon rolled his eyes. 'How?'

'With a rock.'

'And what about the storm window?'

'I guess I'd have to break that too.'

'How brave you are, willing to crawl through all that jagged glass. Shame you're not as good a liar as your grandfather was. Work on it, babe. Takes practise.'

She met his eyes, and he gave her his sternest look. If she thought he was stupid or charmed enough to believe her fables at this point, he might as well summon the sheriff. The little snit had probably had somebody making excuses and covering up for her all her life.

With a disgruntled sigh, she dug the key out of her pocket and held it in the flat of her palm.

Simon lifted it, his fingertips grazing her smooth, soft skin. Holding the key high, he inspected it incredulously.

'Who gave you this?'

'I don't know.'

He shot her an accusing glare.

'I don't know exactly where it came from. Honestly. Someone in your cleaning service maybe.'

Simon gaped at the key. Was there no one in this town he could trust? 'Looks like I need to do some serious house-cleaning of my own,' he suggested. He slipped the key into the pocket of his trousers.

He stood and strode to the hearth, hands in his pockets. He stared into the cold fireplace, the stack of wood waiting to be lit, then crossed the room back to her.

She pressed back against the pillows as he stood over her.

His words were clipped and calculated. 'Just for the record – I'm at a loss as to why I feel compelled to explain this to a sneak thief – your grandfather gave me that mold.'

Yardley stiffened. 'He wouldn't!'

'Why wouldn't he? His only son had no interest in the business. He enjoyed teaching me everything he knew. Think hard about that. You know it's true.'

'He wouldn't have given anything so important to anyone outside the family. Even if he was fond of you. Why should I believe you?'

'I don't care whether you do.'

'My great-grandfather did the sculpture for that mold. He used it to establish Kittridge Collectibles.'

Simon narrowed his gaze. 'And the mold was supposed to be destroyed after the first hundred figurines. A perfect example of your family's long history of deception.'

'My great-grandfather kept it for sentimental reasons, like a shopkeeper framing his first dollar. He had no intention of manufacturing more figurines. Nor allowing anyone else to.'

'Exactly. Jarred wasn't so sentimental, and he thought of anything he couldn't make a profit from as useless junk. He never dreamed some punk from the wrong side of the railroad tracks would ever be able to put it to any use. In his mind, he was doing his civic duty, keeping one of the local hoodlums off the streets and out of juvenile detention. Do you know how much pride I swallowed to sit in his workshop, pretending I looked up to him? I'm not just going to duplicate the figurines, babe. I'm going to enjoy it.'

She stiffened her spine. 'No reflection on your upbringing, I'm sure.'

'I don't break into people's houses.'

She dropped her defiant gaze. 'I was only attempting to recover something that belonged to my family to begin with. There's nothing else I want from you. Surely you can understand why you can't market duplicates. The originals are quite valuable. The Kittridge reputation . . .'

'Is a sham, as far as I'm concerned. Your civic-minded grandfather cared only about promoting his own family's interests. Now I'm promoting mine.'

'I won't listen to you malign him.'

'Did he tell you how he cleverly laid off workers who had been injured on the job, even when his negligence was responsible and those people had families to support? Did he snicker over dinner about doing that to my father?'

Her face blazed bright red, her eyes rounding. In that instant, Simon believed she didn't have a clue as to the sort of man her grandfather had really been.

'No, I thought not.'

'He couldn't have realized . . .'

Simon grimaced. 'Couldn't he? People outside his little circle didn't even have names to him. All those good things you and your sister enjoyed at your grandfather's house, sweetie, came to you courtesy of the sweat of the good citizens of Kittridge. Did you ever have the electricity cut off at your house? Did you ever see your mother cry because she had to accept charity to feed her kids? Or did it occur to you that poor people could have pride?'

Yardley swung her sneakered feet over the side of the bed. 'I'm sorry for your hardships, Mr Blye. Truly. I had no idea. My grandfather would never have intentionally hurt anyone. I think you would be a happier man if you could overcome your bitterness. I am not my grandfather, and if my penance for intruding on your privacy is listening to your ravings, I'll phone the sheriff myself. As you know, I've been in Boston the past several years, and when I was here I was far too young to be allowed any say in the running of the company. But it's unfair of you to slander my grandfather when he's no longer here to defend himself.'

Simon found himself starting down into eyes the color of denim, dark with hurt and anger. He visually traced the hard set of her jaw and those slightly parted lips, revealing a neat row of small white teeth. He swept his hair back with an open hand.

'Your grandfather respected no one. The peasant girl mold was cast from a sculpture *my* great-grandfather made. He was a fine artist, but he had no means to manufacture copies on a large scale. So he was duped into a partnership with your great-grandfather, who was flush with his railroad money and used the peasant girl and other works by my great-grandfather to establish his company. Only, when the profits came in, he forgot it was supposed to be a partnership.'

'That's the most ridiculous tale I've ever heard. Obviously someone in your family made it up to entertain you.'

Simon leaned forward. 'I've never found it amusing. Naturally, the liars would have to be in my family.'

She gave him a blank look. Then her features slackened. 'If that really happened, why didn't your great-grandfather seek protection through the courts?'

Simon snorted. 'You don't get it, do you? Poor people stay poor because they can't afford to hire lawyers and strike back.'

'What do you want from me, Mr Blye? I assume this is leading up to some type of blackmail.'

'Let's call it barter. I need to find out who is handing out my house keys and company files. And I need to infiltrate the close-knit little circle that thinks it runs this town.'

'You're already part of that group.'

'In essence.' Simon intended to not only gain full acceptance but take charge. He heard the whispers behind his back, the speculation that his business was on shaky ground and wouldn't last, that it was only a matter of time before he went broke and retreated to the side of town he belonged on.

Her thin eyebrows purled together. 'You want me to speak up on your behalf?'

Simon chuckled. 'You'd be convincing, I'm sure. No, I don't plan to beg for approval. I have something better in mind. You and I are going to make an appearance together at the autumn charity dance this weekend. I was going to toss those tax – deductible tickets I bought, but since this has come up . . .'

'You expect me to go on a date with you?!'

'Don't be so flattered. I simply want every-body in this town to get a good look at the two of us together. We will have to pretend we like each other somewhat.'

She laughed. 'Maybe you should contact the actors' union. Besides, I made a date weeks ago.'

He shrugged, unimpressed. 'Break it. I'm offering you a deal, not an invitation to the prom. I want people to know I'm taking charge as the leader in this town, and with you on my arm I'll get their attention.'

'You are the coldest, most conniving man I've ever encountered.'

He cast her a long, resentful look. 'Second, maybe.'

'People will assume I approve of your pilfering our design. They'll think I gave it to you!'

Simon nodded sadly, clicking his tongue in mock sympathy. 'You could just explain that you were coerced into attending the dance with me to cover up your attempted burglary. Come to think of it, your timing was nearly perfect.'

Yardley glared up at him.

'I'll have to have your answer before I can let you leave. Do we have a deal, or do I press charges?'

'Whatever you think this will accomplish will backfire on you,' she warned. 'No one will believe there's anything between us. People in this town know me better than that.'

'Do they? Perhaps this will give you a chance to see how many friends you really have here. Commoners love a scandal, especially where the élite are involved.'

Her gaze drifted to the watercolor hanging on the wall.

'All you have to do is go to the dance, and we'll forget this incident.'

She focused on him again. 'How do we bind this agreement?'

'Your end of it is ensured once I take you home. Without you here, it would be your word against mine, and we both know whom the local law will believe. My concern is holding you to your end.'

'My word is good, Mr Blye.'

'All the sincerity of a telephone solicitor. I need more. Give me that necklace you're wearing.'

Looking horrified, she clutched a hand to her neck. 'No – it belonged to my mother. Look . . . here . . . take my watch.' She fumbled to unclasp the gold band.

He motioned for her to stop. 'No. The necklace. You'll get it back after the dance.' He moved behind her and sat down. 'Lift your hair. I need some insurance. It's either this or your underwear.'

'You'd smolder in hell before you got that.' Grudgingly she raised the sheath of silver hair. Despite his thick fingers, he made quick work of unlatching the clasp. He was accustomed to doing intricate work, and his hands were steady. His fingertips grazed the feathery hair at the nape of her neck.

He relieved her of the chain, then stuck it in his pocket. 'I thrive on challenge, Yardley. There, now I won't have to worry about your backing out. Wear something slinky. Low-cut. Black's good.'

Her face was blazing as he stepped in front of her again. She scowled, indicating her distaste. 'Yes, I understand. Something appropriate for an evening in hell.'

Simon nodded slowly. He didn't doubt she'd been raised to believe people from his part of town were devils. 'If you're trying to hurt my feelings, I gave up having any a long while back.'

'Then I'm truly sorry for you, Mr Blye. May I leave now?' she asked.

'Did I give you the impression you couldn't leave? Unless your chauffeur is waiting in the woods, I'll drive you home.'

'That's not necessary.'

'Yes, it is. If you're going to pass out again, I want you off my property first. Besides, you shouldn't be walking alone at night. Criminals lurking about.'

She shook her head. 'You're demented.'

He gave her a harsh look. 'Letting you leave is the probably the only foolish thing I've done tonight.' He pointed her towards the door.

She balked. 'If it's all the same, could we go out the back?'

'The truck's in the front.'

'I don't like your stairs.'

Simon wasn't crazy about them himself, but not to the extent that he'd duck out the back and walk all the way around to the front to avoid them. He wondered if she truly had recovered from her fainting spell. Was she on drugs?

Her problem wasn't his concern. And he knew better than to worry about her. He'd learned a long time ago that concern about anyone or anything was a dangerous mistake, and he'd trained himself to spurn attachments. He fully intended to spend Saturday evening making everyone in town believe he had Yardley Kittridge contentedly sharing his bed. That accomplished, he'd take her home to fume alone while he reveled in a new level of credibility.

Yardley couldn't have sat farther away from Simon in the extended cab of his truck without opening the door and jumping out.

She cringed silently in the darkened interior – the brim of her baseball cap slanted low over her

forehead so no one would see her with him –
trying to sort out how she was going to explain to
Mimi why she was returning without the mold.
Worse, why she was going out with Simon
Saturday night. Yardley didn't want to ponder
that awful reality. How would she endure an
entire evening of his goading over her publicly?
Why would a man like Simon want the company
of a woman who detested him?

He drove on the speed limit, cautiously but
with an aura of self-assurance, the window
rolled down and one arm resting on the door
frame, eyes focused straight ahead.

With the safety of his attention riveted else-
where, she surreptitiously studied him. His
granite profile was breathtakingly handsome,
even more so now than she remembered. The
rough edges that had so intrigued her years ago –
faded jeans, worn T-shirt, shaggy haircut,
whisker shadows – were trimmed and po-
lished. He must be in his early thirties, she
calculated. The wind blowing in through the
open window ruffled his dark hair, and he could
well have posed for a movie poster.

What a waste. All that masculine magnifi-
cence with nothing but arrogance and rudeness
beneath it. He truly believed her family had
wronged him. Perhaps, since she'd be forced

to spend time with him, she could make him realize her beloved grandfather was not the kind of man who lived off the misfortune of others. Jarred Kittridge had been a compassionate, generous soul. If he'd known about Simon's family, he would have immediately found another job for Mr Blye.

'Men make their own bad luck,' Granddad had said. Still, he'd always opened his heart to donate to the toy fund at Christmas, to raise money for the food bank. Why, Granddad had once spent his own money to hire a clown to visit a seriously ill child he'd never even met!

Yardley couldn't understand why Simon's father hadn't gone directly to Granddad with his problem.

Forcing this hardhead to see the truth was her only hope of persuading him to abandon his scheme to duplicate the peasant girl figurines. He was doing it for spite. From all appearances, he didn't need the money! His brand new house still smelled of fresh lumber and paint. But Simon didn't seem inclined to want to get past his deep resentment of the Kittridges. And tonight she'd only made things worse.

'They won't come out the same, you know,' she warned.

Simon turned as though suddenly remembering she was with him.

'The figurines,' she added. 'The mold has deteriorated over the years.'

'There are ways to fix that. Good of you to worry about it, though. Your grandfather was an excellent teacher.'

'I think you're bluffing. I don't believe the mold can be restored.'

'I never bluff.'

'I can take you to court.'

He shrugged as he rotated the steering wheel. 'Call your lawyer. Shame a mold so precious was never registered.'

Yardley sighed heavily. 'My great-grandfather was just starting out. He overlooked including a trademark.'

'Or was too arrogant to believe he needed one. Bad mistake. Maybe he was too busy rubbing out *my* great-grandfather's signature. A good thief covers his tracks. Guess all you Kittridges lack expertise in that area. If you're going to do something, babe, make sure you're good at it.'

'My name is Yardley.'

'I know what your name is.'

'Speaking of mistakes, don't underestimate me because I'm a woman. You don't want the

Kittridges as your enemies now any more than you would have when Granddad was alive.'

He rolled the pick-up to a halt in front of a majestic white frame Victorian-style mansion. 'Well, your private school education may have taught you to add up columns of numbers, Yardley, but I've dealt with characters you'd cross the street to avoid. If I set out to steal something, I'd damn well come home with it. I notice your hands are empty.'

Her glance fell to her lap.

'Mimi put you up to this, didn't she?' he pressed.

Yardley shook her head. 'Don't you dare start in on my grandmother. God knows you've defamed everyone else in my family. No one forced me to do what I did. And doesn't our bargain include your silence on this matter?'

Simon hesitated, but she could feel his intense glance searing her. 'I'll pick you up Saturday at eight.'

'Here?' She glanced anxiously towards the house to see whether her grandmother might have heard them pull up and come to the window. Relief filtered through her as she saw that none of the front lights had come on. 'I'll meet you . . .'

He shook his head. 'No. This has to look real. And try to feign a little enthusiasm. Believe me, I don't plan to enjoy the company any more than you do.'

Yardley shot him a fiery scowl. Opening the door, she burned with an urgent need to get away from him. 'Goodnight, Mr Blye,' she shot back at him over her shoulder.

'Sweet dreams, babe.' His answer floated tauntingly through the night.

Yardley balled her fists at her sides as she marched towards the house without looking back. Her anger ricocheted from him and his insolence to Mimi for inciting her to do this, then back to herself for being so easily swayed into doing something she knew was wrong.

She wanted her mother's necklace back, and she dreaded the prospect of spending one more excruciating minute in Simon Blye's presence. If anyone in this town or the whole universe for that matter assumed she liked that cretin . . . In frustration, she kicked the porch step.

From behind her, she heard Simon's laughter rumble through the night before the truck pulled away.

She who laughs last, she thought. Simon Blye

was in for a big surprise and a lesson he severely deserved. *I don't bluff either.*

Mimi was waiting up in the den, curled on one end of the couch in her jade-green velour robe, staring into the fire. When Yardley smelled the woodsmoke and watched the dancing orange flames, she immediately contrasted the image with Simon Blye's cold, dark hearth. As much as his arrogance infuriated her, something about the man moved her where she didn't want to be touched. How sad it must be to cut oneself off from all feeling except bitterness. And under all that macho sarcasm, she sensed he longed to be free of his self-imposed isolation from the human race. She reminded herself for her own self-preservation, she shouldn't acknowledge glimpsing anything in him beyond what he wanted her to see. Such probing would bring her only trouble. If there was a gentler, more human side to Simon Blye, the beast she'd encountered tonight would never reveal it.

Mimi turned to her. With her small frame and immaculately styled bleached blonde hair, she hardly looked as old as she must be. Mimi never revealed her exact age, nor did she let anyone forget she was more than a decade younger than Jarred.

'Thank God you're back, dear.' Mimi declared, getting up off the sofa and walking towards her. A half-full teacup smelling faintly of vodka, a glass ashtray holding one skinny cigarette butt, and an open copy of the latest issue of *Vogue* sat on the coffee table before her. 'I've been worried sick. Did you get it?'

Yardley shook her head.

Mimi stopped short. 'What went wrong?'

'Everything.'

Mimi's hazel eyes widened in alarm. 'I never should have let you go over there. He didn't hurt you, did he? Oh, God, if that demon put one hand on you . . .'

Yardley did not remind Mimi that she had sent her on this mission. Now, listening to Mimi, she realized that considering the circumstances Simon had been almost kind to her. Except for the manhandling. Even that had been restrained. A warning. How many people would have given a burglar a lift home?

Why was Mimi so quick to believe he would have harmed her?

'People get shot breaking into houses, Mimi. I was lucky tonight, and I'm not going back.'

Mimi rubbed her temples. 'So he still has the mold?'

'Yes, I'm sorry about that. But I don't think stealing is the way to get it.'

Mimi stiffened. 'It's ours to begin with. He was in the workshop the day your grandfather noticed it was missing.'

'I can't imagine Granddad not confronting him, then. Mimi, Simon Blye says Granddad gave him the mold.'

'You discussed it with him? What did you do, go over there and ring the doorbell?'

'Well, I wish I had.'

Mimi crumpled into a heap on the couch.

'Of course, he'd say anything. A man like that has no scruples.'

Yardley stepped closer. 'Are you all right?'

'Oh, I'm getting another migraine. Change in the weather coming, you know.' She looked up at Yardley. 'I feel so lost without your grandfather here. All those years he worked to make sure we'd be taken care of after he was gone, building a solid business with a sterling reputation. And now this upstart is bent on destroying it all.'

Yardley leaned over her, setting a hand on Mimi's frail shoulder. 'Simon Blye is not going to destroy anything, I promise you. But burglarizing a house is more complicated than a trip to the mall, and I was crazy to have attempted it. Let me do this my own way.'

Mimi looked up with a horrified expression. 'You're not getting involved with that awful man, are you? Oh, I should have known better than to let you of all people go anywhere near him . . .'

Yardley sighed heavily. She would find some gentle way in the morning to break it to Mimi that she was going to the dance with him. At the moment, she was too tired to be able to explain it to herself.

'I'm a grown woman, Mimi, and I've dealt before with men who thought they were shrewd. At least I'm not in jail.'

Mimi hooted. 'Do you think he'd call the law and have to explain how he got our mold to begin with?'

Yardley grew nauseous. Had she agreed to something she really didn't have to do? Maybe he had bluffed and she'd been too dense to call him on it. Had he kept laughing all the way home? Was he laughing now?

Her head ached from thinking about him. 'It's late, and you need to get to bed.' Yardley helped her grandmother up. With Jarred gone, she felt doubly protective of the woman who'd always pampered her and made her feel special. As Yardley had proven tonight, she would have done anything for Mimi.

Slipping an arm around the smaller woman, and leading her toward the stairs, Yardley cast a glance back at the littered coffee table. 'Last I heard, vodka and cigarettes weren't antidotes for headaches.'

'Well, I'm too old to change, deary.' At the foot of the stairs, Mimi turned to her. Tears pooled in the corners of her eyes. 'God bless you. I'm so glad you've come home. I don't know what I'd do if I were rattling around this big old house by myself. And I'm lost at the factory. People asking so many questions I can't answer. Jarred and I have always been so proud of you. You understand, don't you, why we can't have the peasant girl resurrected on store shelves? Why, the owners of the originals might sue! The public embarrassment!'

Yardley gave her a hug. 'I do understand. But with a mold so old, wouldn't they be obvious fakes?'

Mimi's look hardened. 'In the hands of a master craftsman, the figurine could be duplicated almost down to the finest detail. Your grandfather could have accomplished that, and he taught the Blye boy well. He once said that boy had more natural ability as a sculptor than he himself had been born with.'

Yardley gnawed her lip. She wondered whether her Granddad had ever conveyed that to Simon himself. Her quick empathy alarmed her. What was she doing now, taking Blye's side?

Simon was dreaming of sweeping back a tumble of white-gold hair, smiling into adoring blue velvet eyes and pressing his mouth hard against yielding lips that tasted like tart cherries when the buzzer woke him.

'Hell,' he muttered groggily, opening his eyes to find himself hugging a pillow scented with white ginger. The face in his mind had disappeared, and with gut-wrenching disappointment he realized he'd been about to make love to Yardley Kittridge. Damn, he'd stayed away from women far too long.

He punched the pillow.

The buzzer whined insistently. He sat up, rubbing the bridge of his nose, and pressed a button on the panel on his wall. It was still dark out. Through the window, he saw stars twinkling in a clear sky, and the read-out on his radio said four-fifteen. He pushed the button for the intercom.

'This better be good,' he announced.

'Simon?'

'Who else?'

'This is the sheriff's department. Need to see you a minute.'

Simon snapped into full wakefulness.

'What's the problem, Jeff?' he demanded.

'Let me in, Simon. We've got a situation here.'

'Give me a minute. I'll be right down.'

Exhaling deeply, he keyed in the codes to admit Jeff Wilson through the gate. He'd recognized his old schoolmate's voice, despite the official-sounding inflections.

Dazed, Simon groped for the terry cloth robe he'd tossed aside earlier and wrapped it over his bare chest and flannel boxers. What the hell was Jeff doing here? He wondered if maybe a passing motorist had seen Yardley trying to break in and reported it, but that had been hours ago. A real burglar could have cleaned the place out by now.

Curious enough to be awake, he padded downstairs barefoot.

He opened the door and found Jeff in uniform, looking solemn and official.

'Come on in, Jeff,' Simon said. 'What's up?'

Jeff stepped inside. 'Got a call from Ms Kittridge reporting that you took her necklace.'

Simon nearly laughed out loud. The woman had grit, more than he'd anticipated.

'Am I under arrest?' he asked.

'Hell, no, Simon. She just wants her necklace back. You know Sheriff Crane is a friend of her family and he's coming up for re-election. Do you have it?'

'Yeah, I have it. She left it here. You know how women are, having a great time one minute, then some little thing sets her off and the next thing you know she's pulling herself together real quick and storming out without everything she took off.'

Jeff exchanged a sympathetic but mildly shocked glance.

'No kidding? How long has this been going on?'

'Is that an official question?'

'No, it's a question between old friends. God, Simon, have you forgotten who you are? The fact that I'm here right now should tell you you're sniffing up the wrong tree.'

'I'm sure Yardley and I can depend on your discretion. I'll get the necklace.'

CHAPTER 3

'You've fainted twice now?' the young doctor asked, focusing on the chart in his hands.

'Yes,' Yardley replied, struggling to read beyond his averted gaze. Why wouldn't he look at her? 'Twice in a week. What's wrong with me?'

'Nothing much, most likely.' Finally, he set the metal clipboard down and swiveled his head to look at her, studying her as if she were a malformed piece of a jigsaw puzzle. 'How did you feel, right before you fainted?'

Like a limp noodle. Yardley exhaled impatiently. She'd already related this information once to the nurse. Didn't these people talk to each other? 'As if my head's full of helium and I'm about to float off the ground,' she replied.

'Hmm,' he said, glancing at the chart again. 'Do you remember the situation you were in when it happened?'

This was a new question. 'The first time, I was at work. I'd gotten up to check something in the stockroom, and the next thing I knew I woke up flat on the floor.'

'What about the second time?'

Yardley drew her shoulders in and hesitated. She wasn't about to admit she'd just been caught committing a burglary.

'I was having an argument with someone . . .' she ventured.

He nodded as if he'd anticipated this. 'Your tests will tell us if there's any physical cause, but I'd guess your problem is stress-related.'

She frowned. 'I'm not a hypochondriac, Dr Stevenson.'

He gave her a serious, patronizing look. 'Of course not. These episodes are very real, and your tests will show whether a physical problem is causing them. But you're awfully young and outwardly healthy to have any serious condition. Didn't you just move back to Kittridge and take over the family business? Changes in your lifestyle can cause stress that manifests itself in strange ways.'

'So what do I do?'

'Avoid the situations that bring on these attacks. Just take things slow and easy for a while.'

Yardley eyed him skeptically. Doctors detached themselves from reality so neatly. Nothing could have created more internal stress than the prospect of her date tomorrow night with Simon. Would he let her off the hook if she produced a doctor's excuse? Fat chance. He was determined to have his revenge, even if it entailed wheeling her into the dance on a stretcher.

'Isn't there some prescription that can stop it?' she asked.

The doctor shook his head. 'Pills don't solve everything. I'll call you next week with your test results. Until then, just be careful. Your biggest risk right now is falling down and hurting yourself. If you start experiencing light-headedness, nausea or blurred vision, lie down immediately. If you can't lie down, sit down and put your head between your knees until the sensation passes.'

Yardley hesitated. She was convinced that more than simple stress was causing her problem. 'What kinds of things might the tests show?'

He shook his head. 'Let's see what they indicate first before we start worrying about that, Ms Kittridge. Believe me, there's no need for alarm. Do you have any other questions?'

'I've taken enough of your time. Thank you.'

Yardley drove the fifty miles back to Kittridge deep in thought. She had never been a weak person who shunned work or responsibility. Why would she suddenly start crumbling under pressure?

The beauty of the golden autumn afternoon nearly escaped her as she drove past rolling fields, pastures, and barns. She'd intentionally taken her complaint to an out-of-town doctor to avoid any local speculation over her health. Stevenson was the friend of a mutual acquaintance in Boston. He'd come with a glowing recommendation, although Yardley wasn't wildly impressed.

By all indications, he must have thought she'd over-reacted. She felt a little foolish for having bothered him with her small complaint. But at least neither he nor his nurses would be sitting in the local restaurants discussing her visit with the town fathers.

She thought of her grandfather, who had always prided himself on never being sick a day in his life. Watching the strong, vital man she'd looked up to since childhood reduced to a tortured shell who couldn't lift a spoon had made an irreversible impact on her. Quickly, she dismissed the haunting memories. If she kept internalizing, over-reacting, she'd soon be languishing in bed suffering some imaginary malady. Still, she nearly turned the car around to beg Stevenson to just please check everything.

Avoid stress. She shook her head. She wasn't about to go home and cower in bed.

Simon Blye was stress personified. She raised a hand to touch the chain at her neck. Simon was an angry man to begin with, and she knew calling the sheriff to retrieve her necklace had certainly intensified his anger.

Yesterday morning the local florist had delivered a dozen white roses to her at work. 'Secret admirer?' her secretary Lisa had commented slyly as she set the bouquet on Yardley's desk. In her bad mood the morning after the encounter with Simon, Yardley had viewed the flowers as the boost she needed. Her first thought was that Jack Warren had sent them. He was the only man in Kittridge who had caught her interest since her return, and despite their growing casual friendship she'd been disappointed he hadn't invited her to the dance. She'd lied when she'd told Simon she had a date. As if that would have dissuaded him from his plan.

When the roses arrived, she'd wondered if Jack was too shy to make overtures in person. Opening the card and seeing Simon's bold signature was like having a coiled serpent spring out at her. 'Saturday. Eight p.m. Yours, Simon.' was all it read. Yardley had tossed the crumpled card in the wastebasket and without explanation given the flowers to Lisa, who had eyed her as though she'd lost her mind. Yardley did not call Simon to thank him. She just wanted Sunday morning to come so she'd have Simon Blye behind her.

The familiar arches of the Parkway Bridge spanning the East Arrow River loomed on the horizon, heralding her approach to the city limits of Kittridge. She slowed as she crossed the bridge, then followed Center Street into the downtown area, three blocks of upscale colonial-style white frame shops and offices. She pulled her BMW into the angle parking at the curb in front of Sophie's Boutique and killed the engine. Stepping out, she tried to muster some enthusiasm for her errand.

When the bell over the door clanged to announce Yardley's entrance, the dark-haired woman sitting behind the counter sipping coffee looked up with a grin and closed her puzzle magazine.

'Caught me slacking off,' Sophie confessed with a smile, silver lattice earrings dangling and sparkling in the light.

'Got time for some coffee? I was beginning to wonder if you'd forgotten your dress.'

'Sure, thanks,' Yardley accepted. 'I hadn't forgotten. I got sidetracked.' When she'd purchased the dress weeks ago and left it for alterations, she'd hoped she'd be attending the dance with Jack. Caffeine and company sounded pretty darn good right now, and she was in no hurry to return to Mimi's big, empty house.

Mimi, lamenting her first autumn dance without Jarred, had unexpectedly jaunted off to New York for the weekend. Yardley had secretly welcomed her grandmother's absence. For now, the inevitability of explaining her date with Simon was postponed. But Mimi was certain to hear of it upon her return and demand an explanation. The whole town would be buzzing.

Yardley considered maybe she should just start packing and slink back to Boston. Adrenalin and stubbornness kicked in. As much as she'd been shuffled around as a child, Kittridge, where she'd spent her summers with her grandparents, was her real home, and she wasn't about to let the likes of Simon Blye drive her away. Especially now that Mimi depended on her. The only way to save face was going to be to pretend she was with Simon by choice.

Afterwards, she could simply tell everyone she'd made an error of judgement. But then there was that nasty business with the figurine. She'd promised Mimi she wouldn't let Simon copy it. The problem was, how was she going to stop him?

'Milk, sugar?' Sophie asked, returning with a steaming mug in one hand.

'Black's fine,' Yardley told her, accepting the mug. 'Thanks.'

Sophie dragged up another wooden stool beside hers and gestured for Yardley to sit. Yardley took a sip of the hot, bracing liquid.

'This is exactly what I needed.'

'Playing hooky from work today?' Sophie asked. Her long, curly hair was tied back with a paisley scarf and she wore an embroidered denim shirt, the sleeves rolled up to her elbows.

Yardley shook her head. 'I had an errand to run in Wellstown. Just got back. I guess having flexi-time is a perk of being your own boss.'

Sophie nodded. 'When you have somebody who can take over. Me, I'm married to this place. This is really the first free moment I've had since everybody began ordering their dresses for the dance. I don't anticipate much of a breather until after the holidays. But believe me, I'm not complaining. I like having a bank account.'

Yardley laughed along with her.

'So,' Sophie asked, 'who's your big date for the dance?'

Yardley nearly choked on her coffee. 'No big date,' she professed. 'Really.'

'Hmm. Thought for sure you'd be going with Jack Warren. Guess my instincts are off these days.'

'Yeah, mine too,' Yardley said with a chuckle. 'How about you? Who are you going with?'

Sophie shook her head. 'I'm not into the gala scene. Craig and I will probably snuggle up with a couple of videos and a bowl of popcorn.'

Yardley smiled. 'Sounds cozy,' she remarked wistfully. She would trade her evening with Simon and Kittridge's most self-righteous for a quiet evening at home with a man she loved in a heartbeat. If such a man existed. More and more, she doubted that. 'I'm jealous.'

Sophie dismissed her with a wave of the hand. 'Not while you're stopping traffic in your new dress. I'll go get it.'

She disappeared into the back room and returned quickly with Yardley's dress suspended under plastic on a hanger. Upon seeing her selection again, Yardley's spirits lifted briefly. A simple scoop-necked plum-colored sheath, it boasted swirls of matching sequins across the bodice. Yardley had known the dress was perfect for her the moment she'd set eyes on it. The day she'd bought it, she'd entertained high expectations.

Seeing it now, she remembered dully that she'd be wearing it for Simon. To satisfy his vengeful ego. She ought to have Sophie send him the bill, but the implications of that action would really send shock-waves through the town.

'Wonder how it would look with a turtle-neck?'

Sophie's gasp was audible as she shifted the hanger into Yardley's hands. Then she sputtered a laugh as she realized Yardley was joking. 'Hang in there,' she advised. 'Maybe Jack will show up and the two of you will have a great time. I think he needs a little coaxing. He took losing his wife pretty hard.'

Yardley quickly paid her bill and left.

Although her stomach was in knots, with Mimi gone there was no point in cooking to-night. As she was carrying the plastic-covered dress out to the car, she decided to dash into the deli and grab a sandwich to take home.

She locked the car with the dress hanging inside and walked down two doors to the deli. A bell rattled overhead as she entered, assaulted by the smells of barbecue sauce and exotic mustards. She hadn't expected a line at the counter this early, but she remembered it was Friday, and even a tiny town like Kittridge experienced its rush-hours.

Patiently, she stepped into line.

She smiled at the elderly woman who turned briefly to look at her, then stared into the glass case full of food and studied a posted menu she knew by heart.

'Hello, Yardley.' A hand on her shoulder startled her. She whipped around to find Jack standing behind her, his pleasant, rectangular face red from the chill outside and green eyes shining. His brown hair, graying prematurely at the temples, was neatly combed in place.

'Jack, hi!' she greeted him. 'How are you?'

He shook his head and shrugged. 'Too busy for my liking. Been working all week on a big proposal, and the client called this morning and said they've gone with another agency.'

Yardley nodded sympathetically. 'Rough going.' Jack ran Kittridge's only advertising agency, and she knew he depended on his out-of-town clients to stay in business.

'I'll get over it. But there is a silver lining: I find myself free this weekend. I know this is the last minute, but I was wondering if you'd be interested in going to the dance. I'm a pretty fair amateur chef, and I thought I'd fix us dinner at my place first.' He bowed his head, then looked up with a sheepish grin. 'I'm not very good at this. I haven't dated much since Chrissie died. Oh, heck, I haven't dated at all.'

Touched, Yardley smiled sweetly. 'You're doing fine, Jack,' she assured him. 'And I'd love to sample your cooking, but I'm afraid I have other plans.'

'Damn. I knew I put off asking too long. Some days I'd sell that darn agency for a nickel. I should have guessed you'd have plans. Sorry if I was out of line to ask.'

'No, you wouldn't – you love that place. And I'm glad you invited me. I can't get out of this, Jack. I'd like to go out with you. Ask me another time, okay?'

'Sure. Look, are you eating here?'

Yardley looked into his blunt, handsome features. Jack had married Chrissie Perkins, a local woman, and moved here from Ohio. Chrissie had died a couple of years ago, and Yardley had met Jack at the Chamber of Commerce meetings after she'd moved back to town.

He was always outgoing and friendly and struck Yardley as exactly the type of man she needed in her life – hard-working, intelligent, steady. The steady part was the most important.

And now that he'd finally asked her out, she was having to turn him down because of Simon Blye. Yet another strike against that arrogant barbarian. Would Jack be interested enough to ask again once he thought she was the kind of woman who would turn him down to date Simon Blye?

She reflected that this mess was her own fault, breaking into Simon's house. But she'd been desperate. He was about to ruin a business her family had made a success of for generations.

Her great-grandfather and her grandfather had kept it thriving over the years, even through the Depression. She couldn't let all that crumble just because the company was in her hands now. She would outsmart Simon Blye, and she would pay him back for playing havoc with her life.

'I'm taking a sandwich home with me,' she said regretfully. 'I have some reports I have to go over tonight.' She would have loved to spend a few hours in Jack's company, but didn't want to have to offer further explanations about tomorrow night.

'Sure,' he said.

'Call me, okay?'

'All right.'

It was her turn to be served, and she quickly got her roast beef sandwich and potato salad and left clutching the white deli bag in one hand.

The sun was already setting as she got back in the BMW and drove the two miles from town to Mimi's house. She smiled as she approached the majestic white house with its sprawling garden bordered by a white wooden fence. The shade trees were nearly bare and the ground covered with red and gold leaves. A wooden swing sat in the front yard. Two giant pumpkins and an assortment of colorful potted chrysanthemums flanked the steps to the long porch, and a scarecrow sat sentinel in one of the porch rockers.

Over Mimi's protests, Yardley had impulsively decorated the porch after a visit to a local nursery. She loved this time of year, just as she in turn wholeheartedly loved winter, spring and summer as they came. Her powerful zest for life sometimes outdid her, as she was prone to put too much of herself into everything she did . . . sometimes ending in disaster.

Looking at the porch now, she could almost see the kids in their costumes on Halloween night, showing off their masks and plastic swords and yelling, 'Trick or treat; smell my feet!' as though the phrase were highly original. She could almost smell the candle burning in a jack-o'-lantern and hear the leaves rustling under pint-sized tennis shoes. The simple stuff, that was all she wanted. Home and a family and all the glorious little rituals that went with that. All she'd missed when she was young.

At the moment, she just felt exhausted. Nerves, she told herself. Too much worry over the business and the doctor's appointment and Simon. Dr Stevenson had made her feel like some fussy little old woman, worrying over nothing. Maybe if he fainted a few times, he'd understand how scary it was.

Especially waking up and finding herself in Simon Blye's bed.

She needed to take the doctor's advice and chill out. How long had it been since she'd spent any time just enjoying herself? Not since Boston. Too bad she couldn't go to the dance with Jack. With him, she might actually have a good time.

Coming around the side of the house, she discovered an old red Sundance streaked with road dirt parked in the drive. Realizing who the car belonged to, Yardley grinned. She couldn't unbuckle her seat-belt and get out of the car fast enough.

Crashing through the unlocked door, she burst into the house.

'Serena?'

Her two-year-old nephew Casey toddled out of the kitchen to greet her with upraised arms. Yardley rushed to meet him, scooping him up and lifting him to her, nestling her cheek against the tiny bib of his denim overalls.

As she pulled him to her chest, something funny happened inside her, as though she were walking on a carousel and it suddenly started moving. Wobbling, she whipped a hand out to brace herself on Mimi's piano.

'You okay, Yardley?'

She looked up and found her half-sister standing in the archway between the living and dining room, her slim body clad in faded jeans and a tight rose-colored sweater, her straight shoulder-length brown hair falling in wisps around her face.

'Yeah,' Yardley replied. But her heart was racing at the thought of how nearly she'd dropped Casey. 'Just overexcited at finding

this Munchkin and my favorite sister here.'
Casey cooed and giggled as she gave him a
big smooch on his soft cheek and inhaled the
soft scents of baby shampoo and graham
crackers.

Reluctantly, she set him down.

Serena wiped her hands on the sides of her
jeans. She walked over to Yardley and gave her a
hug. 'I'm making coffee. Is there food in that
bag? I tried to order a pizza but nobody delivers
this far out of town.'

'Maybe if you had let someone know you were
coming today . . .'

Serena frowned, scrunching her dark brows
and tossing her head back. 'I talked to Mimi on
the phone the other night. Where is she, by the
way?'

Now Yardley was puzzled. 'Well, you know
she's kind of self-absorbed these days. The
autumn dance was coming up and she got the
blues, with Granddad being gone. She took off
to New York.' Watching her sister's crestfallen
expression, Yardley forced herself to lie. 'And I
would have sworn she'd said you weren't coming till Sunday.'

Serena's brown eyes drifted to watch her son.
'Nice try, Yardley. She didn't say a blamed
word about our coming at all, did she?'

Yardley stiffened. 'It was an oversight, Serrie. Nothing intentional, so don't get all ruffled. There's been a lot going on around here.'

Serena looked amused. 'In Kittridge? Snooze capital of North America? I can't wait to hear this.'

'Come on in the kitchen. I've just got a sandwich and potato salad, but I'll share. How's Dad? How's Francesca?'

'Mom and Dad are fine. Don't change the subject. What's going on around here?'

'Well, the business is the main thing.'

'You are a sly one, Yardley,' Serena added, darting into the living room to snare Casey. 'So how come Simon Blye phoned you a couple of minutes ago?'

Yardley's smile dropped.

'Hey, don't look so devastated. You could do a lot worse. This is me, not Mimi. Tell me something exciting, like you're sleeping with him. As I remember, he's quite a hunk. Is he as good as he looks?'

Yardley rolled her eyes. Only Serena could inflate a phone call into an affair in a single breath. Finally, she let her shoulders drop. Serena was the one person she could confide in without fear of repercussions, and she needed to pour this out. 'I'm glad you're here, Serrie. I hope you made a big pot of coffee,' she began.

Yardley took a last critical look at herself in the full-length mirror behind the closet door.

'You're gorgeous,' Serena approved. 'Got the game plan down?'

Patting her upswept hair, Yardley nodded. She was twenty-seven years old and constantly battling against looking seventeen. Tonight, she did not look seventeen.

Her blonde hair was piled into a honeycomb of wide curls atop her head, her blue eyes widened by virtue of variegated eye shadow and Serena's raven-black mascara. Her lips appeared perfectly shaped under artistically applied deep rose lipstick, and a light coat of foundation obliterated the light but infuriating smattering of freckles across the bridge of her nose. Amethyst studs sparkled from her earlobes, accenting the matching necklace at the base of her throat.

Sophie's dress hugged Yardley's curves, dipping low in the front and lower in the back to expose a generous expanse of Yardley's creamy skin. Her high heels and upswept hairdo added several inches to her height, and she reasoned it might help her stand her ground against Simon.

'You're gifted,' Yardley praised her sister. 'If I tried putting so much make-up on on my own, I'd look like a hooker. Definitely not the image I'm after tonight.'

'You'll drive him wild.'

'Not the desired result. I thought I explained this to you, Serrie. The last thing I want to do is seduce him. In fact, he's not getting within a two-foot radius of me.'

Serena smiled. 'I thought you said the mold was in his bedroom closet. Only one way I know to get into a guy's room.'

'He probably moved it to a vault somewhere by now. And even if he didn't, I'm not going to have sex with him just to get it. I'm going to convince him to return it because it's the right thing to do.'

'Where better to get his attention than in his bedroom? You'd be far more convincing bypassing his principles and appealing to his baser instincts. Those are usually more readily accessible.'

Yardley bristled. 'I'm never setting foot in his bedroom again.'

Grinning, Serena folded her arms and leaned against the wall. 'Again? You've already been there? This gets better with every telling. Do go on, Sis.'

Yardley's face burned. 'Nothing to tell . . . Nothing along the lines you're thinking of happened.'

'Then what were you doing in his bedroom with him? Helping him dust under the bed?'

'Really, Serena.' Yardley frowned. She couldn't tell Serena Simon had carried her in there after she fainted. Ironically, Simon was the only person who knew she had fainted, and she preferred to keep it that way. She didn't want her family to worry there was anything wrong with her. Simon didn't count. He didn't care. 'You're hopeless.'

'Sometimes I think you are. Wouldn't be the worst thing that'll ever happen to you . . . In fact, maybe if you'd forget about the silly mold and leave that particular problem to Mimi, you wouldn't have that bad a time tonight.'

Yardley glanced thoughtfully at Casey, but she refrained from stating what was on her mind. 'I tried that live-for-the-moment stuff back in Boston, and I'm not sleeping with another man unless I'm in love and probably not until I'm married. Besides, this is Simon the ogre we're talking about. He's not a nice man. It's not simply because Mimi wouldn't approve.'

'You don't think he's attractive?'

'Sure he is.' Yardley dropped her voice, realizing she'd answered a little too quickly. 'But he's very snide and abrasive. You don't know him. And he hates our family.'

'You said he has a grudge against Granddad.'

'He hates all of us. Trust me on this.'

'I remember sneaking around the studio and watching them that one summer when I was a kid. Granddad acted like he really liked Simon. When Granddad wasn't around, Simon would let me come in and watch him work. He used to give me bubble gum.'

Yardley turned to her sister. 'Really? Granddad wouldn't let me go anywhere near the studio.'

'I think it had something to do with your having a bust while my chest still looked like an ironing board. Granddad figured anyone who lived in Simon's neighborhood spent their free time doing only one thing – rolling around in the dirt making babies.'

'Serena!'

'Don't pretend it isn't true. They were so afraid you'd be tainted by someone who wasn't worthy of you. Now me, as long as I wasn't underfoot, they didn't pay much attention to. I guess they figured I was already tainted because of Mom.'

'That's ridiculous. Mimi loves Francesca. So did Granddad.'

'Really? Then why is Dad and your mom's wedding picture in the living room instead of theirs?'

'They never gave Mimi one. She's always complaining about that.'

'Loudly, I'm sure. Dig through the attic some time. You shouldn't have come back here, Yardley. Look at what she put you up to already. Go back to Boston and live your own life.'

'My life is here now. Why don't you stay and work for Kittridge Collectibles? God knows there's plenty of room here for you and Casey.'

'The space will fill up when Mimi gets back.' Serena shook her head and snickered. 'But I would have loved to see you playing burglar.'

Yardley laughed lightly. At least with Serena she could laugh about it. 'How could I have done something so stupid?'

'Sometimes I think she hypnotizes you.'

Yardley jumped at the sound of the doorbell. She and Serena exchanged startled glances.

'I'll get it,' Serena volunteered. 'I want to get a close look at Simon. It's been a few years since I've seen him.'

74

She grabbed Casey and raced downstairs before Yardley could stop her.

As she gathered up her coat and her handbag, she heard the door opening, Serena's bright chatter from downstairs.

'Hi, Simon. I'm Serena, Yardley's sister. She'll be down in a minute. Come on in.'

Yardley rolled her eyes. Typical of Serena. She was talking to him as though they were high school chums leaving for homecoming. Yardley loved her sister, but she wished Serena would act more responsibly, weigh the consequences of what she did.

'This is my son, Casey. Say hi to the nice man, Casey. Can I get you something to drink?'

'No, thank you.'

'Mimi's not here, so you can relax and stop watching for her to jump out at you.'

Yardley smiled upon hearing the rich boom of Simon's startled laughter. It had a nice ring to it. She envied Serena's automatic ease with people. Even a grinch like Simon couldn't resist it. Two minutes and already Serena had him laughing.

Coat tucked under her arm and purse in one hand, she paused in the open bedroom doorway, craning her head to listen to the exchange of voices below.

'I haven't seen you around town since I moved back, Serena.' Simon's voice floated up the stairs.

'You remember me?'

'I used to see you around when I was working for your grandfather. You were just a kid.'

'Just got back. I don't know what's taking Yardley so long. She spent hours primping. She must really like you.'

'That so?'

Yardley gasped, stiffening with outrage. Obviously, she couldn't leave him alone down there with Serena one more minute. Taking a final deep breath to calm herself, she headed for the stairs. She resolved to be civil and endure these hours with Simon Legree. A shudder coursed down her spine as she remembered Simon's menacing glance and tone as he'd unhooked her from his fence, the mocking sneer in his eyes. But she conceded he'd had every right to be angry with her. Moreover, she remembered the warm, languid sensations he'd triggered inside her. Maybe the intensity of those scared her more than anything.

For some perverse reason, the more wrong a man was for her, the more he turned her on. Well, she'd given in to animal attraction once and the emotional deprivation had torn her apart. She needed a man who could be good to her in all ways, despite her wanton impulse to go after the wicked ones.

God help her should Simon discover that impulse.

Sullenly, she descended the stairs, bracing herself for Simon's wrath. She was sure he'd lord it over her all night and derive strange pleasure from that.

When she reached the foot of the stairs, she stopped dumbfounded at the sight of Simon in his dark suit and silver vest, looking more dashing than any man had a right to. He was stooped down, playing and laughing with Casey, his expression relaxed, a sparkle in his eyes Yardley would have believed him incapable of.

At her entrance, his head shot up. He looked up at her, started to turn away, then didn't, although his easy smile immediately tightened to a grimace.

'Ready?' he asked, not commenting on her appearance although she'd seen the flicker of approval light his expression. Had he expected her to appear wearing fatigues?

As she caught a whiff of soap and sandalwood, she was loath to acknowledge the quickening of her heart-rate and the simmering in her belly, the strain in her breasts. How could she physically crave a man she detested? Well, it had happened before with a man she should have stayed away from.

Serena was standing over to one side with her arms folded, grinning.

Simon slipped Yardley's coat out from under her arm and draped it over her shoulders. His warm, steady hands brushed her bare shoulders, radiating ripples of warmth through her chest. For a split second she forgot what a boor he was, how he hated her and her family, that she was doing this only as punishment.

For just an instant, she was the fair maiden finding her prince.

Reality kicked in real quick.

'Have some fun, Yardley,' Serena called as they were leaving. Yardley cringed, wanting to punch her well-meaning but out-of-line sister.

'Is having fun a problem for you?' he asked as soon as they were out the door and on the porch with the door closed.

'I rob for kicks, remember? I'm going to have a good time tonight, despite the company,' she warned.

'Glad to hear it. After all, you may as well. Your sister tells me you like me.'

Yardley marched toward the car. The silver Jag was miraculously back. 'My sister OD'd on cough syrup as a baby and has never been right since,' she shot back. 'You can't believe a word she says.'

Simon halted, gaping at her.

Reaching the car, she turned. Oh, brother, he believed her. 'Serena and I make up stories about each other. It's a little game we play. Are you coming?'

As he condescendingly opened the car door, she knew the longest evening of her life was just beginning. She resolved to remain aloof and graceful. This was a battle, and she would not allow Simon Blye to best her again.

CHAPTER 4

The band lit into an old sixties rock song, and a few middle-aged couples drifted on to the dance floor, grinning and joking as they gyrated to the music.

Standing along the sidelines, Simon cast a slanted glance at Yardley beside him. The woman was a masterpiece, flaxen hair against the intriguing planes of creamy skin her low-cut dress revealed. Her light, floral scent, a fragrance reminiscent of spring flowers and youthful innocence, wafted up to infiltrate his senses. He hadn't for a moment guessed she'd really wear something that would drive him wild all evening. Another payback?

He longed to lean over and nuzzle his face against the back of her neck, bury his nose in her soft hair and skin, inhale his fill of her enticing scent, kiss her all the way down those smooth, bared shoulders.

His muscles tightened beneath the stiff fabric of his suit. Pity almost that this wasn't a real date, leaving some anticipation and mystery about how the evening might end. The thought of taking Yardley, conscious this time, to his bed tormented him. For a short while, he might be able to overlook her family ties. Long enough, at least.

He smiled as he noticed that, even though she stood as still as a marine at attention, her foot inside its sling-back high-heeled shoe was tapping in time to the music. She must be having a miserable time, he realized. Sweet, stoic Yardley, keeping her word while detesting herself for it. Loathing him.

She'd scarcely spoken to him since they'd arrived. He told himself her opinion shouldn't matter. Maybe she was as tough as her grandfather. She'd been a soldier since they'd arrived, forcing a glorious smile and meeting curious stares with a recriminating look of her own, daring anyone to comment on her choice of escort. Much as he wanted to, Simon couldn't hold back his admiration. The woman had grit as well as grace.

He began to wonder if this were indeed the

same flustered and frightened young woman he'd caught burglarizing his house.

After all, she could have dressed like a hag or taken off and left him standing alone all night. Her display of integrity chipped at his self-esteem. He was starting to feel like a heel for forcing her into this. Only when he reminded himself that she'd instigated this by breaking into his house did his conscience ease. She deserved this. And considering she'd committed a crime, she was getting off lightly.

The Kittridges had dual sets of values, one for how they treated those they included among their own and a second for the others of the world. He ranked among the latter. And always would. No matter what. In dealing with Yardley, he was better off remembering it.

Still, he felt a pang of sympathy. While the town fathers were greeting him with a new respect, he heard the hushed whispers at their backs. He didn't care what anyone said about him, but the gossip about her grated. He'd meant to humiliate her, and now that his plan was working he felt protective. As if a Kittridge needed shielding by him! Hell, in that number she was wearing, protection *from* him might be more appropriate.

Seducing her would only add to his guilt. But didn't he owe it to himself to try? What was the harm in it? With her he wouldn't have to worry about any sticky entanglements later. He'd thought he'd sworn off one-night stands long ago, but for Yardley Kittridge he'd make an exception. A man could only deny his needs so long, and a dream woman in whom he could place absolute trust had yet to enter his life. Women changed like chameleons, and Yardley seemed adept at role-playing. She'd called the law on him and he suspected she was up to something still.

He glanced again at Yardley. He always had loved a challenge, and the prospect of bringing out the inner woman tantalized him. She was exquisite. So what if she was a Kittridge? He realized the nasty demon arguing against it in his head was his conscience. God, he must be getting old.

He reached down and relieved her of the punch cup in her hand, the touch of her small, warm fingers against his hand shooting lightning bolts up his arm and all the way down into his midsection. Once Simon committed himself to a conquest, he pursued it wholeheartedly.

He set the cup on a nearby table and caught hold of her wrist, leaning close enough over her shoulder to feel her against his chest.

'I thought you were going to have a good time. Let's dance,' he said.

To his surprise, she nodded without hesitation, allowing him to escort her on to the dance floor.

Facing him, she began moving gracefully to the music. Simon took hold of her hands, enjoying how he towered over her. He spun her under his arm, and she took his cues perfectly. She glanced up at him briefly with pleasant surprise, then graced him with a startled smile.

She fell into the bop, whirling and spinning. She swayed nicely, reminding him of one of those little porcelain ballerinas in music boxes, only the tune was rock 'n' roll instead of classical. He could not take his eyes off her.

As her impish grin broadened, it invaded the depths of Simon's heart. It was the first time she'd directed any degree of warmth towards him. So why was he suddenly feeling like a Boy Scout with a new badge? Whatever she felt towards him didn't matter, he reminded himself. He wanted to make love to her, not get all sappy and involved.

But he found himself smiling back as she kicked off her high heels and people around them began clapping in time to the music.

Some of the older people starting bopping around them.

As the song ended, Simon twirled her up against him.

Sliding along the floor, she stumbled slightly and fell up against his chest. Reflexively, he tightened his hold to catch her. She tensed in his arms. Puzzled, he glanced down.

Her breathing ragged, she was smiling as though nothing unusual had happened. He glimpsed a hint of worry in her eyes, a chalky undertone to her flushed face. Well, naturally, she was embarrassed at having slipped, he assumed. Odd that a woman who displayed such poise and rhythm should suddenly trip, but then she was in stockinged feet, and the floor was slippery. And maybe he'd spun her too fast, made her dizzy.

'Sorry,' she murmured, not looking at him.

He braced her shoulders as she shifted away. She looked distracted and unsettled. Because of the contact with him? He recalled her fainting at his house, how bleached white her complexion had gone, her clumsiness in getting over the fence. He'd seen a lot of things in his life, but he'd never actually seen anyone faint before. Maybe he hadn't spent time around anyone as highly strung as Yardley Kittridge.

He leaned down close to her. 'Are you all right?' he asked. If she wanted to play sick to make him take her home and end the date, he'd go along with it, even if it meant abandoning his other plan. Which was probably best left unexecuted. By now, he'd made his impression on the town's upper crust. His reluctance to end the evening had nothing to do with vengeance.

She brushed back a loose tendril of white-gold hair. 'Too much wax on the floor,' she said quickly, catching her breath.

As the band began playing a slow ballad, he sidled up close to her, drawing her into his arms before she could protest. She followed his easy rhythm as he meshed his body snugly against hers. Nestled to him, she felt delicate and warm and womanly, and, God help him, he wanted her, more than he could remember ever wanting one woman specifically.

He looked down into a face intriguingly blending aristocratic and girlish features. Part woman, part the wide-eyed innocent teenager he'd remembered watching him through the doorway of Jarred's shop. Even back then, dressed in her preppie little summer outfits and wearing her hair in a braid, she'd stirred something alarming and powerful inside him. A need so raw and urgent controlling that it had been torture.

No matter what degree of interest he'd read in her small features while she'd thought he hadn't noticed her standing there, he'd had to remind himself she was as off limits to him as a rare doll under a glass case at a museum.

Never mind that she'd been still a kid, jail bait and most likely a virgin. A rare status in his world. Her being Jarred's granddaughter set her beyond his grasp. Simon had worked too hard to convince Jarred to teach him how to sculpt to blow everything by making the old man mad enough to kill him.

Simon didn't doubt that Jarred would have actually either killed him or made him wish he were dead. The old man had gone livid the few times he'd caught her hanging around the studio, shooing her away and trumping up chores for her inside the house. Simon had pointedly ignored her.

'She bothering you?' Jarred would ask.

Simon had been smart enough to know Jarred was trying to find out something entirely different. 'Who's that?' Simon would reply without looking up from his work.

And the old man would sit down, clasp his hands on his knees and grunt, apparently satisfied that his granddaughter hadn't been soiled by exposure to Simon's coarseness. But Simon didn't forget the way she had been staring at him.

Hard to believe this was Jarred's precious granddaughter he held now.

He bowed his head, brushing her cheek with his as he lowered his mouth to her ear. 'Where'd you learn to bop like that?' he asked.

'Playing around in college. Where'd you?'

'My mom taught me when I was a kid. She loved to dance more than anybody I know. You're good at it.'

'You're not bad yourself. Pity we'll never be friends. We could start a club or something.'

'I'm not a joiner.' Shaking his head, Simon pressed his face close to hers. Her cheek was smooth as satin against his skin. He closed his eyes and let the music drift through his mind. If she knew his thoughts right now, she'd probably run for cover, and, knowing what was on his mind, he couldn't say he would have blamed her. He wanted to peel back that slinky little frock she was wearing and unravel the secrets of the universe. How could any creature so soft and beautiful have evolved from a man as cold and cruel as Jarred Kittridge?

As the music stopped, he reluctantly released her, but he did not lead her off the dance-floor.

Leaning over her shoulder, he whispered, 'Thank you,' into her ear.

Her forehead crinkled as she nodded and looked up at him as though seeing him for the first time.

The microphone on the bandstand crackled as Warren Riddley, Kittridge's current mayor, stepped up to it. 'Ladies and gentlemen, could I have your attention for a moment, please?'

'Sing!' a heckler in the crowd yelled, drawing a scowl from pompous, pudgy Mr Riddley, who shuffled the file cards in his hand and cleared his throat loudly into the mike. Simon heard Yardley chuckle beside him. Ah, they did share one common bond – a lack of fondness for Riddley.

Riddley infuriatingly stood silent, waiting until the room was quiet to get on with his business. Finally, he held the cards up to his face and stuck his nose to one. Too vain to get glasses, Simon noted. A few months ago, he'd given in to the necessity of adjusting to contacts. Wearing them had been hell at first, but glasses just seemed too old and stodgy for his liking.

'Welcome to the forty-fifth annual Kittridge Harvest Gala,' Riddley announced, as if everyone had come here specifically to hear this from him. The first attended by anyone from my neighborhood, Simon noted with satisfaction. And aside from Yardley's company, what a bore it was. 'As you know, proceeds from this ball benefit the local food bank, and tonight we'd like to take a moment to honor the founder of this fund-raising event.'

To Simon's surprise, Yardley's hand dropped into his. He wrapped his hand around her smaller one and felt her shaking.

Her glance shifted sidewise to him, her expression widening as though she suddenly realized what she'd done. The delicate hand was quickly retracted.

'Although this plaque is being presented posthumously . . . '

Suddenly, Simon understood. They were honoring Jarred. Was she that excited at yet more acclaim for that scheming, conniving old fraud?

Anger flamed inside him. Would the good people of Kittridge be so charitable after his own death? Or would he forever be a kid from the wrong side of town who through some quirk of fate got hold of some money and refused to stay where he belonged?

He glanced down at Yardley, and saw her staring into space, her face colorless against the deep hue of her lipstick. He realized now she did not seem overjoyed about this presentation. Clearly, she hadn't expected it. Strange; he wouldn't have supposed even Riddley would make a gesture like this without consulting Jarred's family in advance.

In no mood to listen to what he knew was coming, he tugged gently at her hand, leading her towards the doorway. Looking puzzled, then slackening her features as she understood, she followed him.

'I could use some air,' Simon suggested when they were far enough from the crowd not to be overheard. 'How about you?'

'Yes, thank you,' she agreed, letting him usher her to the door. Her shoes were still in her hand. She paused to bend and stuff her feet into them.

'Want your coat?'

'No. It's not that cold out.'

He pushed open the door and they stepped out on to the terrace overlooking the golf course. The air was chilly, a cold breeze blowing. The sky was dark and star-studded.

He walked her over to a café table, gesturing for her to sit down. He sat in the chair beside her.

'What's wrong?' he asked.

'I . . .'

He set a hand on her arm to silence her as another couple approached, staring as they walked by. In the darkness, Simon couldn't tell who they were. 'Hello,' he greeted stiffly as they passed.

They mumbled hurried, undiscernible greetings and walked on, shifting their curious glances.

'Sorry,' he said, as though he had caused the interruption. He should have seen it then, that he was starting to assume responsibility. A dangerous sign. 'The town's canonizing your grandfather; don't you want to make a speech?'

When she turned to him, Simon was startled to see her eyes glistening with tears.

'Hey,' he said, leaning closer. 'I knew you'd hate coming here, but I didn't think you were having that lousy a time.'

She started laughing, but the effort shattered into a sob. 'It's got nothing to do with you.'

'That's a relief.'

She raised her tear-streaked face defiantly. 'I don't have to listen to them. Do you think I'm so naive and sentimental that I believe they all loved him? Kittridge Collectibles is important to this town, and every person in that room wants to maintain our goodwill. It's like a pageant they're staging for my benefit. A mockery of my grandfather's good name.'

Simon groaned.

'I don't have to listen to you berate him either. Please don't pretend to know me. You don't at all. You wanted me to come here with you so everybody would stare and talk about us, and I've given you what you wanted. I was ready for all that. I wasn't prepared for that plaque for Granddad.' She gazed off across the pond. 'I know you hated him, Mr Blye, and I don't care. My grandfather lived a long time, and I'm sure you're not the only enemy he made. No one lives that long without making mistakes, making people mad. Whatever you believe he did, I don't know enough about it to explain or make excuses.'

Simon edged closer. 'So if you don't care, what's the problem?'

'It just suddenly hit me. He should have been up there, making corny jokes and laughing. And he's simply not here any more. My Granddad was always there for me, even when my mother died and my father was too concerned about his professional and social life to pay much attention to what I did. There was always my Granddad, strong and in control and advising me about what to

93

do next. He was there for me when no one else was. I wasn't ready for him to die, and I haven't completely let go of him yet.'

'You have no choice.' Simon reached out, gently taking hold of her forearms and pulling her close against him. She resisted at first, then sank against his chest, crying softly.

Feeling like the world's biggest cad, he held her tentatively, as though afraid she might break. Then he hugged her tighter, gently stroking her hair. At the feel of feather-light silk between his fingers, his chest constricted. He wasn't much good at comforting crying women, but he understood loss. Even as he embraced her, his muscles tensed as though bracing for the moment she would transform into a cackling witch and twist a knife into his heart.

Watching a Kittridge come apart wasn't so much fun as he'd anticipated.

Where was the strong, sassy woman he'd met the other night? The cool, distant one he'd brought to the dance tonight?

She looked up, dabbing at tears with her fingertips, and shifting away from him. 'I'm spoiling your evening,' she apologized.

Simon stared at her, dumbstruck. 'Why the devil should you care?'

'Because I owe it to you. I invaded your home, and I was out of line to do that, even to recover something that belongs to my family.'

Simon wasn't up to arguing the last point. 'Do you want to go back inside?' he asked.

She shook her head. 'Not really.'

He searched those big blue eyes, his gaze dropping to the pouty mouth slanting up at him. He ached to distract her from her pain. And yet using her to his own ends would sink him to Mimi's level. Now, he had no doubt Mrs Kittridge had preyed on her granddaughter's grief and confusion to force her into committing a crime she would never on her own have resorted to. God help him, for once in his life, tonight he would behave as a gentleman. Although he was certain he'd regret it.

'Wait here,' he instructed. He stood up and headed back inside.

Yardley shivered in the cool breeze, realizing how little she was wearing. When Simon had disappeared into the clubhouse, she'd assumed he'd gone after her coat so he could take her home. Some date she was, breaking into tears over a stupid plaque. He was probably sorry he'd forced her to come. She should have

95

gloated over that, but she felt only empty. It was such a beautiful autumn night.

Purely and simply, she missed Granddad. Maybe Simon couldn't understand that. He acted such a tough guy, he probably didn't know what needing and depending on anyone was like.

A warm, strong hand lit on her cold shoulder. 'Come on, let's go for a walk.' She looked up and found Simon standing over her. In one hand, he swung a bottle of Jack Daniel's by its neck.

She knew she should make some excuse about going home, but she didn't want to. All she'd done since she'd come back to town was spend long hours in the offices of Kittridge Collectibles and longer ones rattling around in that big empty house.

And as infuriating as Simon could be, something about him fascinated her. Besides, he seemed a little gentler tonight, more approachable. Almost as if he regretted forcing her to accompany him tonight.

Nothing could justify being so reckless as to stroll across an unlit, deserted golf course with him and a bottle of liquor. But she knew he wasn't the kind of man who would physically hurt a woman. She'd sensed his restraint even as he'd bullied her at his house. How much he'd hate her knowing this struck her suddenly. She refused to give him the satisfaction of declining.

Besides, this might be the perfect opportunity to appeal to him to return her mold.

She got up, falling in step at his side as they set out across the endless darkness of the deserted golf course. Strains of music from inside followed them through the night.

'Should have brought our clubs,' she noted.

'I don't own any. Golf's about as exciting as checkers,' Simon retorted, uncapping the bottle and raising it to his lips. Lowering it, he wiped the mouth of the bottle with the heel of his palm and handed it to her.

Yardley faltered as she reached to take it.

'You'll feel better,' he predicted. 'You seem to be in the mood for venting. So go on. Nobody out here but me and the woodchucks. Or are you afraid of getting too relaxed in my presence?'

Yardley swilled the warming liquor. 'I'm not afraid of you. You're not as tough as you pretend. Granddad didn't teach me how to sculpt figurines, but he did teach me things he neglected to tell you. It's not the game, Mr Blye, it's the wheeling and dealing on the course he enjoyed. I suppose you like football.'

'And baseball.' He relieved her of the bottle and took a long drink. 'Jarred wasn't interested in my succeeding. Teaching me his craft fueled his ego, and that was the only reason he gave me the time of day.'

'For someone opposed to all he was and all he did, you try awful hard to be like him.'

She felt the scorching recrimination of dark eyes aimed at her.

'People who don't take control of their lives end up with nothing. Either you struggle for what you want or you accept what you get and settle for it. That's what life is all about, babe. I bet you've never had to fight for anything.'

'Oh yeah, I had it all. Except what I really wanted.'

Simon handed the bottle back to her. Yardley hesitated. He was challenging her to keep up with him on his own terms. She took another drink. It went down easier than the first.

'Shetland pony?'

'I wanted to be like the other kids – ride my bike downtown, go to the carnival. My grandparents wouldn't let me act like any ordinary kid. If you knew how many times I heard I had to "behave like a Kittridge", that I couldn't be friends with someone I liked because their family wasn't at the proper social level . . .'

'You let them pick your friends?'

'I needed their approval. I hardly remembered my mom, she died when I was younger, and my father was always busy trying to prove to Granddad he could be a success without working for Kittridge Collectibles. Dad did try working for Granddad, but he was never happy. Then Dad remarried. His wife, Francesca, was always good to me, but she and I never pretended to be mother and daughter. My real family was here in Kittridge. With Granddad and Mimi, I always felt I belonged.'

Simon took another drink but held on to the bottle.

Absently, she pried it from his hands. 'I don't like being set apart from everybody else. It's a lonely place. That's why I moved to Boston. I thought things would be different there. Tell me, Mr Blye, now that you've gotten what you thought you wanted, are you enjoying your new status as much as you expected? Or do you find it incredibly boring?'

Simon reached the edge of a deep sand trap. 'When I'm bored, I redirect my attention.'

'Don't you get tired of being bitter?'

'Don't you get tired of trying to please everyone but yourself?'

She didn't answer. He stepped down into the bunker. 'Almost like the beach,' he mused. 'As close to one as we'll get in Kittridge.' He sat down in the sand.

Yardley stood at the edge of the sand trap, gaping at him. He couldn't be drunk yet, so he must be mad.

Resting his back against the wall of the trap, he looked up at her.

'Come on, Yardley. Grandma's not watching. Be a little naughty.'

She stepped carefully into the bunker, sliding down in the loose sand. Simon watched her with amusement but did not move to help. She sat beside him, careful to leave a full foot of ground between herself and him, then leaned back on her palms and stretched her legs out in front of her and crossed them.

'We'll ruin our clothes.'

'Send me your cleaning bill. It's actually peaceful down here. Shuts out the rest of the country club.'

'You work hard at that, don't you, shutting people out?'

'I spent a lot of time dreaming about having my own company when it seemed so far out of reach it was impossible. I promised myself a long time ago I was never going to be in a position where someone else was going to determine the direction of my life.'

'Don't you ever stop fighting? Don't you get tired of it?'

'No.'

'So you must understand then how I feel about what you're trying to do to my company.'

'I could bankrupt Kittridge Collectibles and you'd never miss a meal.'

'You could not sell the copycat figurines and never miss a meal,' she retorted.

Simon sighed heavily. 'You're an enchanting woman, despite your family background and your sordid criminal past,' he told her. 'I could give you the mold, but as I've already explained, my family was cheated out of it to begin with. Why in hell should I give it to anybody?"

Yardley leaned forward, biting her lip and trying not to wonder too much whether he truly thought her enchanting. 'If you want money for it – '

'You can be as insulting as Jarred was. I don't want your money, Yardley.'

She shivered. He raised his fingertips to her bare shoulder, drawing a blunt line over its slope. 'You've got goosebumps,' he observed. 'Why didn't you say you were cold?'

Shedding his jacket, he draped it over his shoulders. His unexpected chivalry touched her more than it should have. She suspected

Simon would know how to treat a woman properly, if he ever found one who made him want to be good to her.

'I didn't expect you to give up your jacket.'

He slanted a sly grin at her. 'You can't keep it.'

She smiled back almost shyly, a warmth bubbling inside her that had nothing to do with the whiskey. Maybe he was wicked, but she enjoyed the challenge of figuring him out.

'So was the poor little rich girl happy in Boston?' he asked.

'No,' Yardley replied, surprised how little thought her answer required. No, in Boston, she'd realized only how foolish she could be when left on her own. She'd been like a canary let out of a cage, a domesticated creature incapable of fending for itself, one who would have fared better within the protective confines of its cage. 'I should have come back sooner, before Granddad died. I visited a few times, and he was always worse. I think I stayed away more than I had to because I couldn't bear to watch him deteriorate. The way he died, well, it was a hard way to go. Mimi . . . she had to witness it all.'

Simon put his arm around her and pulled her closer to his side. It was a sweet, friendly gesture, and Yardley rested her head against his side, forgetting briefly who he was and what he represented. He felt so strong and good. She envied the power he exuded.

And she was a little tipsy – the world had grown fuzzy around the edges.

'And now you're flogging yourself with guilt over that.'

'My family needed me, and I made excuses.'

'You're not responsible for anybody but yourself, babe. I figured that out long ago.'

'If you hated my grandfather so much, how could you stand working in the studio with him day after day?'

Simon was silent for a long moment. 'Sometimes I forgot who he was. Sometimes I almost found myself liking him. But then I remembered.'

'You let him down too, you know. He was disappointed my father wouldn't come into the business with him. He was grooming you to work for him, then you turned around and refused him. Don't you know how much that hurt him?'

Simon brushed his hair back. 'Excuse my lack of tears. A limited opportunity at best. I'd never have been granted any real responsibility. I'd learned all I need to know from him.'

'You used him.'

He gave her a long, hard glare that made her heart clench. 'And you Kittridges are such experts at that. He intended to use me, place me where I could do him the most good without threatening his control, his authority. I wouldn't stay where he wanted me, and that infuriated him. What I don't understand is why Mimi sent you to try to steal the mold. Seems she could have hired a professional instead of sending her beloved granddaughter.'

'Yeah, some lug who would drop the mold.' She froze, realizing what she'd confessed.

'Hmmm. I didn't think you came up with that crazy stunt on your own. Aren't you in the least offended that your dear grandmother would put you up to a robbery?'

'She's lost her husband, and she's struggling to preserve the reputation of the company he built.'

Simon chortled. 'Clawing to hang on to the family fortune, you mean.'

'I can't explain loyalty to you if you've never felt any. And the burglary wasn't her idea, it was mine. Just leave her out of this. You and I have settled our score now, haven't we?'

Simon gave her a daunting glance, slowly rubbing his jaw.

Yardley shifted away from him. 'I could teach you how to play golf,' she volunteered. 'You really should learn if you intend to be king of Kittridge.'

Simon laughed. 'Kittridge is only a start. There's a big world out there. Kind of you to offer, but I just can't see myself pretending to be Arnold Palmer.'

'I thought you said you had an imagination.'

'Fine. You give me golf lessons, and I can teach you how to climb a fence.'

She shot him a caustic look.

He ignored it. 'When I was a kid, I'd stand outside the fence and think this was some magical place, like Disney World. A jail with the prisoners locked out instead of in. My little brother and I used to comb through the fields across the pond and collect lost golf balls, sell them back to the guy in the clubhouse, who paid us squat, but I'm sure made a killing selling them back to their rightful owners.'

'I didn't know you had a brother.'

He snorted. 'I still do, somewhere. I haven't seen Glenn since the night my mother left with him.'

'Your mother took him away?'

He hesitated so long, she wondered whether he was going to answer at all. Then he shrugged. 'Dad and I woke up one morning and they were gone.'

Yardley leaned back to gape at him. 'Just like that?'

'I suppose Dad must have sensed it coming. I didn't. She left a note telling my Dad she'd always love him but she couldn't take scraping by any more. He never let me see the note, he just told me what it said.'

'Why did she take your brother?'

He shrugged. 'While leaving me behind? You can say it. Not exactly a slant I've never considered before. I don't suppose I'll ever know. If she tried to explain, my Dad never would tell me. Sometimes I think she said why and Dad's trying to protect me by keeping her note from me. You know, if she'd just said, "I've had it, *adios*," Dad would have gotten over it. It was that "I'll always love you" jab that ate at him. He was sucker enough to believe it. Hell, he still believes it. To this day, he's never really given up hoping she'd come back.'

Even through the darkness, Yardley read the pain in his eyes. Her heart wrenched, and she understood why Simon was so hard and bitter and afraid to care about anything beyond his control. She ached for the little boy who'd awoken one morning and found his family, his whole life shattered.

'It must have hurt very much to feel so betrayed.'

Simon did not meet her glance. 'I scarcely think about it.'

She pressed her palm against his chest. 'She left you because you're strong. She probably had no job, no real place to go . . .'

Simon stared off into the distance. 'You say you can't make excuses for your grandfather, and yet you're making them for a woman you've never met. Stop consoling me, please. I shouldn't have told you this. I don't know why I did.'

Yardley placed a finger across his lips. Reluctantly, he shifted his glance to settle on her face, his eyes searching hers. She saw past the insolence into his confusion and deeply buried pain.

Probing past all the anger and arrogance, she saw a man who was capable of feeling far too much and far too deeply for his own comfort. He had endured the ultimate betrayal and had forever closed himself off to any feeling opening him to vulnerability.

She raised her hands to his cheeks, liking the roughened feel of them against her palms. Rising up on her knees, she ignored all rational caution and leaned forward to swing her mouth up to meet his.

CHAPTER 5

Yardley was as unprepared for the urgent crush of hot, hard lips bearing down on hers as she was for the surge of raw, liquid heat flooding through her. Devouring her lips, Simon pulled her to him, his hands searing her torso like irons. He tasted spicy and wild.

Shameless and forgetting all caution, she moved her lips against his with an insistence paralleling his own, as though she could never get her fill of his exotic, intriguing taste. He was as male and commanding as he'd always appeared to her, and the contact overpowered her senses. Simon raised a hand to cradle the back of her head, as though she might have tried to pull away. Her hands clasped his rough jaws.

He pried her lips open with his, filling her mouth with his probing tongue, tickling the roof of her mouth with its whiskey-tart tip and licking it against her own. Starbursts of giddy sensation exploded inside her.

Easing farther down in the sand and taking her with him, he pulled her body across his chest. The jacket he'd draped over her shoulders fell aside, but at the moment she wasn't lacking for body heat. Sprawled across him, she felt every hard muscle, tense and coiled. His hips arched, grinding into hers. Feeling the evidence of his immediate arousal both frightened and excited her. As he continued kissing her senseless, she longed to feel his skin against hers.

Her breasts ached and strained beneath the delicate fabric of her dress. Simon plunged a hand inside her bodice, capturing one mound in his hand. Yardley whimpered as his fingers folded over her sensitive skin. He massaged it so masterfully he might have been shaping clay. Yardley shivered at the exquisite pleasure radiating through her chest.

She closed her eyes, delighting in the sensations, molding herself against him. He felt so damn good.

Still kneading her breast, Simon broke off the long kiss.

'Yardley?' She heard her own name whispered in the night air.

She opened her eyes and found herself looking down into his dark ones, glazed now in a way she understood. The corners of his lips were curled into a faint smile conveying an astonishing tenderness. The birthmark to one side accented this impression. With one look he promised her something beyond all reason, something his actions and words contradicted. Yardley knew that surrendering to him could be the most reckless action of her life. But her instinct, what she felt in her heart, ran strong.

She wanted Simon Blye in the most intimate, animal way. She had wanted him like this since she had been too young to express it, even to herself. Did she dare entrust herself to a man who professed nothing but contempt for her? He'd told her he hated her and her family; why couldn't she believe him?

Maybe in her own way she was as stubborn and idiotic as he was.

She drew in a deep breath, her eyes held captive by his. She suddenly realized she was returning his intimate smile with one of her own.

Apparently, he wasn't inclined to give her a lot of time to make up her mind. Reaching for her shoulder, skating his fingertips across its smooth slope, he pushed aside her dress strap, then freed her breast from its confines and bared it to the moonlight.

'No bra, sweetheart?' he asked, rubbing her hardened nipple beneath his thumb. 'Living dangerously, are we?' Yardley's lower regions softened like wet clay and she reflexively pushed her thighs against his. Simon raised one leg, wedging it between hers, forcing them apart. His leg muscles pressed tantalizingly against her feminine core as he continued stroking her nipple. A faint mewing sounded, and Yardley realized it had come from her.

'Oh, lord, but you're soft,' he murmured. 'Like I always thought you would be.'

Only fleetingly did Yardley comprehend his admission. Her world was growing increasingly dim and feverish. Until tonight, she'd believed she'd experienced passion and was, in every way, a woman. Never had she been so aroused as this.

Planting his hands just below her bosom, he hoisted her easily, sliding her above him, then bringing his mouth up beneath the bud he'd been so thoroughly caressing.

A scream of delight caught in Yardley's throat as he snapped his mouth up to capture it, nipping with a surprising, precarious gentleness to evoke sensations new and intriguing and irresistible. His lips were as ravenous as they had been against her mouth.

Suspended in what felt like mid-air by his strong arms, she squirmed in his grasp, burning for more. She planted her hands on his shoulders. He suckled her mercilessly, and warm fluid flowed between her legs. His tongue teased the tip of her nipple, and she cried softly from the intensity.

He kissed the fleshy part of her breast, then lowered her back down to rest her chest across his own. 'Shhh,' he murmured. She started to remember they were out in the middle of the golf course with Kittridge's refined movers and shakers in a building several hundred yards away. She should have worried about their being discovered. The prospect loomed vaguely in the recesses of her mind. They. She and Simon . . .

Then he took her lips between his again and not much of anything mattered except this urgent need she hadn't known she harbored. The rest of the world melted away.

When he rolled them sideways, it seemed the most natural progression in the world. The sand shifted beneath her. Her body dug deeper into the soft earth as he covered her body with his own.

His hardened manhood poked at her belly through his trousers. She looked up into his dark eyes and felt the moist heat between her legs. She saw her own naked breasts bleached pure white by the moonlight.

Never in her life had she been so carried away by passion that she lost all reason. Simon was staring down at her with a jarring intensity.

She had no doubt he intended to make love to her. She was neither young enough nor naïve enough not to believe anything less was going to happen here. And for a reason she couldn't define, she needed this.

Idiot! She suddenly snapped.

'I can't,' she asserted through her fog, her voice so low and raspy she scarcely recognized it. 'There's no protection.'

'No. No. I have it.' Like a magician, he produced a foil square in his palm. For all Yardley knew, he'd pulled the condom out of his sleeve. At the moment, his having it mattered more than where it had come from.

He leaned back, trailing his hands across her chest and tummy as he moved, then tucking both hands under the hem of her dress and scooting it up around her waist.

The night breeze played against her skin through her thin panty hose. Yardley watched him and drew in a sharp breath. There was no pretense left.

Simon made short work of his belt and zipper, shedding trousers and boxers in one swoop. Yardley watched as his swollen member sprang free. Raising up, she reached out and wrapped one hand around it. It moved and stiffened yet more in her palm.

Simon groaned. Yardley began rotating her hand, but he reached down and politely disengaged it.

Taking this as a rebuff, Yardley frowned.

Looming over her, Simon grasped her ankles, splaying her her legs and pinning them apart with his own. He planted a palm on the flat of her belly, and she felt herself softening down lower. He massaged leisurely, then wrestled down the panty part of her hose. Yardley obligingly raised her hips and tugged at the waistband.

Simon stroked the insides of her legs, skimming the smooth expanse of delicate skin, working her with the skilful, patient hands of a sculptor. Her skin quivered beneath his touch, each stroke a little harder, a little longer, a little higher.

Yardley grew mad with fever. She forgot everything except the quiet night, the cool air, and a burning need only Simon could sate.

Without warning, he dipped his finger into her wet core. She quivered.

'Good God, Yardley.' Slowly, he moved inside her. She bubbled from within, gripped by pleasure beyond endurance. Her fingers raked the sand.

His thumb ruffled her patch of kinky yellow curls. Throbbing at her core, she sobbed as he lightly touched the source of her distress.

Yardley buckled beneath him as unendurable fire flashed through her, ripping her apart. His hands were hard as leather against her fragile femininity. Yet he gauged his movements as carefully as if she were made of porcelain.

She suddenly understood the extent of her vulnerability, and despite the power she'd given him, his immediate concern was her pleasure.

He leaned down closer, his breath hitting her skin in hot puffs.

'Hold on, babe,' he whispered, stroking her faster.

At last, she gave in to him and all the wicked sensations he'd stirred inside her. The world exploded and with a tortured cry, she writhed mindlessly as spasm after spasm shattered her from within.

Simon held firm to her, but wrapped one arm around her shoulders to clasp her to him. Yardley gradually grew aware of the distant music, the cool air, being sandwiched between Simon and the sand.

Something inside her had changed forever. Acknowledging that, she almost felt afraid, but it was too late for fear. Why did she care so much about understanding him?

Simon linked himself inside her, and Yardley gasped as the fire she'd thought was extinguished raged anew.

Simon's mouth dropped over hers, claiming her lips again. Each thrust of his hips pushed her a little farther beyond herself, and she threaded her fingers through his thick hair, arching her hips to meet his.

Her flesh clamped around him, and a low growl sounded from his throat.

He wedged one hand between their kissing bellies, pressing it lower until he was stroking between her legs.

A current shot through her, and she twisted beneath him, racked with pleasure beyond any she'd imagined.

'You're not through yet, babe,' he whispered, meeting her throes with deeper thrusts. Yardley pushed harder against him, the hot, unexpected rush of release draining her.

Simon shuddered into his own wrenching release, grinding his taut muscles against her and clinging to her.

Everything went black and silent and still.

Yardley opened her eyes, aware of Simon's weight over her, of the ragged rise and fall of his chest as he breathed, of him still nestled between her legs.

What have I done?

Simon raised his dark head off her shoulder to look at her. She caught the worry in his eyes and wondered whether his thoughts mirrored her own.

Oh, God, what now?

Simon brushed her cheek with the backs of his fingers. 'You're exquisitely beautiful,' he said, his voice low.

Yardley swallowed hard. She suddenly felt shy, for Pete's sake, and the position she was in was anything but modest. Dazed and drained, she doubted she could have moved. Her body was thoroughly satiated and peaceful, but her brain was starting to kick in.

Awkwardly, she struggled to yank her dress up to cover her exposed breasts.

Simon brought his hand up to assist her. Then, propping himself up on his hands as though he were doing push-ups, he disengaged himself.

Yardley reached for her hose, quickly pulling them up.

She had no idea what to say to Simon, so she waited for him to speak first. The distant music reverberated in the air between them.

The sound of other voices caught her attention. She rolled over, raising her head to peer over the rim of the sand-trap, but Simon roped an arm around her back and pressed her down.

'Stay low. The dance is letting out,' he informed her in a hard whisper.

The sound of conversations, car doors slamming and engines revving brought home the reality of what she'd done. Now, she was condemned to hiding out here with Simon until the last of the townspeople went home. Her hair and clothes were infiltrated with gritty sand, and long strands had come free from her neatly styled hair.

Straightening her clothes as best she could, she reached for Simon's jacket, tossing it again over her shoulders because she now felt cold. Huddling inside, it, she finally glanced over at silent Simon. *God, what he must think of me now? Bunny rabbits show more restraint.*

Mercifully, he'd retrieved his trousers and was fully dressed except for the jacket. He was sitting across from her, stretched out across the sand, staring at her and straightening his bow tie.

Yardley tensed under his silent scrutiny, waiting for him to make some caustic remark capable of ripping her heart in two. She recognized that her alarming need for him ran deeper than a physical craving. What happened now depended on how much, if anything, he was willing to give.

'Are you waiting for an apology?' he asked finally.

She swept loose hair out of her face and raised her head, determined to maintain her last shred of dignity.

'You don't have to say anything.'

'Really? You are an unusual woman, then, Yardley.'

She leveled her gaze at him. 'I never meant for this to happen.'

'Yet you're assuming I did?'

'You don't feel the least bit smug about it?'

He slunk over closer to her. 'Smug? I feel like I've been run over by a train and am trying to figure out what hit me. I'm so unsure as to my opinion, I'm wondering if we might try it again.'

She shrank back. 'Stay away from me. I can't think properly if you don't.'

'Maybe you're thinking too much. Fact is, we seem pretty compatible in this one respect.'

Yardley felt her face heat. 'I don't jump into bed with just anyone. Normally.'

Simon's expression tightened. 'The theory being I would now assume you did?'

'That's not what I meant.'

'Hard as this may be for you to believe, I am particular about whom I make love to.'

'And now you've gotten back at my grandfather.'

'Dammit. Your grandfather has nothing to do with what just happened between you and me.'

Yardley stiffed. 'What's that supposed to mean?'

His dark eyes narrowed. 'I thought it meant this was about a man and a woman enjoying each other. Or is this another ploy to try to get the mold?'

Her mouth dropped open in horror. She wanted to slap him.

'If that's what this was all about to you, Mr Blye, I feel sorry for you. You'll never trust anything or anybody. And you've gotten more than you bargained for tonight, so you can thrive on your so-called victory now. You'd better hurry home and make sure the precious mold is safe. I wouldn't dream of keeping you from your chance to publicly humiliate my family and our business.'

'Maybe you could call me by my first name now.'

She clasped a hand to her forehead. 'I must have been mad to delude myself that this would mean anything to you beyond a notch on your belt.'

'Why would you give yourself to a man whom you have such a low opinion of?'

Her expression slackened. 'You won't believe me.'

'Try it.'

'Because I know what it's like to be lonely.'

'I never said I was lonely.'

'I can read it in you like a mirror. You put up high fences all around you, just like the ones other people have built around me all my life.'

He swept his hair back with a brush of his hand. His eyes were mocking. 'Am I supposed to believe my welfare concerns you?'

'Actually, I don't give a damn what you're willing to believe. I'm going home.'

Without thinking, she stood. Fortunately, the clubhouse was dark, the parking lot deserted except for Simon's Jag. Too late, she realized that if Simon had wanted to create a scandal, he would have let her jump up out of the sand trap while everyone was leaving. Drawing his jacket around her like a cloak, she marched toward the building.

'Wait, Yardley!' he called. 'You can't walk!'

'Watch me!' She did not look back. Damn him anyway. Arrogant bastard.

Aware of her disheveled appearance, she walked past the clubhouse, relieved to find the front gate unlocked, and headed home at a brisk pace. The cold seeped through his jacket, and as she bunched the lapels together, she realized she should have given it back. Pride and the cold prevented her from going back and returning it. She'd have it cleaned and sent to his house later. Her high heels kept skidding and wobbling on the loose gravel in the parking lot, threatening to fly out from under her.

'Come back here, Yardley!' he called through the night.

When she failed to turn around she heard a string of low curses being muttered. For a moment, she feared he would come after her. She knew all too well that he was capable of overpowering her. Not hearing any rush of footsteps behind her, she breathed easier. She heard a car door slam.

When she reached the road, she spotted the headlights of a slow-moving car following her at a distance. She knew it was Simon. He did not catch up with her and beg her to get in his car.

Her fury kept her moving and she staved off a threatening swell of tears, blinking them back. After her affair with Grant back in Boston, she should have known better than to succumb to Simon's brute masculinity. She'd ignored all the warning signs in Grant, the mood swings, the cold temper, and followed her physical attraction into his bed.

Grant had happily relieved her of her virginity, and Yardley had believed she was in love with him. But bed was the only place where they could get along. It had taken her far too long to learn he wasn't interested in changing and, while he enjoyed having her around, commitment was the last thing on his agenda.

Was she some insatiable whore, that she couldn't control her lust when she found a man who turned her on, lost all sense of judgement? Simon Blye was crude and cruel and despicable, but all that had evaporated from her mind when he'd kissed her. When she'd kissed him. Oh, hell.

She and Grant hadn't even been all that good together in bed, but until tonight she hadn't been experienced enough to know that. Grant had never made her see stars scattering inside her head as Simon had tonight. Grant had never left her feeling as relaxed and weak as a dishrag.

Her body perking with fresh arousal, she pushed the memory away. Good grief, she wasn't ever going to repeat this mistake.

Silently, she acknowledged that she'd always been lonely. She'd lost her mother, and in essence her father had left her as well. Even her own sister came from a family she only vaguely belonged to. Mimi and Granddad had showered her with love but kept her set apart from everyone else. And that feeling of watching from the sidelines had never really left her. She masked her emptiness with a show of independence but it never went away. And perhaps that gnawing hollowness had driven her to Grant and now to Simon.

The least likely man to fill it. *The galaxies collide between us and all he's thinking of is safeguarding the stupid mold?* She folded her arms across her chest, huddling inside his jacket. His accusation stung all the more because it contained a shred of truth. She had hoped to persuade him to relinquish the mold. But she hadn't made love with him in hopes of accomplishing that. How could even he think she would? It would serve him right if someone did steal it from him.

When she finally reached the long drive leading to Mimi's house, the Jag shot past her and disappeared into the night.

Good riddance, she thought. Maybe after a long, hot bath she'd be able to sleep tonight. Thank God Mimi was in New York.

Seeing a light on inside the house, as well as the porch light, Yardley remembered Serena. Surely her sister hadn't waited up for her?

As she reached to retrieve her house key, she realized she'd left her coat and pocketbook checked in at the country club. While she was confident they'd be kept safely until morning, she could have kicked herself. How was she going to explain running off from the dance and leaving her belongings behind?

And now she was going to have to ring the bell and come up with something to tell Serena.

Miserably, she climbed the porch steps and pulled Simon's jacket off her, folding it in half and draping it over one arm. She tried to push her loose hair back into place and brush sand off her dress and skin.

She rang the bell, then stood shivering as she waited for Serena to answer.

Serena shuffled to the door dressed in red fuzzy slippers and an oversized flannel get-up that looked suspiciously like a man's pyjamas.

As she pulled the door open, she looked Yardley up and down, her smile broadening.

'Have a good time?' she asked.

'I don't want to talk about it.'

'You look like you were mud-wrestling and lost.'

Flashing a caustic look, Yardley pushed past her, tossing Simon's jacket on the first chair she passed.

'Come on, Yardley, I've been waiting here all night to hear how Cinderella enjoyed the ball. Casey's sound asleep upstairs, and I made us a pot of tea and everything.'

She steered Yardley toward the kitchen.

'You hate tea,' Yardley muttered.

'I would have made us something to eat. Doesn't Mimi keep groceries in the house any more?'

Yardley frowned at her sister, wondering why she didn't just take her car to the supermarket and buy what she wanted, then she realized Serrie must be broke again. What else would have brought her here?

'We'll go shopping tomorrow and pick up some groceries,' Yardley promised.

Serena had the teapot, cups and saucers, spoons, and sugar bowl arranged on the kitchen table. She pulled out a chair and urged Yardley to sit.

'I didn't hear Simon's car pull up,' Serena noted. 'Nice wheels, huh?'

Yardley stared blankly at the china teapot. Mimi would have strangled Serena for using it.

'I walked home,' Yardley confessed.

'From the country club? And Simon let you? Where was he?'

'I don't care.'

'Don't tell me you two started fighting over that useless mold again.'

Yardley laughed bitterly. 'I could handle that.'

With a sudden gasp, Serena set the teapot down on the table without pouring a drop of tea. She set a hand on Yardley's shoulder.

'Why, you and he made love, didn't you?' Her voice rippled with incredulous admiration. 'I underestimated you, Sis.'

Yardley dropped her head into her hands on the tabletop and finally allowed herself to crumple like a wad of foil. 'I'm surely a genius. A man committed to destroying my family catches me breaking into his house and blackmails me into accompanying him to a dance where I sweeten his prize with some hot and heavy sex in the sand trap.'

Serena, standing over her, drew in a sharp breath.

'You, Yardley? Upstanding, conservative. . .'

'Shocking, isn't it? God, Serrie. I don't want to believe it myself.'

'It happened because you're so much like Granddad. You pretend you don't need anybody, that you're in control of everything. When you don't admit to what you need, it surfaces in strange ways. The man I saw here tonight could charm the pants off a vestal virgin. Sometimes two people are so overwhelmingly attracted to each other, restraint is impossible.'

'Oh, please. I'm old enough to know better. Simon's the last man I have any business being with.'

'So when you least expected it, the passion you repressed sneaked up on you.'

'Thank you, Professor Kittridge.'

Serrie waved off Yardley's sarcasm. 'So you had a better time with him than you planned? The world hasn't ended. You did protect yourself, didn't you?'

Yardley nodded dully. 'He had a condom. I wish he hadn't. At least that would have forced us to stop. He must tuck them in his cuffs before he goes out at night.'

'Well, certain men should be required by law to do so. So maybe you'll feel uncomfortable over it for a while, but you will get over it.'

Yardley shook her head. 'No.'

'You're scaring me.'

The tears Yardley had been holding back so long poured out. 'I feel too much for him, Serena. When he's near me, I'm hypnotized. He's bitter and cruel and sarcastic, but I understand beyond what he's saying. Is that crazy or what?'

'Okay, he's good in bed, or in the *sand trap* at least. In the *sand trap*? And you like him. So why do never want to see him again?'

'He quickly reminded me he's incapable of caring about anyone except himself and getting back at this town and especially our family for everything that's gone wrong in his life. I've lost so much these past few months, I can't set myself up for any more heartbreak.'

Serena began clearing away the cups and saucers, pouring the untouched tea down the sink. She shrugged. 'So you don't have to ever see him again. No problem. Why don't you go soak in the tub while I clean up here?'

'I think I will. Thanks.'

The corners of Serena's lips turned upwards mischievously. 'There's just one thing I really want to know, Sis.'

'I'm afraid to ask.'

'How does he look right now?'

Yardley laughed lightly. 'Like a little boy who ruined his Sunday clothes romping in the sandbox. Goodnight, Serrie.'

'Goodnight.'

Realizing that if she could laugh about the incident she would eventually live through it, Yardley headed wearily up the stairs, trying to focus on a hot bath and a warm bed. But Simon stole into her thoughts. She wondered where he was and what he was doing. Was he thinking about her or had he already forgotten? What was it about him that made her so desperately need to tap into his thoughts and his heart – if he had one?

In his presence she grew as helpless as a moth drawn to a hot light bulb. Even now she felt filled with him, connected. As though he'd not only had her but had taken possession of her as well. She did not want to become one of his trophies.

Her only hope of self-preservation was to avoid him as though her survival depended on it.

CHAPTER 6

Yardley awoke to find the first light of morning filtering through the windows. Groggy and disorientated, she was seized by a fleeting panic, assuming she'd overslept and was going to get to the office late.

Her alarm subsided when she remembered today was Sunday, but an awareness that something in her life was off-kilter rippled through her. Miserably recalling last night, she rolled over and buried her face in the quilted pillow sham. She squeezed her eyes shut, trying to will away reality. How Simon Blye must be reveling in his victory this morning!

The chime of the doorbell from downstairs was followed by a sharp series of knocks. The bell. It had awoken her. What in the world . . .? Oh, gosh, had something happened to Mimi? She bolted to a sitting position.

Just as she was pushing a hand through her disheveled hair and reaching for her robe, she heard Casey's soft babbling from down the hall, and Serena rounded the doorframe, entering the bedroom with her son in her arms. She looked as sleepy as Yardley felt.

'Apparently you made quite an impression on your date last night. He's downstairs at the door.'

Yardley rubbed her forehead with her palm and furrowed her brow. 'No! Simon's here? Now?'

'I looked out the window and saw his car parked out front. No mistaking it. Why don't you go downstairs and show him the calendar? Or, better yet, the clock.'

Yardley stared up at the crystal light fixture. 'What could he want?'

'You, I'd imagine.'

The pounding grew louder.

'Answer the door, will you, Yardley? I doubt he's come to borrow sugar.'

'I don't want to see him.' Yardley glimpsed her reflection in the vanity mirror and gasped. 'Besides, my hair's sticking up like cat-tails.'

'And I, on the other hand, wake up looking like Cindy Crawford.' She indicated her baggy PJs and floppy slippers.

'Please, Serena.'

'Don't you owe it to the man to at least hear him out?'

'I owe him nothing. And nothing will undo what happened last night. I haven't a clue as to what to say to him. Serrie . . .'

Serena smiled slyly. 'Pity Mimi's not around . . . she'd send him on his way.'

Yardley cringed. 'Don't remind me.'

Serena dumped a cheerful Casey on top of Yardley's quilt and shuffled towards the doorway. With a playful grin, he scooted towards his drowsy aunt. 'You owe me, Yardley,' Serena muttered.

Yardley pulled Casey to her lap. 'Now that we're all up, I guess it's time for breakfast,' she told him.

'Cereal!' her nephew decreed.

'Hmm, eggs and toast might have to do it today, champ,' she reflected, remembering her promise to shop for groceries. In her rush to get off, Mimi must have forgotten Serena and Casey were coming. It wasn't like her to overlook stocking the cupboard with company due. But Mimi was still grieving, and Yardley realized she must make allowances for her grandmother's lapses.

And why was Serena here? Yardley wondered, realizing that she hadn't asked.

Yardley heard the front door creak open downstairs. Too curious not to eavesdrop, she grinned at Casey and gave him a conspiratorial 'shhh' sign with one finger across her mouth. Taking him by the hand, she helped him off the bed and slipped out into the hall, lurking at the top of the stairway.

Simon's voice, strong and compelling, jolted her. 'Sorry to wake you, Serena. I must see Yardley.'

Leaning forward, Yardley could just make him out in the doorframe, his tall, broad physique. He wore boots, jeans, and a black leather jacket, unzipped over a white knit shirt. A shock of his normally well-trained hair dipped over his forehead.

She glanced down at her plain pastel blue silk nightie and realized she had almost nothing on.

'She's still in bed,' Serena told him. 'Sunrise is a little early for us on Sunday.'

'I'll wait until she wakes up, then.'

Serena leaned against the door. 'Simon, she asked me to send you away. I'm sorry.'

The door swung open wider and Simon glanced up. Yardley froze, hugging Casey to her as Simon's sloe-black gaze settle on her. She felt pinned by lasers.

Without acknowledging her, Simon shifted his attention back to Serena. He picked up something off the porch and placed it in her arms. 'Give these to her, will you?'

Yardley waited until she heard his car door slam and his engine start before she guided Casey downstairs with her, holding his hand.

Serena shrugged as she set Yardley's coat and pocketbook in the armchair. Shaking her head, Yardley clasped a hand to the top of it. 'How on earth did he manage to retrieve these so quickly? Oh, gosh, I still have his coat.'

'If he had immediate need for his wrinkled, dirty coat, he would have requested it.'

Yardley looked upwards. 'He brought my things back, and I wouldn't even go to the door. How stupid can I get? I presumed he was here because he was wild about me.'

'You didn't see his face when I told him you wouldn't see him, honey. He could have sent a messenger over with your things if all he wanted to do was return them.'

'I suppose.'

'Next time you want to hurt someone's feelings, do it yourself instead of asking me. You get more like Mimi every day.'

'I'm not the villain here. Simon has no feelings.'

'Okay, keep telling yourself that. Maybe it's just a dandy excuse to deny your own. If Simon Blye knocked at my door, I'd definitely seize the day.'

'Don't you ever plan anything, Serrie?' Yardley blurted, glancing pointedly at her nephew. 'Life isn't as simple as you make it sound.'

Serena flashed her a wounded look. 'Sometimes I don't think I even know you, Yardley. You're so much like Granddad and Mimi. No wonder Dad could never get close to you. You could call him once in a while, you know.'

'Phone lines have dials on both ends. Look, I'm sorry about what I said. I didn't mean it.'

'You did. For the same reason Mimi tells people I'm divorced.'

'She does it to protect you and Casey. Why do you always judge her so harshly? By the way, why are you here?'

Serena backed off and shrugged. 'Factory I was working at closed down.'

'Look, now that you're here, why don't you stay? I'll find a place for you at Kittridge Collectibles. We'll hire Casey a good nanny and arrange your hours so you can go back to school.'

'Stay in Kittridge? No way, but thanks for mapping out my life.'

'Casey needs a stable home. What kind of life will he have drifting from town to town?'

'Casey and I do fine. Do you really think I'd be happy here – Mimi watching my every move, worrying I'll embarrass her again and working at some menial job while you run our grandfather's company?'

Yardley's hand curled around the edge of the piano. She'd rushed back here to keep the family business on track, never stopping to consider where her sister fitted into the picture. 'Oh, Serena, I'm sorry. Everybody always assumed you didn't care about Kittridge Collectibles.'

'This family's always making assumptions about me and what I want.'

'You're right Serena. It was unfair for Granddad to leave you out, for whatever reason. I'm sure he was thinking about the company rather than us. I'll go to an attorney tomorrow and arrange a three-way partnership so you'll get your share of the profits.'

'It wouldn't be fair for me to take a free ride while you're running the company. And Mimi would have heart failure.'

'Give her a break, Serena. What do you want from her?'

'A little grandmotherliness.'

Yardley shook her head. 'Mimi's never been one to wear an apron and bake chocolate chip cookies. My gosh, Serena, you disappear for months on end without even telling anyone where you and Casey are. You show up out of the blue and expect her to hire a brass band when she's probably worn out from worrying herself sick about you?'

Serena mustered a weak smile. 'Let's not fight. I really can't stay.'

'Where will you go?'

Serena shrugged. 'When the time comes, I'll know.'

'Don't be in any big hurry, okay? It's great having you and Casey here.'

Serena smiled softly. 'This isn't the healthiest place for you to be. If you have to stay in Kittridge, at least get a house of your own.'

Yardley shook her head. 'I will. I just can't leave Mimi here alone right now.'

'She's never going to let you leave. She's already put you up to committing a crime, for cripes' sake!'

'I thought we weren't going to argue any more.'

Serena sighed heavily. 'I know we always danced around talking about Casey's dad, and Mimi assumes he was a wino. Things didn't go as we'd planned, but I don't regret loving him. It was the best time of my life. I still do love him.'

Yardley studied her sister intently. 'Then why aren't you with him?'

Serena glanced out the window. 'Things happen.' She paused. 'Simon looked real tired, Yardley. The man definitely has something on his mind.'

'Gloating, no doubt.'

'He didn't look particularly cocky. Granddad always assumed everybody had ulterior motives rather than just feeling things. I hope you're not like him in that respect.'

Yardley stiffened. 'I let one man hurt me back in Boston. I'm not going to let that happen again. I was hoping here I could find a sincere, settled kind of man.'

'One who puts on his chef's hat and barbecue apron and grills steaks on the patio? He would bore you into an early grave. You look so hard to find the good in people, sometimes you skim over glaring faults. Something about Simon got to you, Yardley, admit it. I'm not telling you to marry him this afternoon and have his kids.'

Yardley averted her sister's gaze. Had Simon channeled the very determination that pitted him against her own family in another direction, she would have found it admirable. She'd never known a man who had pushed so hard to come so far. What she sensed was good and noble in him, he hid beneath his arrogance, probably dismissing his own honor as a weakness. Just like Granddad.

Or maybe her instincts were wrong. Maybe she was seeing more than was there to justify her knockout physical attraction to him.

She glanced up and found Serena studying her. 'Oh, Serrie,' she said, sinking into an armchair and tucking her legs beneath her. 'I want a house and a husband and kids. Normal things other people take for granted. Simon's consumed with conquering the world, starting with Kittridge Collectibles and Kittridge proper.'

'Just for argument's sake, suppose what happened last night confused him as much as it did you.'

'Believe me, he knew exactly what he was doing.'

'So did you, yet you hadn't planned on it either. It's called passion, Sis.'

Yardley groaned. 'Whose pyjamas are those anyway?'

Serena's glance dropped to her attire and she raised her eyebrows. 'Mine,' she clipped with uncharacteristic evasiveness, then scooped Casey up in her arms, nuzzling his neck and making him giggle. 'Come on, let's go rustle up some breakfast, cowboy.'

Yardley leaned over the handle of the increasingly heavy shopping cart as she pushed it through the aisles of the local Kroger's. Studying the shelves and mentally calculating the best buys, she periodically exchanged goofy faces with her nephew who sat facing her, his chubby hands curled around the cart's handle.

Shopping without a list was a new adventure, and with her concentration shattered, Yardley was impulsively picking up items and tossing them in the cart. After awakening so early, she was having difficulty thinking clearly this morning.

Following the initial burst of sunlight earlier, the day had turned gray and drizzly, the overcast sky suiting her mood perfectly. She was determined to convince her sister to stay. Dragging around the country in Serena's beat-up car wasn't much of a life for either of them. She couldn't understand why Serena was so opposed to staying in Kittridge. Especially after living in Boston, Kittridge seemed to Yardley the perfect place to settle down and raise a family. If she was ever to have one.

Mimi had plenty of room, and she needed her family around her right now. Yardley knew Granddad had left her half of Kittridge Collectibles because of her professional and business experience. No one had intended to exclude Serena. First thing in the morning, Yardley was going to have her attorney draw up papers to rectify that. When Mimi realized Serena deserved her share of the inheritance, she'd feel the same way.

'How old is your son?'

She looked up and found a tall sandy-haired woman in maroon windsuit smiling down at her and Casey. In her basket sat a blue-eyed, curly-haired doll in a smocked corduroy dress.

'Two. He's my nephew,' she explained, realizing that Serena had vanished. Glancing at the contents of the woman's cart, she fleetingly envied her the little girl as well as the man she was probably bringing home the Budweiser and pretzels for. 'Your daughter is lovely.'

'Thank you,' she said with the air of someone accustomed to repeatedly receiving the same compliment. She wound off down the aisle and left them alone.

Yardley shoved the cart under a long arch of honeycombed orange and black crêpe paper. A deep, recorded voice crackled a na-ha-ha. Casey swung his head around worriedly.

'Can you say commercialism?' Yardley asked jokingly, steering quickly past shelves dripping plastic sacks of Hallowe'en candy.

Well, gosh, he would be old enough this year to wear a costume and trick-or-treat at a few select places. She felt heartsick at the prospect of Serena leaving again with him, missing all these little milestones, not having him here for Christmas. But he was Serena's, not hers. She pulled the cart over to a rack of packaged costumes, where an older boy and girl were standing side-by-side, doing some serious browsing, handing packages back and forth.

Yardley felt a pang of emptiness, imagining their excitement over dressing up for a school Hallowe'en carnival, their mom sewing costumes and making candy apples. Why was she plagued by these sappy domestic images? She couldn't sew and had never made a candy apple in her life.

She just wanted all the little things she'd missed while growing up. She didn't blame anybody. Her mother had been sick for a long time before her death, and Dad just wasn't very good at that type of thing.

She touched her fingers to Casey's stubby little hand. God, he was so precious. She didn't care how he came to be, only that he was here for her to love. She wanted children of her own, scads of them. And to round out her perfect family, she had to fall in love with and marry the kind of man who would enjoy being a father and doing things around the house. Not a man who, like her own Dad, was busy chasing his dreams and proving himself.

She plucked a cellophane package containing a ghost costume off the rack and started reading the description.

'Yardley, guess what I found in the frozen foods,' Serena's voice broke through her thoughts.

'I was wondering where you'd disappeared to,' Yardley replied, still reading. 'Just toss it in the basket.'

Serena chuckled. 'Okay, then. Can you give me a hand?'

A sinking suspicion tightened Yardley's chest. She swung her head up. Serena stood beaming like a warrior returning with meat from the hunt, one hand on her prize from the freezer – a frowning Simon Blye.

Oh, God, she'd dragged him back here. By his expression, Yardley could tell he was flustered. Nice to see he was to that degree human.

Suddenly standing beside him after last night, smelling his sandalwood scent and reviving the memories she'd been fighting to push aside all morning, Yardley felt simultaneously hot and cold inside.

'Hello, Simon.' She greeted him guardedly.

He nodded. 'Yardley.'

'Thank you for bringing my things over this morning.'

'Sorry I woke you so early.'

Yardley studied his sharp features. His eyes were underscored by dark shadows. 'I should have given you your jacket. I didn't mean to walk off with it.'

'No problem. I'll get it when I come for dinner this evening.'

Yardley stepped backwards, her lips parting in shock and surprise. She swung an accusing gaze towards her sister. But no one was there. Serena, Casey and the buggy had quietly disappeared.

Unsettled, she looked back at Simon. 'Serena invited me. But I won't come unless you want me there. You surprise me, Yardley. I was beginning to think you were the kind of woman who could face up to anything.' Lowering his voice, he leaned closer. 'We can't pretend last night never happened, no matter how uncomfortable it makes us both.'

At his mention of last night, his dark eyes held hers, acknowledging what specific incident they both knew he was referring to. Yardley's chest constricted, her belly warming with fresh desire at just the memory of their passionate coupling on the golf course. Darn if her body wasn't craving him again.

'You expect me to believe you're troubled over it?'

'You're as quick as Jarred when it comes to assumptions. I got what I wanted and should go away now, is that your attitude? I do find that troubling. I do care that I've upset you so.'

'I can't explain last night,' she stated quietly. 'It should never have happened.'

He brushed a hand through his hair, then folded his arms. 'You're right. It shouldn't have happened. But it did.' He swung his gaze around the aisle, moving aside to allow a middle-aged woman in sweatsuit and tennis shoes to pass with her buggy. 'Blazes, can't we discuss this in private? Look, I'm not asking you for another round of golf. Your sister will be there to chaperon if you're afraid.'

Yardley bristled, her face burning. Some chaperon Serena would make; she'd probably

lock them in a bedroom together if the opportunity arose. Still, Yardley couldn't ignore his
challenge. She would prove, to him and herself,
that last night was a fluke and she could very
well resist him. 'Do you like pot roast?'

His magnificent smile stirred her heart.

'My absolute favorite.'

'We'll expect you around four, then. We eat
early on Sunday.'

'Later, then, Yardley.' His tone held a promise she wanted to ignore.

She watched him walk off down the aisle,
then went in search of her sister so she could
throttle her.

'This is insane,' Yardley fumed as she sat in the
kitchen entertaining Casey while her sister
efficiently basted the roast, shredded lettuce
and chopped vegetables for salad, then checked
the potatoes boiling on the stove. Serena might
not be able to balance her own checkbook, but
she was a whiz in the kitchen.

Serena shot her a sideways glance. 'You know
what they say about the way to a man's heart . . .'

Yardley dismissed the adage with a wave of her
hand. 'I'm telling you Simon Blye has no heart.'

'You honestly believe he's coming here for
food? Do me a favor. Look into his eyes the next

147

time he looks at you. Trust me, the man's besotted. You look terrific, by the way.'

'Thanks,' Yardley said distractedly. The rain had turned the weather cool, so she'd put on black velveteen leggings and a long, deep blue chenille sweater that set off her eyes. Her long hair was brushed loose over her shoulders. Definitely nothing low-cut or revealing to-night. 'Think I should light a fire?'

'Good idea.'

The damp gloom outside created an atmo-sphere of early winter darkness.

Yardley rose from her chair. 'You're great to do all this, Serrie. And you've been right all day, I do need to talk to him. It's really frightening to feel so much so fast for someone so obviously wrong. I need to work past it, and confronting him and my feelings is the only way.'

Serena waved the potato masher in her hand. 'Does he really terrify you so much, or is it Mimi's reaction you're dreading?'

'I'm a grown woman, Serena. Mimi doesn't dictate my social life.'

Serena snorted. 'Have you tried to have one since you've been back?'

'Well, no. There were lots of loose ends left to tie up over the business.'

'She's not going to like anyone she believes will

take you away from her now that she's got you back. And she's always felt threatened by Simon. Granddad was actually fond of him, but that summer they worked together, Mimi was constantly complaining that Granddad was wasting his time trying to teach Simon anything when he was likely to end up in jail making license plates. Remember that when everything hits the fan.'

'Serena, I agreed to see Simon tonight to settle what happened, not to start some wild affair with him.'

'That's a shame.'

Shaking her head, Yardley went to light the fire in the living room. She was determined not to let Simon get to her. He was a man accustomed to getting what he wanted. He'd already proven that last night. God help her if he desired more from her.

She lost herself in her thoughts, lighting the fire, setting the table in the dining room, keeping one eye on adventurous Casey.

When the doorbell rang, her heart wrenched. Standing to answer the door, she realized how anxious she was to see him, how she'd feared he wouldn't show up, and how she cared about him already so much more than she'd ever meant to.

CHAPTER 7

Simon tapped the sole of his shoe against the porch planks, half-expecting Jarred's ghost to spring out at him as he stared down the scarecrow seated in the rocker a few feet away. What in God's name was he doing here? He hadn't bargained on this: finding himself on Jarred Kittridge's doorstep.

The afternoon was dark and chilly and miserable. Yellow light beckoned through the windows of the house before him. Irresistible cooking aromas seeped through the walls. But he'd come not for warmth or food. He was standing here at Yardley's front door like some teenager on heat because Yardley Kittridge was the most incredible, intriguing woman he'd ever met, surpassing his imagination, and he couldn't let her get away. He wanted her in his arms, in his bed, wherever he might have her.

She'd always fascinated him. But he hadn't been prepared for the physical and emotional wallop she'd landed last night. No woman had ever felt so soft and totally feminine in his arms. No woman had ever depleted him so thoroughly, only to leave him mad for more of her. He wanted her as desperately as he wanted his success and his power and his money. That she was Jarred's granddaughter was an unfortunate twist of fate. But Jarred wasn't here to shuffle her away or keep him from her.

He hadn't meant to lose control last night. Normally, he possessed infinite patience, reserve. But once things got started, stopping hadn't occurred to him. And he'd expected she'd be as delectable as she looked, but he'd been totally unprepared for an experience transcending animal lust. She'd shaken him to his essence, and he'd been beyond dealing with it. Assaulted by a barrage of protective, tender, possessive feelings, he'd lashed out in self-defense. He'd latched on to an accusation about the mold like a drowning man clutching the side of a lifeboat.

Smoothing his hair back, he wondered whether he should leave now while he still could. Yardley saw far too deeply into him for his comfort. Her refusal to be daunted only fueled his desire for her. Instead of retreating, she fought back. He'd always considered his ideal woman one totally on his side, not one who would stick daggers in his back when he wasn't looking, and Yardley remained too loyal to her grandparents to be trusted, but for a short while last night he'd wanted to share everything inside himself with her. A dangerous notion at best.

An image popped into his mind. His mom, singing and smiling with her dark blunt-cut hair flying behind her as she coaxed him and Glenn into dancing with her. Even when there was scarcely any food on the table, she'd been able to create the illusion that they were all having a good time.

And then suddenly, she was gone and the house was silent, without the constant drone of the local rock station playing on her portable radio. He wondered if she was even still alive. If she was, he hoped she'd found a man who could buy her pretty dresses and take her out dancing in them every Saturday night. He remembered her in faded jeans and frayed sweaters.

He tried to forgive her for leaving, because he'd been too young to know exactly how things had been between his parents. He couldn't fathom what concerns might run through a woman's mind. But she never should have taken his little brother away from him. He couldn't get over that.

The door opened, and Simon snapped free of his thoughts to stare down into Yardley's lovely face. Her yellow hair shimmered under the light. Her blue eyes matched her sweater against her fair skin.

His loins clenched miserably just at the sight of her. All night and all day he'd been trying to talk himself out of wanting her again, and suddenly he realized how futile that notion was.

'Am I too early?' he asked, when she failed to speak.

'No, no. You're right on time.' She moved aside. 'Come on in, Simon.'

He liked the sound of his name from her lips, although she stumbled over it without warmth. He stepped inside and spotted Casey trailing at her heels. For protection, no doubt. The house felt warm and cozy with the combined scents of furniture polish, woodsmoke, and food mingling through its brightly lit interior. Still, despite the welcoming cushioned chairs, massive antiques and tasteful touches of wall sconces and needlework, he found it hard to shake the thought of invading Jarred Kittridge's castle. He'd always imagined the man living in some dark cave as ogres did.

Yardley stood gaping at him like a small bird facing a bobcat.

'Hello, Casey,' he greeted the toddler beside her. 'I brought you something.'

Interest flickered in Yardley's eyes. He winked at her and watched her face light with surprise. 'It's out on the porch. I'll be right back.'

He opened the door and retrieved the thing he'd set down in the chair, lugging in the huge pumpkin he'd brought. He felt ridiculous carrying it in. But his embarrassment evaporated as Casey's small eyes rounded, and he clapped with glee.

'Serena said you were into carving jack-o'-lanterns,' Simon told Yardley.

'I warned you about Serena. She talks too much.'

'Your sister's straightforwardness is refreshing, Yardley. I'll set this back outside for now.'

She raced to open the door for him.

He deposited the pumpkin near the door and found her waiting for him. 'I'm not good at apologies,' he said.

'It wasn't solely your fault.'

'I'm sorry for what I said, not for what we did.'

154

She pushed a strand of hair to one side. 'Make yourself comfortable, Simon. I've got to help Serena in the kitchen. Can I get you something to drink?'

So painfully polite. 'Nothing, thanks,' he said, stretching out in an armchair. He fully intended to keep his wits about him tonight.

The mouthwatering home cooked meal was wasted on him. All he could do was watch Yardley, admiring her graceful moments, her sweet expression whenever she tended to her nephew. Relaxed, she was at her prettiest. When she caught him watching her, she immediately stiffened.

She was right to be cautious, he reasoned. They hadn't gotten off to an amicable start with her breaking into his house, coupled with his anger over her actions. And then those sudden, breathtaking moments on the golf course. His fierce need to bury himself deep inside her. A need he had still. He would never forget the utter joy of watching her smooth features slacken in ecstasy, of knowing he alone was capable of giving her that.

Oh, what he could give her, if she would allow him. They could have a great time together if she'd get over her staunch New England hangups, the curse of the upper classes, he supposed.

Mimi had probably drilled it into her head that only whores had a good time in bed with a man. Upstanding women simply endured.

Or did she just hate him because he was giving Kittridge Collectibles competition they'd never had before? Or because he wasn't the respectable kind of man her family would have chosen for her?

Sitting at the long dinner table with candles burning, making small talk about the weather was driving him mad. He would have been better off if he'd written off last night as a pleasant encounter then gone about his business instead of barging over here like a madman this morning. He wasn't the kind of guy who sent Valentines. He couldn't pretend to be, even for her. Yet he couldn't leave it alone.

'More potatoes, Simon?'

He looked up to see Serena smiling at him over a bowl heaped with whipped potatoes.

'No, thank you. It's all very good, though. An interesting flavor to the roast . . .'

Serena set the bowl down. 'Dash of nutmeg. Yardley goes all out when she cooks Sunday dinner.'

Yardley choked on a mouthful of milk, setting the glass down quickly. She glared at her sister.

Serena smiled sweetly.

Yardley picked her napkin off her lap, wadded it up and tossed it atop the tablecloth. She turned to Simon. 'Serena made every bit of this,' she declared.

Simon met her gaze. 'I didn't come over here to find out whether you can cook.'

Serena rose from her chair, slanting her glance at Casey, who sat propped on a pile of phone books in the chair beside hers. She leaned over and untied his bib. 'Look at you, covered with mashed potatoes. Bath time's coming early tonight.' She scooped him into her arms and rushed off towards the stairs. 'You guys will have to entertain yourselves for a few minutes.'

Yardley stood up, pushing her chair in. 'Why did you come, Simon?' she asked.

His voice was low and deep. 'I'm not sure I know myself.' He got up, moving his chair aside and taking long strides around the table towards her. He had to touch her. When she tried to turn away, he propped her chin beneath two fingers and forced her to meet his eyes.

'Something happened last night. Something aside from the obvious. Nothing horrible, Yardley. I didn't intend for things to go so far either. But for my part, it was kind of miraculous.'

157

Her eyes pooled with tears, and he regretted whatever he might have done to hurt her. That was not his intention.

'This is crazy,' she whispered. 'Yes, okay, it was wonderful. Is that what you came here to hear? You would know I was lying if I didn't admit that. But, no, I'm not going to have an affair with you just because we have some chemistry between us. I want to get married and have children and join the Kittridge PTA, and I came back here to do that. What happened last night was a step in the wrong direction, and that's why I regret it. You and I don't even like each other.'

'I never said I didn't like you.'

'You hate my family, everything I stand for.'

'My problem was with your grandfather. Until you came over my fence.'

'Serena's his granddaughter too. Yet you seem to like her.'

'There's nothing at stake between me and Serena.' He moved closer. 'Tell me last night was ordinary, that it's like that for you every time, and I'll leave. You see, my problem is, I don't understand what's between us any more than you do. And if you refuse to talk to me, I'll never figure it out.'

Her stricken expression betrayed her answer. 'It's never been like that before. I didn't know it could be.'

He smiled seductively. 'I want to make love to you over and over again,' he said. 'You're as passionate as you are beautiful.'

'No, it can't be like that.'

He stroked her chin with the backs of his fingertips. 'You want to chuck the mysteries of the universe for the PTA? I can't believe that's what a woman like you really wants, Yardley. You're far too imaginative.'

Her breathing quickened, and he felt a small tremor course through her. God, she smelled good. A breath of tropical flowers in autumn.

He bowed his head over hers. 'I came over here intending to prove to you that my only motive wasn't to get back inside your pants again. But the effort's pretty useless. Since I walked through the front door, I haven't thought of much else but getting there and staying.'

She tried to move away from him, but she had nowhere to go.

'You shouldn't talk this way, Simon.'

He prodded her chin upward on the palm of his hand. 'Would you prefer to be lied to?' He traced her trembling lower lip with his thumb.

'Do you think I could forget last night? You have a rare, fine quality about you, Yardley. Your misguided nobility only enhances it. You're a keeper. And I don't want to sit here over pot roast and feign interest in discussing the weather. I want to take you home with me and do what we did last night, only without the sand.'

A light came into her eyes, and her lips curled slightly. 'The sand was horrid.'

He smiled back at her. 'You belong on satin sheets.'

Hungrily, he captured her lips between his own, savoring the mellow, minty taste of her. Pulling her lithe body close, he anxiously coaxed her lips apart and searched for her tongue, spearing it with his own. His hand raked down her side, and as he groped to get under her sweater, he stopped himself.

Abruptly, he pulled back.

Flushed and breathless, she stared up at him, her blue eyes dark and rounded.

Leaving unfinished what he started wasn't his style, and he mustered all his willpower to let her go. 'I can't promise to give you your dream of car pools and bake-sales. You're too intelligent to believe such an outrageous lie anyway. Come home with me, Yardley. Now.'

She shook her head. 'I've risked too much already, Simon.'

'Suit yourself, sweetheart. I'd better go home. Thank Serena for the dinner, would you? I can get my own jacket.' He headed for the closet.

'Simon, I'm sorry if I led you to expect I could be what you wanted.'

'This isn't over. You will change your mind,' he predicted.

'I will not.'

'We'll see. Goodnight, babe.'

Still tingling from his kiss, Yardley watched Simon retrieve his jacket from the coat rack and leave. She appreciated what coming over here to eat dinner in her grandfather's house had cost him.

But she couldn't believe he now expected her to go camp out in his bed.

His kiss had left her weak-kneed and wanting. His scent lingered in her clothes, his taste in her mouth. Why was she so afraid of what she felt for him? Because he'd leave her heart shattered in tiny fragments, that's why, she reminded herself. He hadn't even made any pretense of actually caring for her. No, he thought they'd hit it off great in the sack and he'd like to continue that aspect of their relationship indefinitely.

She should have felt insulted. However, considering the source, she was almost flattered. Maybe inviting a woman into his bedroom was the closest Simon would ever come to a declaration of affection.

She turned to the heap of dirty dishes and leftovers on the table. Well, she wouldn't lack for anything to keep her busy the rest of the evening.

Just as she was reaching for the first plate, the phone rang. Knowing Serena must have Casey in the tub, she went to answer it.

'Hello.'

'Hello, dear. How was the dance?'

Guilt seized her at her grandmother's reference to the dance.

'Same as usual, Mimi. I'll tell you all about it when you get back.'

'Well, that's why I'm calling. The Bertrands are here, so we've making a holiday of it. I'll be staying on a few more days.'

Yardley lowered her voice. 'Mimi, Serena and Casey are here.'

'Oh, that's right. I packed in such a hurry I forgot to leave you a message. I hope you're all having a nice visit.'

'It would be nicer if you were here.'

'Honestly, getting out of that house has done me a world of good. So many memories stored there. I haven't had a single headache since I arrived.'

'Well, I'm glad you're feeling better. But I hope you won't stay too much longer. Serena wants to see you.'

'Oh, don't worry about me. Serena's not in the way, is she?'

'What? Of course not. It's good to have company. And there's something I need to discuss with you in person.'

'Nothing that can't keep, I'd imagine.'

'No. It will keep.'

'Did you get the mold yet?'

'No. Mimi, Simon thinks it's his. There's not much I can do.'

'Well, heavens, child. Don't come out and beg him for it. Make him think giving it to you is his idea. It's your company he's out to ruin, don't forget.'

'No. Have fun.'

Yardley set down the receiver down. If Simon cared about her to any degree, it did seem he might slacken his stance on getting revenge against Kittridge Collectibles.

But then, he hadn't professed to even the smallest degree of caring, had he? He'd been forthright in confessing he simply wanted her presence in his bed.

Yardley staved off the shivery sensation that image provoked, the physical delights she well knew he could provide. Could he sense how much she wanted him? She refused to steer her life down such a reckless path. After Grant, she knew better.

Simon disappeared from Yardley's life as suddenly as he'd invaded it. Four long days went by without a word from him. Yardley convinced herself she was relieved. She supposed he anticipated she'd go to him. Well, he was just making the monumental task of forgetting what had happened Saturday easier for her, she reasoned. She couldn't have cared less whether he ever called her. He must have realized she'd meant what she'd told him Sunday: she wasn't about to assume the role of his personal sex kitten. Obviously he didn't want her badly enough to pursue her. He must have given up and found another outlet for his urges. Perhaps the pretty brunette she sometimes saw him around town with.

What did she care? At least with Mimi away, Serena had settled in to stay for a while. Yardley apologized to her about needing Mimi's signature to transfer her rightful shares in Kittridge

Collectibles and lent her several hundred dollars to cover living expenses until she could start collecting an income from the profits. She remained determined to convince Serena to stay and work for the company. But Serena refused to believe she was truly welcome. Yardley knew Serena wouldn't take the offer seriously until she heard it from Mimi herself, so she wished Mimi would hurry and come home.

On Thursday evening, Yardley came home to find Serena had been shopping.

'I've got fabric to make Casey's Hallowe'en costume,' she announced, pulling a square of orange broadcloth and a pattern out of one bag.

'You're going to make him a costume?' Yardley asked, disappointed Serena wasn't going to allow her to buy Casey a costume. But then, Casey wasn't hers.

Clutching the envelope, Serena blinked excitedly. 'Sure. Would you mind entertaining Casey for a while so I can get this thing cut out? It's hard to keep track of him and pins at the same time. I thought maybe we could go for pizza later.'

'Glad to,' Yardley agreed. 'I'm not hungry just yet anyway. Give me five minutes to change.' She glanced down at her matching light blue wool city shorts and blazer and white silk blouse.

Serena grinned with a mischievous sparkle in

her eye. 'I've brought you a surprise too. Check out the bathroom.'

'What have you done, Serena? There's not a thing I need.'

She walked upstairs to the bathroom, bursting out laughing at the sight of a huge box of condoms on the shelf, nestled between the stacks of color-coordinated magenta towels matching Mimi's chenille throw rug to a T.

'Do you get a discount for buying in bulk or what?' Yardley asked, holding her sides. 'These should last you at least through Thanksgiving, Sis.'

Serena stood in the doorway with Casey at her heels. 'They're not for me. I've sworn off men. I told you, they're for you.'

'Thanks, I guess, Serrie. But you may have noticed Simon hasn't been back since Sunday. Not that it matters.'

'Oh, he will be. That man's got it bad, even if he may not know it yet.'

'Even if he does come around, I won't be needing these.'

'Better safe than sorry, sweetie. And I'm betting you will.'

Yardley turned to her sister. 'And since when have you sworn off men? You know, you haven't told me anything about where you've been or what you've been doing since you got here. What gives?'

Gnawing her lower lip, Serena shook her head. 'Nothing I want to talk about. And don't start feeling sorry for me. I've got Casey, and we'll be okay.'

Yardley studied her sister, noticing that, despite her stiff shoulders and brave smile, her eyes were misty. How terribly lonely it must be to love someone enough to create a child with him, then raise the child without him there to share the joy and the worries.

Yardley exhaled deeply. 'I'll go change so you can get started on your sewing. You know whatever's wrong, Serena, I can take hearing it if you change your mind. I know you too well to think you want to be alone the rest of your life. And please get that box out of the bathroom before Mimi comes home.'

'Why are you so worried she'll discover you have a life?'

'One indiscretion is not my life, Serrie. And if I met someone and fell in love, I'm sure Mimi would be happy for me.'

But as she walked upstairs, she admitted Mimi would be far from pleased if she gave her heart to the man who was out to destroy their business.

CHAPTER 8

'Yahoo!' Yardley shrieked, chasing after Casey and the rolling soccer ball. She dove alongside him into a drift of dry leaves to retrieve it.

Casey, laughing, came up hugging the ball. Yardley lunged at him, then wrestled her nephew back down in the leaves.

'I win! I win!' he decreed.

Lying on her back in the leaves, Yardley stopped laughing as she spied a strange, rusty red truck rattling up the drive toward the house.

She released Casey and sat up to brush fragments of leaves off the legs of her jeans. He tugged at the sleeve of her sweater. 'Play again, Yawd-ley,' he urged.

'In a minute, honey,' she told him, swinging a glance towards the house. Serena's face appeared in the upstairs window, disappearing quickly. Yardley looked back at the old pickup and wondered if her sister was expecting company. When she glanced back up at the window, Serena wasn't there any more.

Yardley stood. The pickup clattered to a halt, and Yardley saw it had out-of-state tags. Stooping down, she told Casey to go in the house.

'Wanna play,' he argued with an endearing smile.

He would pick now of all times to be difficult. Holding fast to Casey's hand, she walked towards the truck.

The man who jumped out of the driver's seat was big as a bear although only a few inches taller than her. His straight sable-brown hair skirted his neck, and he wore hunting boots, faded jeans, and a green flannel shirt unbuttoned to expose a plain white T-shirt. An arrowhead pendant dangled from his thick neck on a silver chain, and his rolled-up sleeves revealed a collage of tattoos beneath the dark hair on his muscular arms.

Yardley was careful not to get too close. 'Hello. Can I help you?' she asked.

He looked at her, the house, then her again, like someone emerging from a space capsule on a foreign planet.

'Beau!' Casey shouted gleefully, jerking free of her hand and racing with arms outstretched towards the hulking stranger. The man's brooding dark eyes lightened, and he stood to open his arms, sweeping the boy up in a bear-hug and kissing him soundly on the cheek with a loud smack.

'Hey, slugger. I missed you.'

Despite Yardley's uneasiness over the stranger's unexpected appearance, she couldn't help smiling. Such a tender gesture from such a burly man.

Still, her heartbeat didn't slow to normal until he set the boy down. 'Yes, ma'am,' he answered in a thick drawl with a quick nod. 'Serena Kittridge live here?' He glanced down back at Casey. 'Well, I reckon she must.'

Yardley's gaze drifted towards the upstairs window. Her sister wasn't showing herself. That she hadn't come out to greet this man indicated she didn't want to see him. Judging by his size and the urgency in his tone, Yardley mentally paired him with the pyjamas her sister had been wearing.

'She's been staying here, but she's not in at the moment.'

He frowned.

Yardley stood straighter, wishing she'd had time to send Casey into the house. Wishing Casey would come back beside her before this conversation went any further. Was this, she wondered, the boy's father? She saw no resemblance.

'Where'd she go?'

Yardley stepped closer. She extended her hand. 'I'm Yardley Kittridge, Serena's sister. I didn't realize she was expecting anyone.'

He wiped his beefy hand on his shirtfront, then clenched her hand in a powerful grip.

'I didn't mean to be rude, ma'am, but it's taken me a week to find out where she'd gone to. I've been driving all day.'

Yardley glanced ruefully at the truck. It didn't look as if it could have held up through such a long drive.

She reached for Casey's shoulders and subtly drew him back against her legs.

'You haven't been rude, Mr . . .'

'Jennings. Folks just call me Beau. I guess since we're all family . . .'

Yardley staggered backwards. The big stranger reached out and caught her.

'No, I'm okay,' she insisted, fanning her neck until she remembered how many times she'd seen Mimi make the same gesture and stopped herself. 'But I'm not sure I follow you . . .'

The sound of a car racing up the drive caught her attention, and she watched in astonishment as Simon's Jag skidded to a stop and Simon emerged, looking angrier than he had when he'd caught her climbing his fence.

'Take your hands off her,' he snarled at Beau.

Yardley's glance dropped to her shoulders, then to Beau's face, and his own surprise at seeing he was still holding on to her mirrored her own.

Beau immediately jerked back his hands. 'Hey, wait a minute. I wasn't hurtin' her, mister.'

Simon loomed tall and dark and menacing as he advanced. He looked murderous.

Yardley stepped between the two men and shielded Beau with an outstretched arm. Simon halted.

'What's going on here?' he asked.

Yardley drew in a deep breath. 'If I understand correctly, Mr Jennings is my brother-in-law.'

Beau grinned, puffing his chest. 'That's right.' He offered Simon a handshake. 'Just call me Beau. When people say Mr Jennings, I keep lookin' around for my Daddy.'

'How long have you and Serena been married?' Yardley asked.

'Goin' on two weeks. Serena ran off on our wedding night, and I've come to take her back to

Nashville.' He frowned as he looked towards the house. 'I swear, I didn't know she lived in a mansion.'

'This is our grandmother's house,' Yardley explained.

'I can show you our marriage certificate. We got hitched in a wedding chapel in Gatlinburg.'

Yardley hoofed at the dirt. 'Something must have happened to change her mind.'

'Well, I'll be damned if I know what. Oops. Sorry, ma'am. She just sneaked off in the middle of the night. I woke up and she was gone. I'm taking her back home.'

'When she gets back, I'll tell her you were here.'

'I don't mean to call you a liar or nothin', ma'am, but that's her car in the driveway.'

Yardley glanced again towards the house. This man seemed harmless and sincere. But Serena wouldn't have left him without a reason, and she wouldn't be inside hiding behind the curtains if she wanted to see him. Yardley's protective instincts and loyalty kicked in.

'She's gone to New York with our grandmother,' Yardley lied, her face heating as she glimpsed Simon's shrewd smile. 'When she returns, I'll certainly tell her you were here.'

'When's she gettin' back?'

Yardley forced a shrug. 'I'm not sure.'

'Well, I'm not going home without her and Casey, here.'

'That's your choice. If you call once you find a hotel, and leave your number, I'll call you after I talk to her.'

'I'd appreciate that, ma'am.' He went to his truck and returned with a hamburger wrapper and a ballpoint. 'If you don't mind giving me the phone number, I'll call as soon as I get settled in. Or maybe I should just drive on to New York.'

Yardley glared at Simon as he chuckled. 'No sense in doing that. I'm sure she'll be back within a day or two. You must be very tired from your trip.'

'To tell the truth, I am,' he admitted. He grinned wearily. 'Nice to meet y'all.'

Yardley stood watching as the truck took off, aware of Simon beside her. When it was out of sight, she turned on Simon.

'I didn't need rescuing, thank you.'

'Looked as if you did, sweetheart. You looked scared.'

'Well, I wasn't.'

'Did you know your bottom lip quivers when you're lying? If you're gonna tell lies, do it with conviction, slick.'

'Thanks, I'll jot that gem in my Dayrunner.' She eyed him thoughtfully. 'Would you have really beat him up for me?'

'Sure. If he'd been trying to hurt you or Casey.'

She shuddered. 'Nice to know we were all spared the bloodshed. What are you doing here, Simon?'

Smiling down, he reached towards her. Liquid heat trickled into her belly. Grazing her cheek lightly with his hand, he came up with a fistful of dried leaves.

'You said you wanted to go to a carnival. I've found you one.'

Yardley blinked with surprise. 'You want me to go to a carnival with you? Now?'

He held his hands in the air as if she had a gun on him. 'I swear I'll behave myself, if you will. Don't you want to see what you missed during your youth?'

Yardley laughed. Every rational nerve in her body told her to run from him as though her life depended on it. Still, learning he'd paid sufficient attention to her ramblings to remember what she'd said surprised and moved her.

'I can't just leave, Simon. My baby sister's married to that man who just left!'

'Your sister's no baby. Seems like she's made up her mind what she wants to do. That guy looks familiar.'

Yardley shook her head. 'I don't see how. He's never been around here before.'

'Isn't this Serena's problem and not yours?'

Yardley shook her head, unwilling to explain how Serena had been dragging around the house in Beau's pyjamas. If she wasn't in love with the guy, she would have borrowed night-clothes from her or Mimi or slept in a T-shirt. What had happened between her and Beau that she wouldn't even talk to him?

'I just don't understand. It doesn't make sense to deny yourself being with someone you care about.' She dodged Simon's intent gaze. 'I have to go inside and find out what this is all about.'

'I'll wait.'

She looked back at him.

'You are coming with me, aren't you?'

'What if he comes back?'

'Serena can lock the doors. Stop making excuses, Yardley. Will you come with me?'

Yardley swallowed hard as she stared into his dark, hypnotic eyes. The late afternoon sunlight played in their depths.

'I'll bring you straight home,' he promised. His brisk, masculine scent permeated her senses, and she felt the heat of his body simmering between them. When she opened her mouth to claim previous plans, she heard a voice that sounded remarkably like hers saying yes, she'd love to go.

Shocked to realize how much she wanted to be with him, she turned away and raced into the house.

Serena was pacing through the dining room like a wild mustang.

'Thank you, Sis,' she said, opening her arms to Casey. 'I can't believe Beau tracked me all this way.'

'Well, if you actually left him on your wedding night without saying goodbye, it's not an irrational action. He says he's your husband.'

Serena nodded. 'Theoretically. I'm divorcing him.' She scrunched her forehead thoughtfully. 'I guess it's too late to get an annulment if you get physical with him after the wedding?'

Yardley hesitated. 'I haven't a clue, Serrie. Did he hurt you?'

'Beau? He wouldn't hurt a cricket.'

'Then why aren't you with him? You must still care about him – you've been parading around here in his pyjamas. Or is this just another tactic designed to shock Mimi? So help me, Serena, if you've been toying with that man's feelings . . .'

Serena blinked back tears. 'Everything's not about Mimi. Just because your world revolves around her, it doesn't mean mine does. Beau and I had a real good time together. We just sort of wound up married and when we went up to Gatlinburg, everything got really intense and I realized how unfair I was being to him. I'll never love him the way I loved Casey's dad, okay?'

'Serrie, I hate to point out the obvious, but Casey's dad abandoned you.'

Openly weeping, Serena shook her head. 'Yeah, he abandoned me all right. Got himself killed before I even found out I was pregnant.'

Yardley froze inside.

'Oh, Serrie, why didn't you ever tell anyone?'

'What difference does it make? You all believed what you wanted to believe.'

'You didn't have to have Casey alone. And you don't have to be alone now. You do have to talk to that man. He's obviously crazy about you and Casey both. He doesn't have a clue as to what he's done wrong. And he's driven all the way from Tennessee in a truck hanging together with duct tape.'

Serena laughed through her tears. 'That's Beulah. He swears she's his good luck charm. I didn't think he'd find me.'

'Serrie, if you really didn't want to be found, this isn't where you would have come.'

Serena brushed back a strand of straight hair and sighed heavily. 'I don't want to break his heart.'

'Sneaking off in the middle of the night wouldn't destroy his pride? You must have crushed his ego, Serrie. He probably thinks his performance in bed disappointed you.'

'Beau knows better. I wouldn't have married him without knowing what to expect on that score. I know I have to talk to him. But not now. Not tonight. I need to sort out what I'm going to say to him.'

'He'll be calling later with the number of his hotel. You might want to let the machine pick it up. Unless you have a change of heart.'

Serena nodded. 'You're going with Simon?'

'To a carnival,' Yardley qualified. 'Why don't you and Casey come?'

Serena was shaking her head before Yardley finished getting the words out. 'No way. You're on your own tonight.'

'I won't be gone long.'

'Famous last words.'

'I won't. Oh, gosh, I forgot about the pizza!'

'Leave it forgotten. Casey and I can rustle up sandwiches. Stop making excuses and go. Simon's waiting for you. Hey, I saw how he came charging up to defend you. I'd say the man's in love.'

'Simon doesn't believe in it.'

'But you do, Yardley.'

'Is he going to leave us up here forever?' Yardley mused, peering over the safety bar of the Ferris wheel basket to view the operator straight below them. She shifted slightly. The metal seat left her little room to retreat from Simon. Why had she let him talk her into riding this contraption?

'He's got to stop the cars to let more passengers on,' Simon explained, sitting back calmly. The night breeze ruffled his inky hair. He looked as out of place here as a polo player at a wrestling match.

Gazing past him to a star-studded sky of diamonds against black velvet, she inhaled deeply. The air was cold and crisp, smelling of caramel and popcorn. Tinny music blared from below.

She focused on Simon again. 'How do you know so much about these things?'

Briefly, he looked perturbed. 'I used to run one of these. Back when I was a kid.'

'Really?' She glanced down again at the shaggy operator in his ancient jeans and once-white, now-gray T-shirt. He was indeed changing out the passengers.

Looking back up at Simon in his tailored clothing and precise haircut, she realized even his appearance was designed to shut out the harsh reality of where he had come from. A place where the need for money to buy food, clothing, and shelter dictated who you were and what you did. Yardley had never had to do without anything she needed, and she began to understand why he viewed her as soft, complacent and pampered. She'd taken for granted all the choices she'd had. Maybe Simon had seen only one for himself.

'Really. Are you afraid of heights, babe?'

'No.' She looked down at the bar and realized the knuckles on the hand she grasped it with were white. In truth, she felt little queasy, but until recently heights had never bothered her. She'd ridden ski lifts higher than this without a qualm.

'Must be me then. You're pale as a ghost. Why don't you sit back?' One hand planted on her shoulder, he drew her back more against him than the seat, casually draping an arm over her shoulders.

She was keenly aware of Simon beside her, his long legs stretched out in front of him. The heat of his body warmed her side.

His strength and intensity no longer frightened her, she realized. Even his arrogant demeanor didn't intimidate her now that she saw through it. Her irrepressible longing for him terrified her, however. After having Simon, how was she ever going to muster any enthusiasm for that safe, sane Mr Right when she met him? Or was she forever condemned to find passion while love and marriage eluded her?

Even now, her belly churned as though made of melting butter. She risked the luxury of leaning against him.

'I never had a job until after I graduated from college,' she admitted. 'Was it awful, working for the carnival?'

Simon laughed. 'At the time, I thought it was great. I was going to quit school and travel around the country, get the hell out of Kittridge.'

'But you didn't go.'

'My old man told me I was better than that, that after all he'd gone through to bring me up, if I threw myself away on some two-bit carnival he was washing his hands of me forever. And he meant it.'

Yardley refrained from noting that she was beginning to understand where Simon had inherited his single-mindedness.

'Where is your father now?' she asked.

'Florida. He wanted to live someplace warm.'

He didn't have to tell Yardley he'd financed his father's move. She heard the affection in his voice and instinctively knew it.

Suddenly the car lurched forward, beginning its descent and swinging to a stop as the operator unloaded yet another carload of passengers. Yardley pressed closer against Simon, and he instinctively tightened his grasp on her.

'And you came back to Kittridge.'

'There's no point in accomplishing something unless the people who said you'd never amount to anything are watching.'

'Pleasing yourself should be far more important than what anybody thinks. It is to me.'

'Because you're accustomed to people holding you in high regard. My own mother . . .' He broke off his words.

'Made a terrible mistake,' she finished for him. 'And I'm sure she's suffered for it. Love means nothing without loyalty behind it. Maybe that's the only way I can explain how Mimi convinced me I had to get that mold back.'

'And now? Do you still want it?'

'I honestly don't know. Breaking into your house was wrong. But Mimi was so distraught. I won't do it again.'

'No, please do. Give me a call and I'll unlock the front door for you. Besides, I've fired my cleaning people and hidden it where it will never be found.'

'What does it take for you to trust anyone?'

He frowned. 'Your calling the sheriff to get your necklace back wasn't part of our agreement.'

'You shouldn't have taken my mother's necklace. It meant too much to me to entrust leaving it with you. I went to the dance with you, didn't I?'

He stared hard into her eyes. 'God, I wish we were both on the same side.'

'There don't have to be sides, Simon. We both happen to be in the same business. We aren't each other's sole competitors.'

'Except we're the only two companies responsible for the exact same figurine.'

'That's your doing, not mine.'

'Suppose our situations were reversed. Suppose my family had cheated yours and for decades wielded money and power to keep your family impoverished. You can't tell me you'd take that in your stride.'

'You have your own money and power now. How much do you need? Why drop the bomb after you've conquered your territory? I think it's cruel and spiteful and you're doing it only to hurt people. To hurt us. I can see how proud you are, but I don't believe you're as callous as you want to be.'

'How do you know that?'

'Because you're too smart. You've invested too much in your company to base your reputation on a rip-off design. I've seen the original pieces you're already offering. You don't need the peasant girl.'

Simon's long silence confirmed the accuracy of her observation.

'Why did you bring me here tonight, Simon?' she asked.

'Because you said it was lonely being set apart. Because I think I understand. And you can see that being in a crowd of people doesn't necessarily make it go away.'

'Does anything?'

'You do.'

Her eyes flared, then collided with his. Their even, dark depths were not mocking own her. His hand found hers and he squeezed her fingers between his own. She understood that this small admission of caring was all he would allow himself. For now, it was enough.

The moment ended as the bucket swayed again and finally, they were released from its confines.

'Thanks, man,' Simon told the stone-faced operator as he unlatched the safety bar. The man rolled his eyes as if he thought Simon must be drunk.

Glad to have her feet planted on the asphalt parking lot of the church sponsoring the carnival, Yardley swung her glance around the maze of metal beams and multicolored neon. Since they were about thirty miles away from Kittridge, she saw no one she knew and was glad to be spared curious eyes. That Simon had brought her here proved his purpose tonight was not to parade her around like some prize he'd won.

Simon came up beside her when a boy about ten came barreling at him, his head turned around to watch the friend chasing him. Simon caught the boy by the shoulders, steering him to one side before he collided with his legs. 'Whoa,' he cautioned the boy who looked up at him, startled.

'Sorry, mister,' he muttered, then scrambled away.

'So,' Simon asked her. 'What do you want to

do now? Bumper cars, carousel, tilt-a-whirl, cotton candy?'

'Your lack of enthusiasm is obvious. I'm not a child you have to entertain.'

'Sorry. I've been to these things before.'

Yardley pointed to a tent off to one side. 'Look! A fortune-teller.'

Simon stiffened, attempting to draw her away. 'They're all con artists, sweetheart. No one can predict what's going to happen.'

'It's for charity, Simon. I want to hear what Madame Zoe has to say. Too chicken to hear what's in store for you?'

'All she's going to tell you is a load of nonsense.'

'Don't be such a skeptic.' Yardley was already at the entrance tearing off two dollars' worth of yellow cardboard tickets when he caught up to her.

The girl sitting at a card table outside the tent flap took Yardley's tickets, then held out her palm to Simon.

'No, thanks,' he said. 'I like surprises. I'll take my future as it comes.'

'He can go in with me, can't he?' Yardley asked.

The girl studied Simon as though deciding. 'Sure. I guess it'll be all right.'

'You really want me to hear this?' he asked.

'Yes,' Yardley said over her shoulder as she pulled pack the tent flap. 'Just don't start arguing with her.'

Adjusting her vision to the darkness inside required a few minutes. The tent's interior smelled like moldy canvas and strong rose-scented potpourri. All the activity outside suddenly seemed very far away.

The woman seated behind the black draped round table nodded like a toy with a spring in its neck but said nothing. A huge crystal ball sat on the table before her. She wore a cheap, flowing black wig and heavy theatrical make-up. A red veil shrouded the bottom of her face. Huge almond-shaped eyes topped by shaggy black brows danced above the scrap of fabric. The darkest eyes Yardley had ever seen. While Simon's were such a deep brown they sometimes appeared black, this woman's irises were like coal. Must be trick contacts, Yardley reasoned, not liking the effect. The fabric of her black gown was imprinted with iridescent gold moons and stars.

With a toss of her head she motioned for Yardley to take the chair opposite her. Yardley sat. Simon stood behind her.

Her dark gaze riveted on Simon, the woman finally spoke.

'You want your lover in here with you? It's not a good idea.'

Discomfited, Yardley gaped at her. How did she know? She couldn't. A lucky guess, it had to be. The woman was putting them on. Or good at reading body language? Was their previous intimacy so transparent?

'He's okay,' Yardley assured her, playing along.

Beside her, Simon struggled to suppress a slanted smile.

The woman nodded without argument. 'Place your hand on the crystal, and I will gaze at what is forecast,' she instructed.

Yardley inspected the glowing orb, which looked to her like an upside-down light fixture, and wondered if it would feel hot like a light bulb. Tentatively, she set a hand on it, surprised by its coolness, although it held her hand like a magnet locking metal.

The woman dropped her gaze idly into the glowing ball, and Yardley caught how her face froze in horror and alarm before she masked it.

Arrows of dread pierced her heart. This was no longer fun. 'What's wrong?' she demanded. She felt Simon's hand pressed on her shoulder.

The woman stared at her with a bland expression, but Yardley saw sadness in her eyes.

The fortune-teller locked her hands together and dropped her gaze back into the crystal. She cleared her throat.

'Soon,' she predicted, 'you will know great happiness.'

'How? What kind of happiness?'

'It has already come into your life, but you have yet to recognize it.'

'That's all? You saw something else first.'

'No. There is no more.'

Simon was gently nudging her to her feet. 'Come on, Yardley. I warned you it was all a hoax.' He pulled her to her feet, shot a fiery glance at the woman behind the table, then ushered her outside.

The fresh air cleared her head slightly. 'I've had better fortunes from vending machines,' she complained.

'Don't tell me you believe this hocus-pocus.'

Yardley squinted at him. 'Did you know her?'

'Yeah, I paid her off in advance because I looked in my magic crystal and knew you'd insist on going in there.'

'She saw something she wouldn't tell me about.'

'It was darker than midnight in that tent. You're imagining things.'

'What could she have seen that she wouldn't tell me?'

'That you were about to regret having wasted two bucks? Who would want to know the future anyway? It'd make life as dry as reading through a play. She's not even a real gypsy, probably some housewife from down the street. Can't you tell when someone is acting? It's all part of the show, babe.'

Yardley locked her gaze on his. 'How did she know about us, Simon?'

He shrugged nonchalantly, but she could tell it bothered him too. 'Damned if I know.' Quickly, he changed the subject. 'Come on, I'll win you a teddy bear.'

She laughed. 'This I've got to see.'

'Hey, I'm rusty, but I used to be good at shooting ducks.'

'Winning your girlfriends teddy bears?'

'Won their undying devotion every time. I guess I was pretty cocky back then. Come on, Yardley. I wouldn't do this for just anyone.'

Walking beside Simon towards the midway, she wondered just how many girls he'd won stuffed animals for and how many had pledged more than devotion. How many hearts had he broken over the years?

As a breeze blew over her, she shivered and crossed her arms. Her encounter with the make-believe fortune-teller had left her haunted and uneasy. Even as Simon was leading her away, she was staring back at the tent.

CHAPTER 9

Half an hour later, Yardley was standing in the midway with a black and white plush panda tucked under her arm. 'I assume this is supposed to make you irresistible,' she told Simon, straightening the red bow around the panda's neck.

'Come on, babe. I sweated bullets to win that thing for you.'

'I hope you won't be too offended if I give it to Casey.'

'Does this mean we're not going back to my place?'

'We never were. Straight home. As you promised. Would you mind if we left now? I'm worried about Serena.'

'All right. You're not responsible for the welfare of your entire family, you know.'

'Someone's got to hold everything together.'

His Jag was waiting at the curb. Yardley sat back in comfortable silence as he drove towards Kittridge.

'Have you been feeling okay?' he asked suddenly.

Yardley bristled. 'Of course. Why shouldn't I?'

'It was kind of scary, the way you fainted the other night.'

She sighed heavily. 'It frightened me too. Enough to send me to the doctor, who says I'm fine. Thanks for your concern.'

'I felt responsible. After all, it was my house you were breaking into.'

'I take care of myself. But I'd appreciate it if you didn't mention it to Serena. No sense in alarming her.'

'Discretion is my middle name. I won't tell her about the golf course either.'

Yardley wrung her hands. 'She knows about the golf course.'

'Really?'

'Well, I came home covered with sand. I had to explain.'

'And she still invited me for dinner?'

'Serena likes you.'

'And Yardley?'

She grinned. 'Yardley thinks you're a severely depraved and pathetic individual.'

194

'Warms my heart to know I'm held in such high esteem.' He popped a cassette in the tape player and strains of orchestral music filled the amiable silence between them the rest of the way back to Kittridge. He slowed the car as it approached her house. 'You are inviting me in, aren't you?'

She cast him a sidewise glance. 'For coffee.'

He nodded as he stopped the car and killed the engine. 'I'll settle for coffee. Tonight.'

The downstairs was deserted, although the kitchen and living room lights were on. Yardley set up the coffee-maker, then turned to Simon. 'I'm going to go check on Serena and Casey. I'll be right back.'

She raced upstairs and found Casey asleep in the guest room. She followed the drone of the television to Mimi's room, where her sister was ensconced in Mimi's king-sized bed, propped on a mountain of pillows, eating chocolates and watching an old movie. She was wearing Beau's pyjamas.

'Did Beau come back?' Yardley asked.

Serena shook her head. She lifted a corner of the box to offer chocolates, but Yardley declined with a shake of her head. 'No, but he left a message for you on the machine. Did I hear Simon downstairs?'

'We're having coffee. Care to join us?'

'Nope. I'll have enough trouble sleeping as it is. You'll have to tough it out without a chaperon. And I won't be coming downstairs, so you have complete privacy.'

Yardley quietly closed the door.

She returned downstairs to find Simon in the living room, studying the glass case full of Kittridge Collectibles' finest pieces, the peasant girl at the forefront.

She came up beside him. 'She is beautiful, isn't she? Such a mysterious, wistful expression.'

He glanced down at her, then raised his eyes to the case. 'As elusive as the Mona Lisa's smile. She's thinking of her lover. He's taken her innocence and her heart, and then married someone from his own wealthier class.'

Yardley gasped. 'That's a horrible story! That's what you see when you look at her?'

He turned his dark eyes to her. 'You shouldn't produce art if you don't understand it. The story is true. This girl was my great-grandmother. My great-grandfather loved her so much he married her despite her disgrace, and he took her from her home town here to Kittridge, to start a new life together. It's her he sculpted.'

Yardley's eyes swung from Simon to the tiny statue, then back again. Incredulously, she detected a faint family resemblance in the cheekbones, the nose, the dark hair.

'My God, you were telling the truth.'

'Generally, I do. Quirk of nature, I suppose.'

Again, she studied the statue. On such a tiny figure, the similarities could be coincidental. A skilled craftsman like Simon could have easily picked them out and capitalized on them. He sounded sincere, but she remembered how he'd advised her earlier that when you lied, you must do it with conviction.

'Even if it is your great-grandmother, my great-grandfather could have seen her in town and been so struck by her as to model his sculpture after her.'

Simon shook his head. 'You Kittridges don't budge an inch, do you?'

'I accept, Simon, that you truly believe the mold is rightfully yours. If it was taken from your family without compensation, I'm sorry. I don't agree that entitles you to destroy my company's reputation. Is that really what you want? You'd better make damn sure it is, because if you go ahead with your plans, it will be one blow that can never be taken back.'

He eyed her speculatively. 'This is about me and your grandfather. It's not personal.'

'My grandfather's dead. Why can't everyone just let him rest? Whatever sins he committed in his lifetime, he paid for through a living hell on earth before he died. Isn't that enough? He never intentionally set out to destroy your family.'

'But he never gave a damn who or what he destroyed to get what he wanted. We were in his way, like so many traffic cones he ran over.'

She reached out and set a trembling hand to Simon's jaw. Even with that slight touch, his power raced through her with the force of a shooting star. 'When I look at you, Simon, I see a man who is fine and noble inside and wants to do the right thing, but who is too bitter to follow those instincts. Am I wrong, Simon? Am I seeing only what I want to see?'

A shadow crossed his expression. 'Sometimes I don't know any more.'

'You told me I had to let Granddad go. Can't you do the same?'

'Half my family is missing. I can't just forget about that.'

Yardley tilted her head. 'For richer or for poorer. Your mother took those vows when she married your father. His misfortune didn't absolve her of her obligations. You don't know for a fact that she left because Granddad treated your father unfairly. She might have left anyway.'

Anger flashed in his eyes. His jaw clenched. 'Maybe you should have been selling fortunes at that fair tonight.'

'Things aren't always black and white. Some situations merit a deeper inspection into the shadows. I think I know what that fortune-teller saw to upset her so. She saw you carrying through your plan and destroying forever the possibility of you and I ever trusting each other.'

'We were born to be enemies, Yardley. We haven't made it that way.'

'Couldn't we change it? Or do you even care to try?'

'We already know that's not required for us to have a good time together.'

'I would hope you'd recognize that required, for me at least, the highest level of trust. Did you think I wouldn't go home with you Sunday night because I didn't want to make love with you again? That I was playing some coy little game? I've never learned how to let myself get close to anyone without letting them into my heart. Don't you see I can't risk that with a man who has locked away all feeling that makes him feel vulnerable?'

'Just because someone's hurt you, Yardley, it doesn't mean he and I are made from the same mold.'

'Stupid me. I want to believe that.'

'Because neither of us can deny how good we are together. Why don't you stop analyzing everything and learn how to enjoy yourself?'

'That's how I got hurt last time.'

She tried to look away, but he pulled her into his arms and kissed her hot and hard and heavy. Yardley opened her lips to him, her breasts straining against his iron chest. As his tongue shot into her mouth, she clamped her lips around it.

Her traitorous body grew soft and pliant. His hands cupped the backside of her jeans, lifting her to his hips as his leg jutted urgently against her womanhood. Moistening, she shimmied against him. His hands played against her throat.

He broke off the kiss, but did not release her. 'Let me inside you, Yardley. You're so rare. Exquisite. I'd never hurt you.'

Inwardly, Yardley quivered with longing. But she summoned the last of her resolve.

'I can't think clearly when you kiss me like that.'

'I'm not asking you to concentrate.'

'All the more reason to do it. You'd better leave now, Simon. Please.'

'We will make love again. And we both know it.'

Yardley couldn't argue, but silently, she resolved not to let it happen.

Simon drove with the windows down, night air shrieking in protest as he sped down the highway toward Bentley, the town he'd driven back from less than an hour earlier.

The purpose of his strange errand made him feel foolish. He considered himself a realist, immune to superstition. But he hadn't missed the fortune-teller's initial reaction to Yardley when she'd looked in the bogus crystal.

He knew the whole set-up was a lark. Yet Yardley assumed the fortune-teller's evasiveness indicated the disaster he was going to cause between them by marketing the peasant girl figurines. What exactly there was between them he couldn't say. Great sex once. Different from any he'd ever experienced. And he was aching to give it another shot.

He'd never expected to get involved with her. Sure, he could abandon his plan, but then he would never know whether her interest in him was solely related to convincing him to do just that. She didn't understand, this wasn't about money. He wanted justice. For generations, her family had enjoyed status and prestige at the expense of his family, scraping by and looked down upon. He wanted the world's attention, and this was the only way he knew to get it. He wanted everyone to know that the Blyes were the craftsmen and the Kittridges cheap opportunists.

The only weak link in his plan was his increasing fondness for Yardley. He wanted her so badly he pulsed like dynamite set to go off, wanted to take her home and slowly undress her, kiss and caress her ivory skin until the sun came up.

Reaching the parking lot where the carnival had been, he brought the car to a screeching halt.

'Damn,' he muttered, raking his hair back and getting out of the car. The rides sat motionless and empty, their lights turned off for the night. With quick, clipped strides, he walked towards the location of the fortune-teller's tent, astonished to find nothing there.

'Can I help you, Mister?'

Simon turned and found a wiry bald man in jeans and an NYU sweatshirt standing behind him.

'I was looking for the fortune-teller.'

'Carnival's closed for the night.'

Simon forced down his impatience. 'Yes. But my friend lost her necklace earlier and I was retracing our steps hoping to find it.' The Kittridge influence. Already Yardley had him lying.

The man rubbed the back of his neck, looking Simon up and down.

'Don't know of anything being turned in. Betty Flannigan usually runs that booth.'

'Where can I find her?'

'She's gone home.' Eyeing Simon, he hesitated. 'Her son runs the coffee shop downtown, and I imagine they're still open. Why don't you go by and leave your phone number with him? I'm sure he'll pass along your message.'

'Thanks.'

Flannigan's Coffee Shop was not difficult to find, as it was the only establishment downtown with lights still on. Simon found Evan Flannigan behind the counter. He ordered coffee he didn't want and quickly repeated his mission.

'Wish I could help you, but Mom came down with the flu and missed the carnival tonight. First time in twenty-three years, and she's really upset about it. She loves the kids and all.'

'Do you know who might have taken her place?'

'Sure don't. Sorry. I hope your friend finds her necklace. Might turn up in the car or in her pocketbook.'

'Hmm? Oh, yes. Thank you. I hope your mother recovers quickly.'

Simon walked back out on the street, the overhead bell jangling behind him. Okay, the incident was strange. That he'd come here at all indicated he was getting soft.

Because he feared Yardley would slip away from him, and she wasn't even his at all. Her melodic voice, her breathtaking smile wrenched his insides. He couldn't get her out of his mind, and he would do anything to have her. Anything except concede what she really wanted. Growing up, he'd watched everyone close to him buckle to the Kittridges. If Jarred Kittridge had it in for a man, he simply circulated the word among his friends, the other business leaders in town. And that was it. No job. No credit. No future. And that tradition was ending with him. Mimi was never going to have the hold on this town Jarred had exerted. He would see to that.

Shortly after sundown on Hallowe'en, Yardley stood over Serena's pot of chilli on the stove, stirring slowly with a wooden spoon. Wrinkling her nose, she turned her face away as its peppery aroma assaulted her nostrils.

'Are you sure this stuff's going to be fit to eat?' Yardley called upstairs, realizing Serena would never be able to hear her above the loud stereo. Serena sure seemed to be in a good mood this evening.

Giving up, Yardley set the spoon in its holder. Simon had called her at work and asked if he could come over this evening, so she'd invited him to dinner. Cheerful anticipation buzzed through her. She pushed aside her worries over caring far too much for a man so obviously wrong for her. Simon made no pretense of not wanting to make love to her again, but she was grateful for his restraint in not pressing the issue.

He'd been over almost every evening since the carnival. Sometimes she'd look up suddenly and see him undressing her with his eyes. She knew he was only waiting until her own desires wore her down. That was why he kept coming back.

In time she'd crumble. And he was waiting. Wanting to be nearby.

So sure of himself, so sure of getting what he wanted.

Oh, hell, she wanted it too. She didn't fear intimacy with him. Mercy, it had been glorious!

But getting her heart hopelessly entangled was another story. Damn him. Why did he have to be so attractive and macho and sexy, making her insides melt every time he came near?

Maybe it was just a matter of time.

And jumping off a cliff might be safer.

Glancing out of the window, she saw only a square of black laced with shadows of swaying tree branches. A blustery wind out of the north was beating against the walls. She hoped it wasn't going to rain until after the local children finished their rounds of trick-or-treating.

Not that she was expecting any little ghouls to show up way out here. Too far off the beaten path.

She wished Serena would come downstairs. She was anxious to see Casey in his costume.

The music upstairs cut off suddenly. Yardley went into the den and started the fire in the fireplace. When she looked up, she nearly dropped the still-burning match as she saw a black-haired witch holding Casey's hand. He was dressed in a pumpkin costume, complete with a green felt hat cocked atop his head for a stem. She recognized the beaming witch as her sister.

'Good grief, Serrie, where'd you get that get-up?'

'Like it?' her sister asked, grinning to expose a gaping grin with two blacked-out teeth. She pushed a sheaf of long black hair off her shoulder. 'I made the dress.'

'Think it's short and slinky enough?'

'Adds a nice touch, doesn't it?' Serena asked, smoothing her black tights.

'Why are you dressed up?' Yardley asked.

'I told you I was going to a Hallowe'en party.'

'No. You didn't. Do you want me and Simon to take Casey trick-or-treating, then?'

'Simon's not coming over here to babysit. We're taking Casey with us.'

'We?' Yardley asked.

The doorbell rang, and thinking Simon had arrived, Yardley walked to answer it.

'Why don't you look in the mirror and see the dreamy look in your eyes when that man's around, Yardley?' Serena called after her. 'Why don't you just admit you've fallen for the big bad wolf?'

'I haven't fallen for anyone. What about these horror videos I rented and your chilli? Why didn't you tell me you were going to a party? I could have made other plans.'

'Which wouldn't have included you and Simon having a cozy evening alone here?'

Furious, knowing her sister had set her up without a shred of shame, Yardley swung the door open and came face-to-face with a gorilla. He cocked his head and methodically scratched his armpit.

Yelping, she reeled backwards, the blood rushing from her head, the world swimming around her.

To her horror, the gorilla rushed in after her.

'You okay, ma'am? It's me, Beau.'

Yardley dropped into the chair behind her and ducked her head down between her knees. Her hands wrapped over the back of her head, she gulped long, deep breaths until her dizziness passed.

She brought her head up to find herself staring into Beau's and Serena's concerned faces.

Serena looked up sharply at Beau, then swung a kick at his furry ankle.

'Ow!' he complained, jumping back.

'You nearly scared my sister to death,' she accused.

'I didn't mean to.'

'You should have better sense than to come to the door with a mask on. Not that it looks much worse than your face.'

'Yeah, well, you seemed to like this face fine back in Nashville, sugarpie. And I expected you to answer the door.'

'How could you know who would answer the door? And stop calling my sister "ma'am". It upsets her.'

Yardley raised open palms in the air. She alternated her glance between them. When had this reconciliation taken place? If that was what it was. 'Please, you guys. Stop it. Go to your party. I should have expected as much on Hallowe'en.'

Blinking, Serena stared down at her. 'Are you sure you're okay? Want some water or something or some aspirins or something?'

Yardley shook her head. 'No, really.'

The doorbell rang. Suspecting Simon had arrived, Yardley boosted herself to her feet. She did not want him to know she'd nearly passed out. Remembering she'd fainted at his house, he'd make too much of it. She didn't want people thinking she was sick.

Simon walked through the door wearing, thankfully, no costume, just jeans and a deep blue velour shirt and his leather jacket. Gosh, he looked good.

His eyes played over her appreciatively, and her heartbeat quickened.

'Becoming costume,' he quipped.

Yardley pushed back her bangs, fighting to suppress a smile. 'Come on in, Simon.' She stepped back from the doorway to let him pass. As he brushed by, she smelled soap and leather.

'I can smell chilli all the way to the river,' he remarked, sweeping his gaze across the room. He took off his jacket and hung it on the coat rack. Yardley realized that jacket was becoming a permanent accessory lately.

'Must be the jalapeños,' Serena explained.

'You don't put jalapeños in chilli, Serrie,' Beau countered.

Simon's glance settled on Casey. 'Tell me you're not sending the boy out dressed like a fruit, Serena.'

Serena scowled. 'He's only two, Simon. I don't want him to scare himself. And he's not fruit, he's a vegetable.'

'What about a pirate or a football player?' Beau suggested. 'It's a good thing you have me around to stop you from turning him into a wuss.'

'He's a baby,' Serena insisted.

'I can tell right now, you're gonna need more babies to keep you from ruining him,' Beau said, catching hold of her by the waist from behind and nuzzling her neck. 'Maybe we could work on that later.'

Serena wrenched away from him. 'I didn't ever say I wasn't divorcing you, Beau Jennings. No one said you're going to be around.'

'Oh, hell, Serena. This hot and cold stuff is really getting irritating.'

Simon cleared his throat. 'Maybe Yardley and I should leave for a while,' he volunteered.

Serena shook her head and held up a hand. 'No, we're leaving. The house belongs to you and Yardley tonight, and we won't be back until very late.'

She cast Yardley a defiant look. Yardley glared back at her sister, then reddened as she realized Simon was watching her with mild amusement.

Serena retrieved her and Casey's coats from out of the closet. She pulled Beau towards the door.

'Be careful,' Simon warned. 'There's a severe storm warning out.'

Serena dismissed him with a wave of her black-gloved hand. 'Don't worry about us. You two just have fun,' she said with a wink, shutting the door behind her.

'Save me some of that chilli!' Beau called through the door.

Once they were gone, Simon turned to her. 'I can go if you'd rather.'

Yardley smiled faintly. 'Somebody's got to eat all this chilli. And I've got horror movies. I want you to stay, Simon.'

'You're sure?'

She nodded. He shook his head as he walked towards her. 'I know I've seen Beau somewhere before,' he claimed.

'If you'd met him before, wouldn't he recognize you too? He probably resembles someone else you've met. So do you want to sample Serena's atomic chilli?'

Simon shook his head. 'Not at the moment. But go ahead and eat if you're hungry.'

'No. I'll turn the burner down, and we can watch the movies in the den. I've built a fire in there and set up the VCR.'

'I can't remember the last time I sat and watched a movie.'

'We don't have to. The movies were Serena's idea anyway.'

'What's bothering you, Yardley?'

She shook her head. 'Nothing.' She shrugged. 'I expected we'd all have dinner together and take Casey out. I guess I'm a little disappointed at missing that.'

'Your sister has her own life.'

'Sometimes I envy her freedom. She never plans anything, and yet everything turns out wonderful for her. Maybe being irresponsible is better than it's made out to be.'

'Stop comparing yourself to your sister. Serena's charming, but if you haven't noticed, she's still childishly rebelling against someone or something. Maybe she's even rebelling against you.'

'Me?' Yardley touched fingertips to the front of her shirt.

'You act like her mother at times.'

'Habit, I guess. I was five when she was born. I thought I was really big stuff when Francesca, my stepmother, used to let me help with the baby.'

'I'm sure you'll make a great mother some day. But in the meantime you might want to cut Serena some slack. Especially if you're still determined to convince her to stay in Kittridge.'

'I suppose if she stays married to Beau, she'll be going to Nashville.' Yardley wondered if Beau had a job. If he did, his employer must be quite lenient about his taking so much time off. Her face lit up as a solution struck her. 'Unless Beau had a job here,' she mused aloud.

'Why don't you leave them to work their lives out on their own, Yardley? You mean well, but they might not appreciate your interfering.'

'But it's silly to let Beau take her and Casey all the way to Nashville when I can – '

'Listen to yourself. Your grandfather did a lot of things because he could.'

'I don't want to argue with you this evening. Not about that.'

'I don't either. Sorry. I'll go check the fire while you take care of the chilli.'

Yardley did a quick clean-up, wiping off counters and turning the stove down low. As she stood in front of the stove, she realized she was delaying joining Simon in the den. The plain fact was, she loved him, and she shouldn't.

Through his arrogance, she sensed a bitter loneliness inside him, and she longed to get closer to him, to prove he wasn't alone. If only he would let down those barriers as easily as he'd shed his trousers. Simon was a man who would go down kicking and screaming rather than admitting to needing anyone. She'd thought, by backing off, she was sparing herself.

Now, she realized she couldn't protect herself. He was the strongest, most fascinating man she'd ever encountered. And there was only one way to prove to him that she cared. She was going to have to take all the risks, let down her barriers and hope his would come down with them.

She covered the pot of chilli and stiffened her spine. Was she sure enough of Simon to gamble her heart and soul? She could be dead wrong. Simon could be every bit the cold-hearted scoundrel he professed to being. Hadn't she once believed she loved Grant?

But things had been off-kilter with him from the start. She'd felt it but stubbornly refused to acknowledge it. With Simon, even rolling around in the sand trap had felt like fate. He made love beautifully.

She raised her head and looked up to find him standing in the doorframe, watching her. He was tall and handsome and magnificent. She longed to race into his arms and entrench herself there.

'A thousand dollars for your thoughts, babe,' he said.

Yardley grinned. 'It's supposed to be a penny.'

'By the look on your face, I'm guessing I'd get my money's worth.'

Yardley thought of suggesting that if he truly wanted bargaining power he could call off his vendetta against her family, halt his plans to reproduce the copycat figurines. The first thing Mimi would ask about on her return was the presence of the mold.

She shrugged off the condemning thoughts. Tonight wasn't about corporate warfare. She had to believe Simon would ultimately do the right thing. She did believe it. If he truly cared about her to any degree he would never be able to execute his plan.

The sudden beating of rain sounded against the roof.

Yardley bit her lip. 'Oh, lord, here it comes. I hope Serena and Beau and Casey make it to their party okay.'

Simon caught hold of her hand. 'They'll be fine. Come on, it's show-time.'

He led her into the den. She'd lit orange and black cinnamon and licorice-scented candles around the room earlier to diminish the over-powering smell of chilli.

Simon had dimmed the lights and scattered the throw pillows across the floor. He walked to the sofa, sat down and took his boots off. 'If you insist on spending the evening watching horror movies, we might as well do it proper-ly,' he stated, setting his shoes aside. He rose and turned on the television while she stood gawking.

Settling himself on the floor, he stretched out belly-down, propping his elbows on a pile of pillows. He glanced up at her, nodding toward the stack of pillows beside him. 'If you'd be more comfortable on the sofa . . .' he said.

Yardley kicked off her flats and wriggled down beside him. Simon smiled, then turned his attention to the movie.

Yardley tried to concentrate, but all she could focus on was Simon lying beside her. She braced herself for him to slide over at any moment. But his gaze was directed straight ahead at the flickering screen.

In an instant, the screen went blank and the overhead light went out. Orange firelight and candlelight flickered through the darkness. Rain drummed steadily against the roof, pounding in time to Yardley's own thundering heart-beat.

'Power's out,' she rasped, her mouth suddenly dry. The dim light increased her awareness of him lying beside her. She pushed herself up on her hands and knees. 'There's a flashlight in the kitchen.'

Simon caught hold of her wrist, his thumb resting against her pulse. 'We don't need it. The lights will be back on in a minute,' he said, gently pulling her to him.

Yardley glided into his arms as he rolled on his side. Molding herself against the hard length of him, she savored how good he felt. Brushing her hair back with one large hand, he kissed the underside of her jaw.

'Do you rub flowers into your hair or what?' he asked. 'You smell delicious.'

He scattered kisses across her throat, shooting ripples of delight through her. She looked up into eyes darker than the night, compelled by the passion and tenderness she found there.

'You're driving me mad,' he accused.

'It hasn't been easy for me, either, Simon,' she admitted.

His lips crushed down hard against hers as lightning flashed outside. As he eased her down on her back and glided atop her, she parted her lips to welcome his hot tongue. It whipped into her mouth and she gently clamped her lips together, pressing her own tongue against his.

Her body heated with the frenzied urgency of desire too long denied. With Grant, the only other man she'd had, she'd always felt a strong inclination to please him. For Simon she harbored a selfish craving to feel him against her, take him inside her. But then she was remembering the shattering ecstasy Simon had driven

218

her to once. A release Grant had convinced her she was incapable of.

When Simon's flattened hand slipped beneath the waistband of her leggings and pressed against her bare belly, she shamelessly wriggled her hips under the heat of his skin. She parted her legs eagerly, gasping as Simon pushed his fingers inside her thin panties, dipping down low to stroke the damp delicate point between her legs.

'Oh, yes, babe,' he moaned.

Clutching his shoulders, Yardley arched her hips to him as fierce pleasure seized her. Boldly, he inserted his fingers into her as though they belonged there.

Her eyes popped open in surprise as he suddenly removed his hand.

Dark eyes shining in the firelight, he was smiling down at her. Reaching down, he began unbuttoning her blouse. Her chest heaved, and she felt feverish as she watched him moving over her. The muscles in his arms rippled as he worked her buttons with deft fingers.

Undoing the bottom one, he pushed away both sides of her shirt-front, looking dismayed to discover her lacy little white bra.

Yardley sat up, pulling her arms free of the shirt sleeves, flinging the shirt aside, then reaching behind her to unsnap the bra. As it fell away, his eyes widened as he viewed her breasts.

He moved towards her, but she pushed him back. She grabbed the sides of his pullover, dragging upwards. He raised his arms to accommodate her. Pulling the garment over his head to bare his expansive chest, she threw it across the room.

Reaching out, she threaded her fingers through his coarse, dark chest hair, digging deeper to revel in the texture of his skin, the swell of muscle beneath. Bowing her head, she drew her lips to his flattened nipple, tracing the small red circle with her tongue.

His muscles contracted, and a low, animal groan escaped his throat. Fueled by his response, she skated her cheek across his chest to suckle his other nipple.

Finally, he pushed her back, easing her down on her back atop the pile of pillows he'd been propped on earlier.

Slanting over her, he lowered his head, suckling and kneading her bared breast. He wedged his knee between her legs, forcing them apart insistently, then grinding his muscles against her burning mound.

Yardley wrapped her arms around his neck,

squirming at the barrage of sensations he relentlessly provoked.

Continuing to knead her pliant flesh, he brought his mouth up to her ear, licking inside it to shoot flames down her side. His hips ground against her thighs. He lowered his mouth to capture hers, filling it with his tongue.

Moving back on his knees, he peered back her leggings. 'Trick or treat, sweetheart?' he asked, his eyes glued to her satiny panties.

'No tricks, Simon,' she said, her breathing ragged. 'What are you doing?'

He grabbed a pillow off the floor. 'Shhh. No tricks, babe. I swear.' Kneeling between her legs, he slipped the pillow under her upraised hips. He bowed to kiss her tingling belly, the heat of his skin penetrating her aching womanhood.

When he suddenly dived lower, kissing her aching midpoint and spearing her with pleasure as intense as white flame, she cried out. Pinning her belly to the pillow with one splayed hand, he carefully inserted a roughened finger inside her satiny catacombs.

Yardley's head fell back as spasm after spasm racked her, draining her as she flowed into him.

'Simon,' she cried.

He held fast to her. After she fell raggedly against the pillows, she opened her eyes to see him smiling over her.

'Why didn't you tell me no one's ever done that for you before?'

'You didn't exactly announce your intentions,' she retorted. 'Did I do something wrong?'

He stroked her cheek with the backs of his fingers. 'Not at all.'

She reached down to unsnap his jeans, surprised when he swung his hips away.

'I think we have a problem,' he said.

Yardley tilted her head. 'I can't imagine what,' she offered, etching a line down his midriff with her fingertip.

'Well, first you'd better stop that. I hate myself for this at the moment, but I don't have any protection, Yardley. And I won't make love to you without it.'

She frowned. 'Nor would I let you. Nothing up your sleeve tonight, Simon?'

He looked disconcerted. 'The other night was a happy coincidence. I don't leave home armed with condoms. It's been a very long time since I found anyone I couldn't keep from making love to.'

'Why?' she asked.

'It stopped making sense.'

'And now?'

'I'm trying to make sense out of this.'

She reached for his zipper.

'Yardley, are you mad? I had a complete physical a few months ago and as far as I know I'm healthy, but I'm also dangerously brimming with sperm. You know, those naughty little – '

'Serena's got about a year's supply of condoms in the upstairs bathroom.'

'Why didn't you say so? I'll be right back.'

Yardley shook her head. 'No, I know the way and where they are. I'll carry one of the candles. I can get back faster.'

He grinned. 'No argument from me on that.'

Standing, she retrieved her shirt and threw it over her shoulders. Away from the fire, the house felt chilly and damp from the rain. She trotted up the stairs, humming as she grabbed a handful of packets. Silently, she thanked her sister.

Condoms in one hand, candle in the other, she started down stairs. She was a quarter of the way down when the world started spinning. Looking down, she saw two sets of stairs in front of her, and she couldn't discern which step to put her foot on.

Reaching frantically for the railing, she opened her hand and the glass candleholder crashed to the floor below. Clasping the rail, she eased herself into a sitting position on the steps, propping her forehead in one hand.

Simon dashed out of the den below. 'Are you okay?' he asked, racing into the kitchen and returning with a glass of water. He doused the candle, then set the glass on the floor and rushed up the steps toward her. 'What happened?' he demanded, standing over her, his hands on his hips.

'I was going down the stairs too fast in the dark and nearly fell. My own fault,' she said. 'Sorry if I scared you.'

He stared at her, and she could tell he didn't believe her. She raised her clenched fist. 'Do you think this is enough?'

His deep laugh echoed through the house. 'For starters. Depends what time Serena and her crew get back.' He took her by the elbow to help her up.

At the foot of the stairs, he startled her by sweeping her into his powerful arms and carrying her towards the den.

'Watch the glass,' she cautioned. 'Maybe I should get the vacuum.'

'Later,' he cut her off, taking her into the den and laying her across the rug in front of the fire. As he reached down to shuck his jeans, he hesitated. 'Yardley, maybe you should go back to that doctor you saw. You lose your balance a lot.'

'So I'm clumsy, Simon? I've never felt better in my life, honestly. And he's already told me I'm fine.'

'Never felt better in your life, hmm? I'm going to have to work on that,' he said, stripping off his jeans, then his boxers. His engorged manhood sprung free, pointing toward her. He made quick work of sheathing it, then climbed astride her, prying her legs apart with his own.

'It's all I've been able to think about for days, getting inside you,' he told her, the tip of his erection poking into the soft flesh of her belly. 'You're all silky on the inside and slick as honey.'

He swung his hips, watching her expression as he entered her. Her flesh tightened around him, and he thrust deeper. Yardley raised her hips to meet his thrust. Then again, as he moved in a rhythm as steady yet unpredictable as the rain outside.

He kissed the skin between her breasts, then up the inside curve of each one in turn. His slow heat overpowered her. She breathed in his unique scent of musk and spice and sex, tasted the salt in the toughened skin on his shoulder.

He growled from down deep in his throat. She watched his handsome features slacken in profound pleasure.

She felt him hard and hot and magnificent inside her. Bucking beneath him, she floated away into a swirl of mindless, buoyant delight.

Yardley clung to Simon as he shuddered with the throes of his release.

She didn't move, and neither did he. His head fell across her bosom. He stayed inside her.

Finally he raised his head, stroking her face and her hair and kissing her lips. 'What are we going to do about this, Yardley?' he asked. 'This is too good to let go of.'

She averted her eyes as best she could. He was referring to the physical passion – not her personally.

'If I knew the answer to that I might not be here. Or maybe that's why I am here, Simon.'

She hoped he wasn't noticing her trembling lip. Only one thing had brought her to Simon. She was in love with him. And she knew that was the one wrong thing she could say that would send him fleeing out into the stormy night faster than anything.

He moved off of her. 'It's never been like this with anybody before,' he said. 'Honestly.'

She bit her lip. 'Chemistry, I suppose,' she murmured.

He rose, scooping his boxers off the floor. 'I'll be right back, don't go away.'

Yardley nodded, knowing he was going to dispose of the prophylactic. She pulled the crocheted, cream-colored afghan off the back of the sofa and draped it over herself as she lay back against the pillows. She pushed the incident on the stairs out of her mind. She had just gotten up and started moving around too fast, that was all. Besides, she was fine now.

As she heard the hum of the Dust Buster from the hallway, she smiled to herself. Simon wouldn't leave the glass there for anyone to get cut.

He was good inside. She'd already bet her heart on that. But she wondered whether he could ever overcome his bitterness and mistrust to allow himself to love anyone, especially a Kittridge.

Dread knotted her stomach as she realized Simon might never admit to the feelings for her she read in his eyes but needed to hear him confess to. How long could she endure that?

He reappeared in the doorframe. 'Damn things. I certainly hope twenty-first-century technology can come up with something better. You didn't get dressed, I hope?'

'Already, Simon?'

He stretched out alongside her, wrapping her in his arms and hugging her back to his chest. Yardley closed her eyes. His arms were heaven.

He kissed her cheek, crossing his arms over her naval. 'Soon, I think. God, this is good, just lying here with you. Stay here with me, sweetheart.'

'I'm here, Simon. I'm not going anywhere.'

She closed her eyes and drifted into a brief, peaceful slumber.

CHAPTER 10

Simon locked Yardley's hand in his as he strode across the front section of his property, dry leaves crunching under the soles of his boots. The glorious red, gold and orange hues of autumn shifted under the final brilliant streaks of late afternoon sunlight, and the brisk air filled his lungs.

Yardley walked silently beside him. As he cast a sideways glance at her, slim and fair and blonde and proud, his chest constricted. Simon had always had an eye for uncommon beauty. Yardley Kittridge was forged from no mold. She was an intricate masterpiece, like fine porcelain. Fragile to the touch. Strong enough to endure through time.

She smiled up at him, tilting her face to the sunshine, and he wondered what she was thinking. Hers was a face he would never tire of looking at. And this feeling of treading through midair, never wanting to let go, was foreign and confusing. All his life he'd been careful never to entrust his well-being to anyone but himself. To depend on another person was to give someone power over you, and Simon had vowed never to leave himself at anyone's mercy.

Yet here was Yardley Kittridge, sharing his bed and seeing all this good in him he didn't believe existed, even while he pursued his vendetta against the company she'd inherited. Instead of fighting him, she was trying to understand. He would have been better prepared for an outright battle. Simon had thought of giving it up, but he couldn't let go. This was about him and Jarred and reached farther back than anything between him and Yardley. And despite his mounting affection and respect for her, he couldn't help remembering that she'd been so hot to get that mold back, she'd tried to rob him. Bringing business into the bedroom had ruined better men than him.

If Yardley was being honest, he was beginning to understand why she'd adored her scoundrel of a grandfather. When it came to people close to her, Yardley wore rose-colored spectacles. Otherwise, she wouldn't have been with him. She assumed everyone had good intentions, while Simon assumed the opposite.

After having the incredible luck of sharing his bed with her the entire weekend, exploring and touching inside and out, skin to skin, learning exactly what made her smile and what made her thrill beneath him, memorizing the places where her skin felt the softest, he found her as much of a mystery as ever.

He only knew that waking up with her in his arms, white-blonde hair covering his chest like a silk sheet and sleepy midnight-blue eyes smiling up at him, started his day with a sense of hope and joy that had eluded him all his life. Why the hell was she here with him? He had nothing to give her except a good time in bed. Happy as he was to oblige her on that score, he knew sex alone didn't mean enough to Yardley that she would abandon her principles.

And lord, had he. He'd brought her here Friday evening, and until now they hadn't been out of bed except to bathe and bring in food from the kitchen. Even for him, the experience was reckless and decadent. He couldn't remember the last time he'd gone an entire weekend without turning on his computer. His own state of perpetual arousal had astonished him.

For two and half days, they'd shut out all the world, even Jarred's ghost. But today was Sunday and the inevitability of her departure was encroaching. Simon didn't want her to go. Ever.

A knife jabbed his gut at the prospect of taking her back to Jarred's house. He'd been alone a long time. He valued his privacy, yet he didn't want her to leave. He had the nagging feeling of rendering a task incomplete.

Yardley, kicking at the leaves as she waded through them, slowed as they approached the covered bridge over the brook. 'It's such a gorgeous day, Simon. There aren't many left before winter kicks in. We should have come outside earlier.'

'We were busy earlier.'

Her cheeks pinkened becomingly. Simon grinned. He knew to what heights of abandonment his angel could soar.

His expression grew serious. 'I hate for you to go.'

'Maybe it's best, Simon, that we have to be away from each other for a while, give ourselves room to breathe.'

Stopping beside the bridge, she slipped her hand out of his and perched herself atop the wooden railing at the entrance. She sat facing

232

him, her hands propped on the rail on either side of her.

Simon couldn't help remembering her dangling on his fence by the seat of her pants. Had that been only a few weeks past? Was he mad to be sharing his bed with this woman? He stepped closer, standing inside the open triangle between her knees. His hands rested atop her legs. 'Breathing isn't a problem. Stay here tonight, Yardley. We can go back and get your clothes and your car. The drive to your office is no farther from here than from Mimi's.'

She tipped her head as though he had said something astonishing.

'I have to go,' she insisted softly. Reaching up, she stroked his stubbled cheek, currently in need of shaving. 'My thinking gets muddled when I'm with you.'

He leaned forward and kissed the tip of her nose. 'What's to think about? This has been the most incredible weekend of my life.'

She blinked rapidly. 'Simon, I'm not going to China. I'll only be a couple of miles away. We can't just shuck our lives and spend all our time in bed together.'

He strummed his fingertips over the underside of her chin. 'Call it superstitious. I have a feeling that once you leave this afternoon, everything's going to change.'

'Nothing's ever going to change the way I feel about you, Simon. You're too smart a man not to have guessed that.'

He stared at her hard, a knot forming in the back of his throat. 'I'll never have enough of you.' He ran his fingers along a strand of her silky, golden hair, then slanted his glance to meet hers. 'Everything in my life that's ever meant anything has been taken away.'

'I must go home, Simon. I truly don't know what I mean to you or you to me. Maybe we should try keeping our clothes on long enough to decide if we even like each other. I don't regret having come here, but I honestly can't say it was the best thing for either of us.'

'Can you say it wasn't?' Simon ran his hands through her long hair, remembering how it had fanned across his pillow earlier, how it brushed against his skin when they made love.

Wrapping his arms around her shoulders, he pulled her head to his breast and cradled her against him. Simon didn't believe in love. In his world, you looked out for yourself or you were screwed. But what he felt for her transcended lust.

He knew he should tell her she was precious beyond words. He would never want another woman the way he wanted her. He would have cut his own hand off to protect her and keep her safe and happy. Dangerous, dangerous thoughts.

Raw emotion rumbled inside him like heavy snow before an avalanche. And he feared it would bury him if he tried to release it, if he tried to get those words out. She'd tumbled into his life like a miracle. But he could not relinquish his last shreds of pride and suspicion that dammed the words in his throat. He had come too far to surrender to the command she held over him.

And why should she even want his love? He had no promises to offer with it.

So instead of telling her what was in his heart, he lowered his head and moved her back to kiss red lips as tart and sweet as fresh cider. He hugged her to him again and closed his eyes at the feel of her slender form against him. He inhaled her scent, basked in her feminine heat.

Reluctantly, he drew back.

'Thank you, Simon,' she said.

He gave her a blank look.

'For this weekend. Whatever happens.'

He raised a corner of his mouth in a half smile. 'You forget, I don't let go of anything that matters. Go to China. I'll find you.'

'I wish I could believe that.'

'We'd better go, darling. It's getting late.'

He grasped her waist to help her down, glancing up to find her studying him intently. She quickly averted her gaze, before sailing through the air suspended in his arms.

Yardley gazed out of the car window as Simon pulled the Jag up to Mimi's house. Beau's truck was parked over to the side, and he and Casey were tossing a toy football around on the front lawn. Beau stood poised like a bear as he prepared to throw the ball to Casey. The little ball in his huge hand looked the size of an almond.

'Ah, just in time,' Yardley said, grinning at Simon as he killed the engine. 'Isn't football one of your favorite games?'

Simon raked his hair back with one hand as he pulled the keys out of the ignition. 'Maybe I should just go on straight back to the house.'

She set one hand on his wrist. 'Please stay for a while. Since Beau's here, Serena's probably whipping up something fantastic for dinner. We haven't had a decent meal all weekend.'

With an indulgent flick of one dark eyebrow, he pushed open the car door. Watching him, Yardley felt love so strong surge through her that she ached inside. It brought the sensation of balancing on a highwire. Was she letting herself in for a fall so far she'd never recover? Even if he gave her nothing else, she wanted desperately to hear him say just once he loved her. That alone would carry her through the rest of her life, even if the rest of her dreams never materialized.

Simon shed his jacket and shucked it on the porch rail.

'You're coming up against some stiff competition, Yankee!' Beau challenged as Simon approached, rolling up his shirtsleeves.

'Yeah, well we'll see who's stiff come morning, slick,' Simon shot back, flashing Yardley a wink. 'Looks like Casey here already has you winded. I'll help you out and put him on your team.'

Yardley left them to their game and dashed inside the house. Serena was in the kitchen slicing a steaming ham.

'Hi, Serena,' Yardley greeted her.

Serena cast her a sidelong glance. 'The prodigal sister returns. I don't think I need to ask how your weekend was. If that grin was any bigger, you'd need your face widened.'

Yardley's face heated. She filched a sliver of ham, jerking her hand back as Serena swatted at it.

'I hate Sunday nights,' Yardley proclaimed, blowing on the morsel before popping it into her mouth. 'So, are you going to Nashville with Beau?'

'I'm only trying to convince him why I can't go with him.'

Yardley nodded towards the front yard. 'Seems you're doing a bang-up job.'

'He's so damn hardheaded. Only listens to what he wants to hear.'

'Serena, it's none of my business, but he's real and alive and seems to be very much in love with you. You must care for him if you went through with a wedding. Isn't taking a chance with him better than holding on to old memories?'

Serena wiped her hands on the sides of her jeans. 'You don't know my memories, Sis. Would you mind getting the potato salad out of the fridge? Simon's staying for dinner?'

'I think so. He's playing football with Beau and Casey.'

'Good. There's plenty.' Folding her arms across her chest, Serena paced to the front window. Simon had tackled Casey and was flat on his back in the leaves, dangling the kicking, laughing tot in midair. Serena smiled. 'Grown men and they're all as silly as Casey deep inside. He'd make a good dad, your Simon.'

Yardley raised her eyebrows. 'Well, Beau seems as crazy about Casey as he is about you. And please don't tell Simon what a good dad he'd make or he'll be running into the hills. This is good between us, Serena, but we're not making any commitments. His parents separated when he was young, and I don't think he believes in families.'

Serena turned to her. 'I can't believe the shining star of the Kittridge clan would settle for less than her heart's desire. What happened to the big church wedding and tons of white lace and pink roses you always talked about? And the picket fences and jelly-faced kids?'

Yardley gave her a fierce scowl. 'A couple of weeks ago, you were encouraging me to sleep with him. You invited him over for dinner, for Pete's sake!'

'You of all people should know better than to listen to me. I thought a little fling might be good for you. But all I have to do is take one look at you and see you've fallen for him. He's blind if he can't see it too. You and he have talked through all this commitment business?'

'N-no.'

'Yardley, he's gorgeous, but seems to me if felt the same way about you, he would have stopped plans to reproduce your figurine. I just don't want to see you get hurt.'

'The figurine has nothing to do with us.'

'Nothing and everything. Did you know the Henderson department store chain is already advertising the damn thing? Ads claiming these are exact duplicates of the originals? They were in this morning's *New York Times*. If you read the paper.'

Yardley paled. 'No, I didn't.'

'Too busy, huh? Simon's already taking advance orders. He's going to have lots of cash for Christmas this year. In the meantime, be ready to answer your phone tomorrow morning. I can't say I blame the owners of the originals for being ticked. If I paid thirty-five hundred dollars for a rare figurine and overnight the value dropped to maybe fifty dollars, I'd be indignant about it myself.'

'I didn't know you cared so much about the company.'

'I care about you.'

'Simon has the mold. He doesn't need me in his bed to manufacture the figurines and sell them through Hendersons.'

'If you weren't so distracted, you would have known about those ads coming out and already put out some advertising of your own explaining these are cheap rip-offs and not the originals. And why, Sis, are you too distracted to be on top of these things?'

Yardley inhaled deeply. Was she a complete idiot? 'You think he's just entertaining me?'

'I don't know what to think. Here, go set this out on the table.' She shifted a relish tray into Yardley's hands. 'I'll probably have to throw Casey in the tub before he's fit to sit at the table.'

'I'll get him cleaned up for you, Serena.'

She shook her head. 'No, you go get the troops inside. I have bathing that boy down to a system.'

Yardley stepped out on the porch. 'Casey's being called in to the showers,' she announced. She looked at Simon and Beau, both breathing hard, sweaty, and covered with fragments of leaves. Both wearing sheepish grins. 'Maybe I should make that a team summons,' she reconsidered.

Tossing the toy football aside, Simon scooted Casey up the stairs ahead of him, then came up beside Yardley. A thrill rippled through her at his nearness, and she acknowledged how thoroughly he possessed her. Maybe Serena was right. Maybe she did need some larger assurance that she wasn't repeating her mistake with Grant.

He looped an arm around her shoulders, pulling her closer to his side. Heat radiated from him through rapidly chilling air. The last of the sunlight was fading, leaving them in gray shadows.

He kissed her lips, and an easy warmth spread through her chest. When he drew back, she locked her fingers together to keep from touching him.

Peering at her through dark lashes, he frowned. 'What's wrong?' he asked.

She shook her head, glancing anxiously at Beau, who quickly excused himself and shot inside the house. 'It's the figurine, Simon. I know I don't have the right to ask you not to sell copies, but . . .'

His dark eyes blackened. 'You've known my intentions all along. I haven't lied to you. Babe, if I had any doubts as to whether that mold rightfully belonged to your family in the first place, I wouldn't produce the figurine. Don't tell me you expected that to change.'

She pulled away from him and paced the width of the porch. Then she spun to face him, hair flying. 'Maybe it should. Does it matter who it belonged to sixty years ago? Everybody who had anything to do with sculpting and selling the originals is dead, yet here it sits between you and me.'

He stepped closer. 'I didn't know there was any barrier between us.'

'Your ads, Simon. What am I supposed to tell my family? Even my sister's looking at me like I'm a fool.'

'You think I'm making a fool of you, Yardley? If you believed that, you wouldn't have been at my house this weekend.'

'I was there because I thought I liked you.'

Simon groaned. 'Yardley, I've let you in closer than I've let anybody in a very long time. Please don't turn on me over this. I started it long ago, and I intend to finish it. I spent a summer working with your grandfather, I earned an art scholarship to study in Europe. I built a business men older than I am only dream of running one day, and only because I spent every minute thinking of the day I would pay back Jarred Kittridge for what he did to my family.'

'You're punishing a dead man. If hurting us is going to restore your father's pride and bring back your mother and your brother, then do it. But it won't. You're only going to feel empty inside. You're better than that. Look at yourself, Simon. You're intelligent and talented and compassionate. Not arrogant and detached. No matter how much you want to be like that.'

'I've paid my dues. I'm entitled to my arrogance. I'm not a soft touch.'

'Really? How many people would have carried an unconscious burglar into their house? You could have just called the police and an ambulance.'

'I could see you weren't armed. Besides, I frisked you before you woke up.'

She gasped.

'You see? I'm not as fine and noble as you're trying to convince me I am.'

'I don't believe you.'

'Yardley, is Kittridge Collectibles' reputation so fragile as to be destroyed this easily?'

'No. Of course not. I'll expose you as an exploitative opportunist.'

He smiled. 'I never doubted you would.'

She shrugged. 'Just remember it's nothing personal, Simon. Do what you have to do. But I will too.'

'Can we eat now? I'm starving.'

'Sure.'

Serena had cooked enough food to feed a pro football team, and by the time the dishes were washed, the refrigerator was brimming with enough leftovers to last all week. Yardley and Simon were wrapping the last of them when the strains of guitar music drifted in from the living room.

A deep, soothing voice echoed through the house.

'Beau's singing!' Yardley exclaimed in surprise. 'Let's go listen.'

Poised on the ottoman with his guitar across his lap, Beau nodded an acknowledgment as they came in the room, but after that, his gaze remained riveted on Serena, who sat on the sofa with Casey on her lap. He played several lulling country ballads, songs of hard times and unrequited love.

Yardley dropped into the nearest armchair. Simon sat on its arm. Glancing up, she caught him smiling down on her in a way that made her heart swell. Had she risked too much of herself to him? She didn't know how to love anyone halfway. And God help her, she did love him.

The sound of a car approaching snapped Yardley from the dreamy spell Beau's music had spun. She moved to the window. Pushing aside the drapes, and pressing her face to the glass, she peered into the front yard, surprised to see a cab had pulled up.

The driver came out first, rounding the hood to open the passenger door. When the passenger stepped out, Yardley knew she shouldn't have been surprised.

Still, a panic rose inside her, and her hand trembled against the stiff draperies. She turned, realizing Beau had stopped singing and everyone was looking at her.

'Is someone here?' Serena asked.

Yardley glanced at Simon. He watched her with concerned interest. She cast him a tentative smile.

Pressing her hands together, she approached the front door.

'Mimi's home,' she announced over her shoulder.

CHAPTER 11

The front door swung open, cold wind blasting in along with Mimi.

A sliver of apprehension ran through Simon. He stepped closer beside Yardley, setting a hand lightly on the small of her back. His curiosity got the better of him as he came face to face with Mimi Kittridge. Personally, he knew little about the woman except that she exerted a gripping influence over those close to her. The old-timers swore Jarred had been an affable guy back before he'd brought home his bride.

Mimi flitted her glance over Simon with the small, dark eyes of a raven. Suddenly, his unshaven jaws itched. He grew aware of his wild, disheveled appearance from the earlier football game. Mimi lifted an eyebrow, but quickly dismissed him and returned her attention to her eldest granddaughter. With a single swoop of her hand, she plucked the leopard-print-trimmed hat off her head and beamed at Yardley.

'Hello, dear,' she greeted her granddaughter, sweeping her into a brief hug, leaving Simon holding a handful of air. 'Whatever is going on? Someone's abandoned a horrible old truck in our yard.'

'No one's abandoned it, Mimi.'

Finally, Mimi acknowledged Simon. 'Mr Blye,' she murmured, offering a gloved handshake. 'Jarred would have been pleased you've come to see us again. He always thought highly of you.'

Simon regarded her without blinking. He knew Jarred would have blown a fuse to find him here today, and that inwardly the old woman was seething. Grudgingly, he admired her outward calm and omitted pointing out Jarred's struggle to thwart his business.

'I learned much from your late husband, Mrs Kittridge,' Simon replied, matching her cool demeanor.

As they eyed each other like dueling opponents preparing to count off paces, Yardley broke the ensuing silence. 'I'm so glad you're back, Mimi. But why didn't you tell us you were returning today? We've just finished dinner, but there's plenty left if you don't mind a cold meal. Serena made ham and potato salad.'

Stripping off a black glove, Mimi waved her off. 'Oh, honey, I couldn't eat anything salty. Actually, I'm not hungry. I love New York, but all that smog has my head pounding and my stomach in knots. That's why I decided to come home. I do hope you have everything under control.'

Without waiting for an answer, she stepped past them. 'Serena, I'm happy to see I haven't missed you and Casey. I was afraid you'd vanish again before I got home.'

Serena stepped forward and gave Mimi a hug while Casey clung to Beau. 'No, Mimi, I wanted very much to see you.'

Serena's straightforwardness seemed to distress Mimi more than Simon's presence, he noted. She reached out and straightened Serena's collar. Fidgeting with her gloves, Mimi turned to Casey. 'You're getting so big, Casey. Really, Serena, you and that boy need to get settled.'

'I've been wanting to discuss that with you,' Yardley interjected.

Mimi smiled condescendingly. 'Yes, and we'll talk later, dear. I've had a very long day.'

The door opened again. Harvey Miller, who operated Kittridge's local cab company, marched in, loaded with packages and luggage.

'Where do you want these, Mrs Kittridge?' he asked.

'Just set them down here in the foyer, Harvey,' she ordered, pointing out a spot.

Yardley's eyes widened. 'Good grief, Mimi! What did you do, buy out Macy's?' she asked.

Mimi laughed lightly. 'I couldn't resist all those early holiday sales, I'm afraid. It's impossible to find nice things here in town. The styles are outdated before anything gets here. Wait until you see the beautiful cashmere sweater I found you. Well, it'll keep until later, of course.'

Harvey shook his head. 'I'll go get the rest of it, Mrs Kittridge.'

'I'll give you a hand,' Simon offered, trailing out of the door behind him. He felt Mimi's eyes scalding his back.

The cold air revived him from the shock of her unexpected arrival. Nothing she could think or say could scathe him. But he knew she wielded a strong influence over Yardley. And that bothered him. He felt threatened. Had he found heaven only to have it yanked away from him now by a conniving old woman?

'Thanks, Mr Blye,' Harvey said.

'No problem,' Simon returned, fishing the last of the bags out of Harvey's trunk. 'Working kind of late tonight, aren't you?'

'This is my last run. I've been running overtime since Winnie got laid off from the bottling plant in Westrun a couple months back.'

'Sorry to hear that. Why don't you send her around to my office and I'll see what I can do?'

Harvey's expression narrowed. 'Thanks, Mr Blye, but she already put in an application at Evergreen Images and was told there weren't any openings.'

'Well, send her back around. Tell her to come to my office this time.'

Harvey's grim face brightened. 'She'll be there tomorrow.'

Back inside, Mimi had taken her coat off and was jabbering baby talk at Casey, who cowered at his mother's knees.

Mimi was too distracted to notice Harvey in the foyer. Afraid to interrupt her, the cab driver stood awkwardly with his hands in his pockets. Simon extracted his wallet from his pocket and dug out a bill, shifting it to Harvey's hand.

Harvey's eyes widened as he glanced down. 'Thanks, Mr Blye.'

'Goodnight, Harvey,' he said.

'He needs some time to get used to you,' Serena apologized to her grandmother, ruffling her son's hair.

Mimi looked up sharply. 'Perhaps if you'd stay put I wouldn't be a stranger to him each time I see him.'

'You could try speaking English to him, ma'am.'

A hush fell over the room as every eye turned to Beau.

Mimi raised one eyebrow. 'I don't believe we've met, young man.'

Beau rose, dwarfing her and extending a bearlike paw. 'Beau Jennings, ma'am. I'm Serena's . . .'

'Friend,' Serena blurted.

'Husband,' Beau finished.

A look of astonished betrayal flashed between the two of them.

'Well, which is it, dear?' Mimi demanded of Serena.

'We did get married, but . . . I would really prefer to discuss this with you in private, Mimi.'

'Without even telling your own family?' Mimi asked. 'Of course, we'll have to arrange a proper wedding here in Kittridge. I know you're anxious to make plans, but after that wretched trip, I can't think right now. If you'll all excuse me, I'm going to turn in. Much as I'd love a cup of tea, I'm too tired to make any.'

'I'll bring a cup up to you, Mimi,' Yardley offered.

Mimi smiled wanly. 'Sweet of you , dear, but I don't want to disrupt your evening.' Her eyes drifted to Simon.

'I was on my way out,' he said. He couldn't help noting the satisfied spark in her eye at his announcement. 'Tomorrow's a work day, you know. Goodnight, Serena, Beau, Mrs Kittridge.'

Yardley turned to him. 'I'll walk you out to your car.'

Simon ushered her out the door.

Yardley walked along side of him. 'Thank you, Simon.'

'For what?'

'For being civil to Mimi. I want you both to like each other.'

'Asking a little much, isn't it?'

'She was quite warm to you. As a matter of fact, she didn't seem the least bit upset to find you in her house.'

For an intelligent woman, Yardley had missed a lot. 'Ah, but you expected her to be, didn't you? What if she had known how we spent our weekend? And she was obviously glad to see me go. I'm sorry to disappoint you, Yardley, but I'll never approve of Mimi. Nor understand her. What kind of woman puts her granddaughter up to committing a crime?'

'A desperate one. Look, I take responsibility for my actions. I'm the one who tried to break into your house, so if you're angry, direct it at me, not her. Don't judge her, Simon.'

'Something more terrible than encountering me could have happened to you that night, Yardley. You don't place someone you love in that kind of danger.'

She turned to him with a sly look. 'What do you know about love? You seem to have spent most of your life dodging it.'

He smoothed back his hair. 'I believe it gives you more to lose. My concern is with building things that last.'

'Love lasts forever. My granddad's gone, but I still love him. And my mother.'

He chuckled bitterly and gave her a sidelong glance.

'Wouldn't my mother then have loved me too much to leave? And you're wrong about me, sweetheart. I thought I was in love once, a long time ago. We were students together in Italy. Had a great time for a few months. I asked her to marry me, but she said she had decided long before she ever met me that she always wanted to stay free.'

'And so you closed your heart forever?'

As they reached the car, Simon reached out and caught her hand in his. He halted, and she spun to face him.

'Not forever, it seems,' he conceded. Just looking at her made him ache inside. 'Only until you came along.'

'I don't know, Simon, that I can give you what you need.'

He gave her a slanted smile. 'You can start by coming back to my bed tonight. Doesn't the thought of me there all alone sadden you?'

Yardley laughed lightly. 'I can't pity you, Simon. You're far too good at getting what you want.'

'Not good enough, it seems, since you're denying me your company.'

Her expression grew solemn. 'Simon, I loved this weekend. But I'm not like you. I can't shut off my feelings. They always get the best of me whether I want them to or not.'

'Come back with me, Yardley. Stay with me tonight.'

She shivered. 'And then what?'

'When I touch you, when I'm inside you, nothing matters. It's like the exhilaration after working on a design that refused to take shape exactly as I see it and then in this rush of excitement everything comes together at once. You feel that good to me, darling. Can't we just enjoy each other and go from there?'

'I can't risk any more, Simon. Neither you nor I are the kind of people who leave anything to chance.'

She was leaning with her back against his car, and he stepped forward, pinning her against the metal with his body.

Reaching out, he pressed a hand to her breastbone. He felt her heart drumming beneath his fingers.

She tilted her head up at him, puzzled by the gesture.

'You're as passionate in spirit as you are every other way. There's more going on between us than this wonderful chemistry, Yardley. We both know that. You're not like any woman I've ever known.'

Bowing over her, he nuzzled her neck, drinking in the taste of her skin. He plastered his hips to hers, pressing into her with a howling urgency. At first she stiffened and shifted as if trying to get away. Then she softened against him, raising her hips to meet his.

The thought of any other man ever touching her tore him apart. She wasn't his to keep, yet he wanted her to be. But what could he promise a woman who had always been given everything?

He stared down into her wide sapphire eyes and read in them a profound adoration he didn't merit. Who was this woman who saw more good in him than he did in himself?

'You make me feel things I never wanted to,' he whispered, his voice rough in the night breeze.

'If I didn't care for you, Simon, that first night in the sand trap might have happened anyway. But I never would have made love with you again. Something special happened between us, and if I'm wrong about that, tell me now,' she pleaded.

When she raised her face to him, he kissed her with a restrained tenderness, his fingertips playing over the slope of her jaw, the hollow of her throat. Yes, he'd made love with many other women. None had stayed under his skin as she did. He wanted her now, again, as fiercely as he had that first night. Maybe more.

'It was as though I had never really made love before,' he said, kissing her cheek, his hand slipping inside her sweater to caress skin as soft as freshly fallen snow. He pushed into her skimpy bra to cup her breast. With steadfast gentleness, he began kneading it.

She drew in a sharp breath, her eyes fluttering shut. Simon wanted to make love to her here and now. He kissed her thoroughly, melding himself against her.

As her nipple starched beneath his fingertips, his own arousal flared excruciatingly. If he could bring her home tonight, he would not waste time sleeping.

'You're so warm and sweet and incredibly sexy,' he whispered. 'And we've only begun to explore the heights where we can take each other. Come with me, Yardley. It can only get better. I want so desperately to make you feel good.'

Drawing back, he stroked the backs of his fingers against her temple. Her breathing was ragged, her lips parted to reveal small white teeth. She looked at him through blue eyes hazy with passion.

He realized how afraid he was of losing her. He remembered now the long quiet afternoons he'd spent at home alone after his mother left. He would turn the radio or television up loud to fill the silence and toss his schoolbooks aside while he sketched or painted. And he would pretend he had a big happy family and any minute they would all come home. Over the years, he'd anaesthetized himself to loneliness. Yardley had reawakened his most sensitive, long-numbed emotions. If she turned away, he'd fall again into a pit of emptiness, and he feared this time he'd never climb out.

For a thirteen-year-old, he'd been far too serious, too intense. But his father was working too hard and suffering too badly to pay attention. And he had no mother at home to fret over his brooding. Physically, he could care for himself, so his dad never guessed he needed anything more.

Back then, Simon had swore that when he was old enough he would have a family of his own. And he would protect it from anything outside that threatened to tear it apart. He would stand up to anyone and anything.

How long ago had he abandoned that dream? Forgotten it?

Slowly, he withdrew his hand from Yardley's sweater, adjusting the hem and setting his hand on the fabric over her midriff. He looked down at her, then leaned down to lay his head across her breast. He felt her heart thumping. Her chest fell as she exhaled deeply.

Bringing up her hand, she webbed her fingers through his hair, holding him to her. Simon closed his eyes. His need for her surpassed seduction. He understood now why he fought against his feelings. Bringing them to the surface was painful. Pulling a dagger out of a wound.

'I'm aware of what you can do for me, Simon. Physically, we're like fireworks in a bonfire. It's the part of yourself you hold back that frightens me. Like after we make love and you start talking and then you catch yourself and clam up as if you've suddenly remembered you expect me to take a knife to your back while you're asleep. I care for you too much to ever betray you. Maybe I expected this weekend would prove that. I don't have any barriers left to let down to prove myself to you, and it hurts that I have to keep trying.'

Simon raised his head to look at her. 'You have barriers. I heard your teeth grinding when Mimi and I met at the door.'

'I admit I was tense. But I have to believe this business with the figurine is separate from us. It is, isn't it, Simon?'

'Thank you for finally understanding that.'

'Simon, I can almost appreciate why you feel compelled to duplicate our figurine. I know you believe you're doing the right thing, and I admire you for acting on your convictions.

But we have a problem here that runs stronger than some porcelain doll. I am and will always be a Kittridge. There's nothing I can do to change that, nor would I want to. You're the one who is going to have to reconcile yourself to that. When we're together, you shut it out, then, when it surfaces, I feel your contempt.'

'Not for you. Not now.'

'My family is part of what I am. I know Mimi's no saint, but she's struggling to do the best she can under difficult circumstances. Don't be so quick to judge, Simon. I care about you enough, I want you and her to get along.'

'You'd better go inside. Your grandmother's waiting for her tea.'

'Goodnight, Simon,' she replied, turning towards the house.

He glanced up at the house just in time to see the curtain drop back in one of the upstairs windows. Mimi. She'd been watching them.

Yardley set the teapot on the tray alongside the mug and the neatly folded napkin and the blossom she'd plucked off one of the chrysanthemums on the porch. She worked methodically, trying to blot the misery from her face.

She loved Simon as she'd never loved anyone. She read in his eyes and felt in his touch his regard for her. If he could only say he loved her, nothing else would matter. That he couldn't or wouldn't say it left an emptiness inside her. She couldn't go on endlessly involved in a passionate affair providing her with less than what she really needed. She couldn't love a man who refused to love her back. To her, love involved complete surrender without reservation. She had surrendered, only to be conquered.

Was Serena right? Did Simon merely want to keep her occupied while he set his marketing plans in place?

She knew she would find out when she took her next step to stop him. She loved him beyond reason, yet she wasn't fool enough to sit back and let him destroy her company's fine reputation.

Serena entered the kitchen, Casey tagging alongside her. She glanced absently at the tray Yardley was preparing.

'Mimi's been home an hour and already she's got me in the bridal registry and you sulking here without Simon.'

Yardley glanced up. 'She's hurt to have missed your wedding. To tell the truth, I am too. And I wasn't planning to stay at Simon's tonight.'

Serena wrinkled her brow. 'Why do you both refuse to listen to me? She wants a production to

262

show her friends I've become an honest woman.'

'Serena, why are you even here when you
constantly question Mimi's motives?'

Serena shrugged. 'Maybe I just want to visit
with my grandmother. Maybe I want someone
to talk to. You're both so damn anxious to have
me married and fittingly respectable, nobody
here is willing to listen to how I feel.'

Yardley looked up at her sister. Why did
Mimi's return have everyone on edge? 'I've
been listening, and you're not making much
sense. I love you and Casey and I want you
both to be happy and safe and well. You must
have thought Beau could give you that since you
went so far as to marry him. Personally, I think
you're afraid of Beau, afraid of loving a real live
man who is going to expect you to settle down
and build a stable life with him. Loving memories is safer, isn't it, Serena?'

'Ah, the expert speaks.'

Yardley ignored her barb. 'There's no
reason you and Beau have to run off to
Tennessee. Beau could work here, and the
three of you could stay. Mimi and I could
help you go back to school . . .'

'And we'd be under Mimi's thumb for the
rest of our lives.'

'The three of you could find your own place. I could arrange a job for Beau.'

Serena shot her a look of mild amusement. 'You're going to offer Beau a job? At the plant?'

'Well, sure. He may not have experience working with ceramics, but I'll see to his training myself . . .'

Serena howled with laughter, then patted her sister on the shoulder. 'I love you, Yardley. I guess it's funny we turned out to be so close, coming from practically different families. We should be jealous as hell of each other.'

'I've been jealous sometimes of you and Dad and Francesca.'

'You know why Dad left Kittridge, don't you? It took him a long time to break free and find his own life. He wanted us to grow up in the real world, not Granddad's little kingdom where we always had the right jobs, the right friends, the right connections waiting for us. He wanted us to learn to get by on our own.'

'He never said that to me.'

'He was afraid he'd already lost you to Jarred and Mimi. Even when your mom was alive, they were always trying to take charge of you, spoiling you with expensive toys and clothes, planning what schools you'd go to.'

'They were there for me when Mom died. Dad wasn't.'

'You feel so sorry for Mimi over losing her husband, and you can't relate to how Dad must have felt after your mom died? When it happened to Dad, he was much younger than Mimi is, and he had to face the rest of his life without the woman he'd thought he'd be with forever.'

'I was too young to be thinking in terms of him. I'd better get this up to Mimi before it gets cold.'

'Watch out for her, Yardley. If you're in love with Simon, don't let her come between the two of you.'

'I'm not the dishrag you think I am, Serrie. I know my own mind.'

'Glad to hear it. And do me a favor, Sis. Don't suggest to Beau he go to work for you. Don't you see the prospect of his taking me and Casey far away is the only reason Mimi's so anxious to give us her blessing?'

Wondering how she might do it in a way that wouldn't offend his pride, Yardley carried the tray up the stairs, relieved to scale them without experiencing any dizziness. She pushed aside the realization that she'd come to expect it now.

She tapped on Mimi's door with the side of her shoe.

'Come on in, dear,' Mimi called.

Yardley leaned into the door to push it open. Mimi, wearing her champagne-colored satin nightgown, sat up in bed with her head propped against the pillows. Her face, washed clean of make-up, looked sallow against the gaily patterned sheets.

Yardley set the tray on a side table along the wall. She poured the steaming brew into a mug.

'I brought your favorite, the cinnamon-flavored tea,' she announced.

'Thank you, Yardley,' Mimi replied, pushing herself up higher against the pillows. 'I did want to stay up and chat with you. I just can't seem to keep up these days. It was all I could do to change and crawl into bed.'

Yardley sat on the edge of the mattress. 'We can talk now. Have you taken anything for your headache?'

'Oh, pooh. Those pills never work. And I must say I've been terribly worried about you.'

'Worried?' Yardley asked.

'Yes. Well, when I heard you attended the harvest dance with young Mr Blye, I have to admit I was shocked. Everything that man does is directed against our family. He's the last man on earth I would expect you to be seeing socially. Finally, I calmed down and realized you were simply charming him out of implementing his outlandish scheme to reproduce the peasant girl. I had confidence you would be delivering good news to me shortly. But when I opened this morning's paper I was horrified to see he's actually advertising them! Yardley, don't tell me this cretin has gotten the better of you.'

'He's not a cretin, Mimi. And I told you before you left I was not going to try to get the mold from him.'

'Then what in heaven's name was he doing here tonight?'

'He was bringing me home.'

'Home from where? Why are there suddenly secrets between us? You've always confided in me, since you were a girl.'

Yardley's stomach compressed. 'We've been seeing each other, Mimi. I care very much for him.'

'He's not a decent kind of man, Yardley. You deserve better. Looking at Mr Blye, I can understand your fascination, but you're too level-headed not to see what he's doing. You're just icing on his vendetta against your grandfather.'

'Why did Granddad try to stop the permits for Simon's company? He was so sick then, I wouldn't have thought he'd care.'

'Hard enough to find good labor in this town without another big company competing for it. Your grandfather was just . . .'

Yardley's glance narrowed. 'He was just going through the motions, wasn't he? It was your idea to stop Simon.'

Mimi's expression confirmed her suspicions. The truth chilled her.

'He should have gone somewhere else to build his business. This is our town, and it always has been.'

'It's not just our town. Lots of other people live here and they care about having jobs and good stores and opportunities.'

'Mercy. I can see he's been brainwashing you, turning you against your own family.'

'No. What he's doing isn't right. But he believes he's justified in doing it. Does that make him any less decent than Granddad?'

'So you're going to lie back and just let him walk all over us? Ruin the reputation for quality and integrity your grandfather and your great-grandfather worked so hard to establish? Jarred left the company in your hands because he had faith in you, Yardley. He had confidence in your good sense and integrity. You were never flighty like Serena. Really, Yardley, what would Jarred say if he saw you now?'

'There is a way to stop Simon. And it's the route we should have gone to begin with. I'll take care of it.'

Mimi cast her a beatific smile. 'You have so much of Jarred in you.'

Yardley shook her head. 'I'm doing this because we're in the right. Don't ever ask me to interfere in Simon's business again, Mimi. This foolishness has to end somewhere.'

'Oh, it will, dear. It will. You're young and trusting, but I've seen men like Simon come and go. They fall into a lot of money, and they think they have the world in their hands. They get bold and foolish, and they don't have the stamina to back up what they have or build a future. Their fortunes vanish overnight, just as they were made. Yes, Mr Blye's riding his high horse right now. But when the dust settles, he'll go back to being nothing more than a penniless hoodlum. Perhaps then you'll see him in a clearer perspective.'

Startled, Yardley turned to her grandmother. 'Mimi, I intend to stop Simon from embarrassing us. I have no intention of ruining him. He's worked hard for what he has. And his financial status has no bearing on my affection for him. I wouldn't care if he were broke.'

'Ah, but it would matter to him. At least, I would hope so. Can you imagine him living off Kittridge money? Or is that part of his plan?'

Yardley stood, her face burning. She couldn't believe her grandmother's cruelty.

'How could you even suggest that, Mimi?'

'Jarred and I always wanted the best for you, dear.'

'Simon is the best. Please just get to know him, give him a chance.'

Mimi winced.

'What's wrong?' Yardley asked, stepping closer to the bed.

Still wincing, Mimi waved her off. 'Nothing, nothing. Just a cramp.'

Yardley stared down at her grandmother's pinched face. She did look worn. This wasn't the best time to be discussing Simon, she reflected guiltily.

She took the teacup from her grandmother's hands. 'Get some rest, Mimi. We don't have to talk about this now.'

'Don't fall prey to that man, dear. He used your grandfather to teach him to sculpt, then turned it against him. Do you think he's above using you as well?'

Yardley cast her a worried look as she helped

her slide down in the bed. Lovingly, she drew the quilt over her.

'Goodnight, Mimi,' she said. 'I'll chain the front door when I come back.'

'You're not going to him, are you, dear?'

'No. I'm going to the office for a few hours. I have some catching up to do. Mimi, you will speak to Serena tomorrow, won't you? I think she needs your advice. She's very confused.'

Mimi gave a long-suffering sigh. 'That girl was born confused. Of course I'll talk to her, dear. Not that she's ever listened to me.'

Yardley turned out the light and closed the door behind her.

Until she was out in the hall, she didn't realize she was trembling. If Simon hadn't been using her to enhance his status in Kittridge, she never would have been on the golf course with him. She couldn't tolerate the thought of his love-making being nothing more than a ploy to gain her confidence.

Was that why he didn't say he loved her, because even he couldn't orchestrate the ulti-mate lie? She refused to believe he had deceived her. She recalled how he had unexpectedly dropped his head to her breast earlier, how tense his muscles had felt. In her heart, she trusted and accepted him. In her head, she

271

knew they were business rivals and sparring on that level was a necessary part of survival.

Gathering up her coat, purse and car keys, she went outside and got in her car. The clear sky overhead was black velvet and translucent diamonds.

She started the engine. She could be in Simon's bed right now. She belonged there. She drove along the deserted highway, the short distance to his house. The neatly cut stone and mullioned glass fell in sleek, modern architectural lines. Simon's fortress on the hill. A light burned in the front window. She wondered what he was doing, and somehow, she knew he was working.

She pulled up to the gate and studied the intercom panel.

She leaned back in the car seat, taking a deep, frosty breath. She hadn't run the heater. Her heart and body had betrayed her before. Grant had never moved her soul as Simon did. Her body had never responded to Grant as it yielded to Simon's, had never evoked such fevered responses from him as it did from Simon.

She wanted to share his bed tonight, but she craved more than physical contact. She wanted, God help her, to touch his soul, to pull it out and make him look and see it wasn't charred and cold but good. She closed her eyes. Simon was the man she wanted to marry. It was his children she wanted planted inside her, with him there to love her and watch them grow.

She needed more than he was willing to give. Now that she recognized that, she couldn't go on accepting less.

Backing away from the gate, she pressed the gas pedal to the floor and raced off toward Kittridge Collectibles.

CHAPTER 12

A cold front blew in during the night. The icy snap in the air forecast a hard winter ahead.

Walking out to his car, Simon contemplated the overcast sky and dreaded the inevitable ice and snow of the coming months. Damned inconvenience. He hoped it would hold off until after the holidays when he might be able to sneak off for a few days and visit the old man in Sarasota. Images of sun, sand and sailing on clam-blue waters popped into his head. But as soon as the thought struck him, he realized he wasn't inclined to want to go anywhere away from Yardley.

He arrived at the office around ten. He'd been up half the night at his computer, the other half spent tossing and turning in a bed suddenly far too big for even his substantial frame. Before dawn, he'd given up, making a pot of coffee and sipping it as he watched the sun rise from his front porch. Funny, he'd reflected, how he'd devoted most of his life to creating and producing things of beauty, yet he'd given scant attention to the beauty around him.

Until Yardley had woken him up. Suddenly, the sky was clearer, the sun brighter, what remained of the fall foliage all the more brilliant. As the sun came up, his heart lifted along with it. Why, of all the women he could fall in love with, did he have to choose Jarred's granddaughter? He'd always instinctively followed a path that led him in a single direction. Now, he found himself wanting to pull over and enjoy the view.

Last night he'd seen Yardley's car creep over to his gate. Joyously, he'd waited for her to buzz on the intercom. But she'd driven away instead. A woman like Yardley deserved to be loved and treasured. As no one could do as well as he could. He had never been a coward. Why couldn't he tell her?

He remembered the only time he'd ever told a woman he loved her. Only now did he realize that more than a decade had passed since Monica had simply blinked and replied, 'I wish I had known you were so serious, Simon.'

Yardley had pressed him, not for promises or commitment, simply acceptance of who she was. Could he swallow enough pride to ever warm to Mimi? No way would she ever stop being Yardley's grandmother. Yardley would never abandon her devotion to her, nor would he expect her to. Yardley was right: she came as a package, family and all. He couldn't just pull out the pretties. If he wanted her, he had to deal with the whole Kittridge clan. Lord, he should have thought, back on the golf course that night, how complicated this could get.

Now, he paused at the open doorway of Kay's office, his briefcase in one hand, a Styrofoam cup in the other.

Kay, the phone tucked in the crook of her neck, motioned for him to enter.

'Yes, Robin. I'm sure we can handle that. We'll put a rush on the order. You should have the stock before Thanksgiving,' she was saying as she nodded at Simon. He sat, placing the cup on the desktop and removing the plastic lid.

She hung up the phone. Her office smelled of perfume, and she had a vase full of pink carnations on her desk. The blooms brightened an otherwise dreary day.

She smiled broadly. 'Corrigan's in Atlanta wants to carry the peasant girl. Of course, we'll have to step up production . . .'

'Careful, Kay,' he cautioned. 'We can't sacrifice the quality. This is admittedly an imitation, but not a cheap one.'

'Aye-aye. Simon, the stir over the peasant girl is drawing attention to the whole line. Corrigan's wants to carry it. They want you to come down there for a collectibles open house at their downtown store. Tremendous publicity.'

Simon slid the container to her. She looked down into a mound of whipped cream.

'Hot cocoa,' he explained.

'Thanks. Should I be worried when my boss arrives bearing gifts?'

'No, Kay. You do your job well. So I'm going to Atlanta, am I?'

'I don't think we can pass this up, Simon.'

'Nor do I. Are you sure it's the peasant girl sparking their interest and they're not simply catching on to the line?'

'She's making them take a second look. You know how slow people are to embrace new things, and your designs are a bit avant-garde.'

Simon smiled slyly. 'A blend of the twenty-first century and the nineteenth. You really should learn something about art.'

Kay gave him a serious look. 'You're not backing down on the peasant girl, are you?'

Simon scowled. 'Why would I?'

'Yardley Kittridge. I heard some talk in the diner downtown . . .'

'You shouldn't go to those places. The food's not fit for eating. Yardley Kittridge runs that other company . . . not this one.'

Kay smiled. 'Glad to hear it. But watch out, Simon. Stopping the enemy by luring him over to your side is a tactic as old as time.'

'I pay you well to advise me on business matters, Kay, and you do one hell of a job.'

'But butt out of this? This one's free because we're friends, Simon. My God, don't you see it? Local boy makes good. Comes home. Homecoming queen who never gave him the time of day swoons at his feet. You're too smart to be taken. Can you honestly tell me she hasn't tried to convince you to abandon reproducing the mold?'

Simon couldn't answer.

'And it's not like I'm not jealous,' she added.

'Oh, don't, Kay. We both know it would never have been a good idea for either of us.'

He realized then that a woman totally on his side had been in front of him all along. But she hadn't been the right one.

'Damn shame,' she said. 'At least one of us has too much integrity.'

Simon chuckled inwardly. He'd never been accused of that before.

Proceeding into his office, he studied the expanse of paneling, massive oak furniture and leather upholstery. Only a few weeks ago, he'd felt like a king when he'd sat in this chair and stared out of the long window behind the desk across the meadow behind it.

Now he realized he'd found something that mattered more, something he needed to hold on to beyond his success. Jarred Kittridge was dead, his judgement left to a higher power. The Kittridges had always been shrewd businesspeople. The Blyes were the artists, the craftsmen. He only wanted the truth to be known.

Yardley didn't agree, but she was trying to understand. Mimi, on the other hand, would never forgive him. He hung his head over the desk blotter. Could he go through with this even if it cost him Yardley? Or was Yardley truly his? He had to know. And if he backed down now, he would not only alienate the merchants he had so diligently courted. Evergreen Images was not so well-established that it could survive a blow like that at this point. He'd gone too far to back out.

Maybe carrying out his plan was the only way he'd ever know for sure the extent of Yardley's interest in him, whether he could trust her.

Kay's voice crackled on the intercom. 'Simon. Walter Cartwright, the buyer from Whitwell's, is on the phone. He's very interested in our entire line, but he insists he'll deal only with you. Line three.'

Excitement welled inside him. A major gift store chain on the West Coast wanted his line. He and Kay had nearly given up hoping for Whitwell's.

'Thanks, Kay.' When he reached to push the button on his phone, his ever-steady hand was shaking.

'Goodnight, Ms Kittridge. Be careful driving out there. Weather's getting nasty,' Jake Bellman, the night watchman, told Yardley as she passed him in the hall on her way out of the Kittridge Collectibles plant. 'Rain's supposed to turn to sleet, maybe even snow.'

'Thanks, Jake.' She flashed a smile at the stocky, gray-haired man who had worked for the company since he was in his late teens. 'I'm armed.' She hoisted the umbrella she kept in her office for such occasions.

'Your Granddad never had an umbrella. I used to keep a spare here just in case he needed it.'

Yardley paused under the bright fluorescent lights of the now deserted corridor. 'He worked a lot of late nights, didn't he?'

'Sometimes he'd just stay up here late talking. I think that was his way of working things out in his head. He'd act like he was asking me for advice.' Jake chuckled. 'Like he needed advice from someone like me? Old Jarred was the smartest man I ever met. Nobody could put anything over on him.'

Yardley gave him a long, thoughtful look. 'Do you think my grandfather was a fair man, Jake?'

His smile dropped. 'He always treated me right.'

'But the others? Were the other employees dealt with fairly? You can be open with me, Jake. I'm not trying to trap you. I just really need to know if my grandfather misused anyone who worked here. So I can make amends.'

'People are always going to gripe about something. It's human nature. Nobody can please everybody. Your grandfather demanded a lot from people, and he didn't make allowances for anyone who couldn't keep up.'

Yardley realized this was the most she'd get from Jake. 'Thank you for your honesty, Jake.'

'Ms Kittridge, I see a lot of things that go on around here, and I try to do my job and mind my own business. Everybody can see you've got a lot of heart. Back in the old days, Jarred took responsibility for everybody like they were family. The company got bigger. A couple workers started taking advantage of him. He had to kind of step back and detach himself, be the boss and not some good-natured uncle. He might have stepped on some toes in the process, made some people sore, but he had to put the business first.'

Yardley nodded. 'Thank you, Jake. Goodnight.'

Jake unlocked the front door for her. Six-thirty and it was black as midnight out. Her car was one of only a couple scattered in the well-lit parking lot. Carrying her briefcase and handbag by their straps over her shoulder, she opened the umbrella.

She was halfway to her car when Simon's Jag pulled up. Halting, she watched as he climbed out, smiling at the welcome sight of him. He wore a black trenchcoat over his suit.

Unable to wait, she walked forward to meet him.

'You're getting drenched,' she greeted him, shifting the umbrella handle to his hand and standing close to him to stay under it.

'Who cares?' he asked, surprising her by capturing her lips in a knee-buckling kiss. 'Oh, that's better,' he declared, smiling down on her. 'I was afraid I'd miss you.'

'Miss me?' she asked.

He nodded. 'I've been tied up all day in meetings and on the phone. Babe, doors are opening I'd never dreamed would unlock.'

She lowered her gaze. 'I'm glad for you, Simon,' she murmured.

He lifted her chin with his fingertips. She met his dark gaze, her heart pounding and her belly tingling. He smelled of soap and spice and sandalwood. The rain drummed on the pavement.

'Yardley, backing out of the peasant girl campaign now would be suicide for my company.'

'Do what you have to, Simon.'

'I went by your house and Serena said you were still here. I wanted to see you before I left.'

'Where are you going?'

'Los Angeles. I'm on my way to the airport.'

'How long will you be gone?'

'I should be back by the end of the week. As soon as I can.'

'Will you even be able to get out in this weather?'

'It's not supposed to get really bad until later tonight. Come with me, Yardley.'

'I'd love to go. But you know it's impossible. Even if I could get away, you'll be in your meetings. Do you really want your competition in that close?'

'I want you as close as I can get you, babe. Wouldn't it be wild to leave Kittridge behind us for a while?'

'We'd have to come back eventually.'

'I've got to go. If I miss my flight, I may not get out tonight.'

'Yes, go, then.'

He kissed her again, his lips as hot as the rain was cold. She pressed close to him, memorizing the feel of his body. She didn't want him to go anywhere without her. Yet perhaps his being away right now was for the best. When he returned, he'd be in for the surprise of his life, and guilt stabbed her when she realized what she was doing. He was so elated and optimistic. For once he was happy, and she was wrecking everything for him.

If she didn't come straight with him now, she might not ever have the chance.

He placed the umbrella back in her hand, turning away. She clasped one hand over his, forcing him to hang on. He looked down at her, raising one eyebrow quizzically.

'I love you, Simon,' she blurted, her words tapping with the rhythm of the rain.

A light filtered into his dark eyes, and a smile teased the corners of his mouth. 'It's not as if I'm going to China, darling.' He threw her own words back at her.

Yardley's mouth dropped open. Damn him. Why did she have to love him? Why had she admitted it?

One broad hand looped around the back of her neck, his fingers entwining through her hair. Simon slanted over her, taking her mouth for his own, kissing her until her mind went blank and her knees went weak.

Finally releasing her lips, he kept his face close to hers. 'You don't give up, do you? Maybe you and I are two of a kind after all. How could I not love you, babe? We'll talk when I get back. Dammit, I didn't want to go to begin with. Now . . .'

Yardley stood stunned. By the time she comprehended what Simon had said and realized when he got back he would be as angry at her as a wounded lion, she knew she had to warn him now of what was coming.

But before she could move, she heard the slam of a car door. Simon sped off into the night.

'Are you sure you're up to this, Mimi?' Yardley asked as she straightened the russet bow on the autumn centerpiece of eucalyptus and baby's breath on the mantelpiece. Potpourri oil bubbled over a tealight, scenting the room with a blend of cinnamon, cloves, oranges, and apples.

Mimi turned, looking stately and elegant despite her small size in a deep blue dress. 'Oh, I'm fine, dear.'

'I don't see why you insisted on hiring a caterer. Serena offered to cook.'

Mimi set a dish of spiced almonds on the coffee table. 'I won't have my granddaughter performing menial tasks and showing people how good she is at them. Besides, she always tosses in some odd ingredient to make things taste strange.'

Yardley shook her head. 'She's inventive. It really doesn't feel right having a party here. Don't you think it's too soon?'

Mimi shook her head. 'You have so much to learn. This isn't purely social, Yardley. Entertaining is part of the business. You'll understand the importance of maintaining social contacts when you need a building permit or a delivery made in a hurry. Of course, I always handled that for Jarred, and I plan to continue to do so for you. Lord knows it's the least I can do to hold up my share of the business.'

'Mimi, since you're feeling so much better, we need to go ahead next week and have papers drawn up to make Serena a partner.'

'Yes, we do need to take care of Serena. But a full partnership, Yardley? That's a lot of dead weight to carry. Perhaps there's another way to take care of her financially without compromising our control. Lord knows how that hillbilly she married will ever provide properly for her and Casey.'

Yardley gaped at Mimi as though she were a Martian. 'Serena has as much right to a partnership as I do. I have a hard time thinking of her as dead weight.'

'You earn your way, Yardley.'

'Serena could too if anyone had ever given her a chance.'

'You can't think with your heart and run a business. Your grandfather arranged his estate in the best interests of the company. He wanted you in charge because he knew you could handle it.'

'He slighted Serena intentionally? I don't believe it. Granddad would never do that. He adored Serena.'

'He recognized her limitations. Serena has always been unsettled.'

'Well, I'm in charge now, and I'm not doing things the way Granddad would have done them.'

'But he always . . .'

'Did what you wanted him to? That's what you and he always groomed me for, wasn't it? Someone to take his place in implementing what you wanted? You're afraid, aren't you, that Serena and I together will override you. And to think I was ready to steal for you.'

'You never spoke to me that way, Yardley, before you became involved with Simon Blye. I don't like the way he's influencing you, pitting you against your family.'

'I don't want to take sides. I've half a mind to cancel my plans to get an injunction to stop Simon from selling the peasant girl.'

Mimi's eyes widened. 'You're getting an injunction against him?'

'If it's possible. We've used the peasant girl in so much of our advertising, we might be able to pass it off as a trademark. I'm not going outside the law again, for you or anyone else.'

'Why didn't you tell me?'

'I did tell you I was taking care of the situation. I saw no need to bother you with the details. Didn't you trust I would?'

'Not with the leverage that thief has over you.'

'Simon Blye is no thief.' Serena stood at the foot of the stairs, magically transformed with

288

her hair falling over her shoulders in soft curls and wearing a sleek beaded gown in winter white.

Yardley wondered how long she had been standing there.

Mimi paled.

'I don't believe he is either,' Yardley added gently, alarmed by her grandmother's pallor.

'I know he isn't,' Serena insisted.

'How, Serrie?' Yardley asked.

Serena glanced briefly at her grandmother before she spoke. 'Because I was in the workshop the day Granddad pulled out that mold and showed it to Simon. Simon said he'd always thought the mold for a limited edition was supposed to be destroyed. And Granddad was going to smash it. He said he figured it was too old and deteriorated to ever be used again. Simon asked if he might have it then as a kind of keepsake of working with Granddad. Granddad was flattered and he gave it to him.'

'Why didn't you tell me about this?'

'I thought it was kind of funny, Mimi putting you up to stealing it. As long as you felt you were on a mission to recover it, you had to keep seeing Simon. I knew you used to have a crush on him, so I didn't want to give you an excuse to back off.

And I thought if he fell for you, he'd quit his plan to use the damn thing. Everybody'd be happy. But this has gotten way out of hand.'

Mimi crumpled on the couch. 'Your grandfather told me it was stolen.' She directed her comment to Yardley.

'He had no reason to tell you such a thing, Mimi,' Serena repeated.

Yardley's stomach clenched as Mimi looked up to shoot daggers at Serena. Why couldn't Serena let it go and allow Mimi to save face? Mimi must have assumed the mold was stolen, then embellished her claim by attributing it to Jarred. Serena might as well have flat out called their grandmother a liar.

Then Yardley realized that if Mimi had confessed that she was guessing he might have stolen it, she wouldn't have tried to steal it back. She wouldn't right now be trying to wreck his business and possibly drive away the only man she would ever love.

As she slowly comprehended the implications of Mimi's deception, Serena stood defiantly meeting the older woman's threatening gaze.

Serena was much wiser and more righteous than anyone gave her credit for.

The doorbell shattered the accusing silence. Serena moved toward the door. 'Maybe that's

Beau. I hope you don't mind that I invited him, Mimi.'

Simon drove straight from the airport to the Kittridge house. His meetings had gone well. Beyond his wildest dreams. If things played out as they stood now, he was going to have to expand his plant, perhaps build a second. He realized how vulnerable his own success had made him. When he'd started out, he'd had little beyond pride to lose. The risks were greater now, the stakes higher. Ironically, he owed the attention he was attracting to Jarred Kittridge's father, Wilbur Kittridge, the man who had swindled his great-grandfather. People were noticing him only because of the peasant girl. If Wilbur had paid Simon's grandfather for the design, Simon wouldn't have gone to such lengths to reproduce it. Finally, his months of painstaking work were paying off.

For the first time in as long as he could remember, he felt angry at no one. Yardley hadn't been out of his thoughts all week, and he had missed her fiercely. She stirred a feeling so deep inside him, he ached. Admitting he loved her was like removing a splinter. Only after the pain of pulling it free could the wound begin to heal.

If she hadn't expressed her feelings first, he might never have found the courage to tell her how he felt. Might have kept denying it even to himself. But she dared to love him even when sanity should have driven her away. Only she would have done that for him, risked so much of herself.

She'd given him more than he had ever hoped for. He wanted to give her everything she wanted. The home, the kids, the silly PTA meetings. In the glove box was the diamond and amethyst ring he'd searched the antique stores of LA to find. It suited Yardley perfectly. He had no family heirlooms to share with her, no mementoes from his grandparents, who'd been too dirt-poor to have even a nice wedding ring, and nothing, of course, to symbolize his parents' broken marriage.

The ring was technically new, because everything Simon had in his life he'd built from scratch. Yet it was old and traditional, because Yardley believed in loyalty and legacies.

As he drove, he tried to sort out the proper way to propose marriage. Nothing about their relationship had been conventional so far. Catching her attempting a burglary, forcing her to attend a dance with him, making love to her in a sand trap.

This time, he was going to treat her as she merited, prove he intended to spend the rest of his life making her happy. If they could get away from Kittridge together, only for a few hours.

As he turned down the drive, he was astonished to see cars parked throughout the garden, lights blazing from inside the house. Someone was having a party – Mimi, no doubt. He pulled up and killed the engine. Failure to receive his invitation wasn't going to keep him from seeing Yardley tonight.

Stepping on to the porch, he rang the bell. The door opened, and he was disappointed to find Serena, not Yardley standing behind it. He'd been hoping to draw her out on the porch and elicit the kind of welcome he'd been anticipating.

'Aren't you brave, Simon?' Serena asked calmly. She looked unusually wan, her normally bright expression tired and beaten. 'Come on in. You're just in time for dessert. Let me take your coat.'

As she hung it on the rack, she leaned over his shoulder and whispered, 'Mimi's been hitting the wine pretty hard since the appetizer. Watch your back.'

Wearing a phoney smile a mile wide, Serena took his arm and guided him into the dining room, where she introduced him to everyone at the table. Simon went through the motions of polite exchanges, nods and handshakes, but his attention was riveted on Yardley, sitting at one end of the long table. Her hair was done up in curls with gold ribbons woven through it. Her glittery top crisscrossed intriguingly, dipping low enough in front to taunt him with her cleavage. The color of the fabric made her eyes look lighter.

Surprised to see him, she graced him with a dazzling smile, weaving it quickly into a frown as Mimi sneered in her direction.

'Pull up a chair, Mr Blye,' Mimi slurred, her head bobbing over her ice-cream dish.

Yardley shot him an apologetic glance.

'I ate on the plane, thanks, Mrs Kittridge,' he lied. 'Sorry to crash the party, but I need a minute with Yardley.' He gestured at her with his eyebrows.

Yardley tossed her cloth napkin on the table and moved to push her chair back.

Mimi's voice, uncharacteristically forceful, halted her. 'I insist, Mr Blye. Or does sitting at my table prick your conscience?'

Simon scanned the curious faces around her. Her guests feigned sudden interest in food. He glanced at Yardley, who looked shocked.

'Everyone in this room knows you're stealing our design, Mr Blye. So why don't you sit down and enjoy your victory? Have a drink.'

'Seems you've already had enough for both of us.'

Yardley inched closer on the edge of her chair. Simon saw her poised, ready to throw herself in the line of fire.

Yardley forced a smile. 'I don't begrudge Simon's success, Mimi. We should all be glad he chose to come back to Kittridge and build his headquarters here.'

'Psssh!' Mimi hissed, waving her hand. 'Just this afternoon you were on the phone with a lawyer about getting an injunction against him selling them. Why don't you tell him all about that, dear?'

Yardley swung her glance up to meet Simon's incredulous one. Her face was scarlet. He searched her eyes. Hadn't she warned him she was playing hardball? Had he underestimated her? He reminded himself that he had professed that the business with the figurine stood apart from their relationship. Why, then, did he feel so totally betrayed? Ironic, wasn't it, that the only woman he'd allowed himself to love should pull everything out from under him? But then, he'd known from the start she was a Kittridge.

Mimi continued her tirade. 'You've always been too cocky for your own good. I'll tell you right now, you're mistaken if you think you're going to sell a single peasant girl figurine. You may have charmed my granddaughter out of her wits, but you won't put anything past me, Simon Blye. I knew you'd bring Jarred trouble from the first day he brought you here.'

CHAPTER 13

'Excuse me,' Yardley said, pushing her chair back and zipping past Mimi to catch Simon by the arm and pull him back into the living room and out the front door.

'Alone at last,' Simon remarked once they were safety outside. 'What the hell did she mean? Has she put a contract out on me or what?'

'Stop it, Simon. No one's committing murder here. I apologize for my grandmother's rudeness. But have a little compassion. Her whole life has been turned upside-down these past few months. She's suffering terribly.'

'Are you suggesting I go back in and apologize?'

'No, please don't go back in.'

'What she said about the injunction – it's true?'

Arms crossed, she shook her hair over one bared shoulder.

'It was discussed. I'm not going through with it.'

He studied her intently. Was she backing down? Did she lack sufficient ammunition for that particular battle? Or was she finally understanding his viewpoint, willing to concede he had more right to the peasant girl than any Kittridge ever had?

He realized now how much having her on his side would mean to him. 'Thank you, Yardley.'

She shivered from the cold. In her shimmery knit outfit of loose trousers and a wrapped blouse, shoulders bare and white-gold hair spilling over her shoulders, to Simon she looked like a gift ready to be opened.

She brushed hair off her temple, scrunching her shoulders to ward off the chill. 'I'm tiring of the peasant girl tagging along everywhere we go.'

'It's too cold for you to be out here without a coat,' he admonished her, draping his over her shoulders.

'I don't want to fight with you, Simon. And I don't want you and Mimi fighting either.'

'I knew Mimi resented the time Jarred spent with me that summer I worked with him. Even

298

then I thought it was strange. He would have been away from her, working anyway. And she was busy with her club meetings and bridge parties. I wasn't keeping him away from her.'

'She doesn't know you well enough to hate you, Simon.'

He grinned. 'I'm not sure I appreciate what that statement implies. I'll assume it's poor wording.'

She clicked her tongue. 'Don't make more of this than what it is. Our company's image, our family's image, has always been very important to her. You're threatening that.'

'I can't drop the peasant girl from my line now. I've got commitments.'

'I'm not asking you to.'

'Where Mimi's concerned, I doubt it would enhance her opinion of me if I did.'

'You're wrong about that.' Yardley gazed into the darkness before she shifted her glance back to him.

'God, it's good to see you.' He bunched the lapels of his coat in both hands and pulled her closer.

'I missed you, Simon.'

He shook his head. 'Doesn't begin to describe it.' He bowed to kiss lips still sweet from the dessert she'd been eating. She reached up to wind her arms around his neck, returning his kiss with a jarring passion. He brushed his lips against the soft place just below her ear, nestling his nose under the veil of her hair. He reveled in her light, powdery scent, running his hands through the silken strands.

'You just bathed,' he whispered in her ear, his breathing heavy, his loins pinched.

'Before dinner.'

He kissed the inner curve of her ear, tracing its rim with the tip of his tongue. Her shudder of delight as she pressed closer against him fueled his desire. He'd had a long string of solitary days to spend imagining ways he might please her.

'Stuck up there in mid-air, all I could think of was getting back to you. Making love to you again. I want to be inside you right now.' The back of his hand skated lightly across her tummy.

She glanced toward the house, then speared her bottom lip with her teeth.

'I can't leave now. Mimi's guests – she's not up to handling them alone.'

'Send them home.'

'Wouldn't that be a little obvious? After Mimi's display, I'm sure everyone will be leaving soon anyway. Why don't you go home and unpack? I'll tuck Mimi into bed and meet you at your house.'

'Promise?'

'I swear.'

'Yardley, I need to be with you tonight. I never expected to feel this way about you or anyone else. I've loved you for quite some time now, and I should be horsewhipped for taking so long to tell you. Saying it doesn't come easy for me. The funny thing is how such a grueling admission could feel so right.'

'I understand, Simon. Do you think falling in love with you was easy?'

He smiled. 'Damn near impossible for anyone but you. You have this knack for looking through everything I do and seeing more than I see myself. Perhaps that's part of why you amaze me so.' He rubbed the underside of her chin. 'I know you didn't want this to happen any more than I did. Are you sorry, sweetheart? I'm not the kind of man you wanted. And I know that.'

She blinked up at him. 'You're exactly the man I need, Simon. The man I want. I know that now. No, you don't fit into the scenario I had in my head. But I can't deny what I feel in my heart, in my soul.'

'A precious heart you have, Yardley. You never learned how to withhold love, a survival instinct I developed by necessity.'

She pressed a hand to his cheek. 'Because the one person who should have loved you most hurt you. People do cruel things, sometimes without being aware of what they're doing. When I needed my dad the most, he withdrew into himself. I didn't understand then. When he married Francesca, I believed he was rejecting me, rejecting Mom's memory. Now that I'm older, I see more clearly none of it was about me. I turned to Mimi and Granddad. I turned away from him but accused him of casting me off. It hurts less when you find the strength to forgive, Simon. Sometimes we expect too much from the wrong people. It doesn't mean we're not worthy of their regard. I have to go back inside.'

She stood on tiptoe to kiss him. 'Later,' she promised.

He released her from the confines of his coat. 'Not much, Yardley. I've waited too long already.'

'I'll be there as soon as I can get away. I swear.'

She raced inside the house.

'I acted badly tonight,' Mimi admitted sheepishly as Yardley helped her upstairs. 'I am so sorry, Yardley. Jarred wanted us to be provided for, and I'm afraid I get overly defensive when I see someone trying to undermine what it took him years to build. And Serena is so angry with me.'

'Serena will get over it, Mimi. I'm not angry. I know how much you miss Granddad. I miss him too.'

'Where is Serena?'

'She's gone to bed already. And it's time for you to turn in too.'

'I can't imagine why she would lie to protect Simon Blye.'

'She's not lying, Mimi.'

'So I suppose now everyone thinks I am?'

'You probably assumed the only way Simon could have gotten the mold was to have stolen it. Maybe you didn't realize how proud Granddad was to have a protégé, especially after Dad left the business. You forget, back then Granddad expected Simon would be working for him one day. What harm could he have seen in giving him a deteriorated old mold?'

Reaching the top of the stairs, Mimi stiffened. 'Well, you can't just pick up a surrogate son off the streets. If that boy had had a proper upbringing, he wouldn't have been scheming to recreate the peasant girl and sell her as his own. Imagine the gall! People of the lower classes have the morals of alley cats. Nothing like this has ever been done before!'

They reached the doorway of her bedroom. Mimi scanned the interior. 'Where are my cigarettes? I left a pack in here somewhere.'

Yardley led her inside. 'It's late, Mimi. You can find them in the morning.'

'Hmph. Serena probably crept in here and snatched them.'

Yardley steered her toward the bed. 'Why would she do that? Serena doesn't smoke.'

Mimi sat on the edge of her bed. 'Seems there's no one you won't defend lately.'

'Simon wants to right a wrong he believes was done a long time ago. You could at least try to understand him. He knows the kind of strain hardship puts on people, how they act out of desperation and let things slip away because they're trying so hard to get what they need to get by. He wants to be in a position where he can help people be secure in their jobs as long as they work hard, to help other people starting out with nothing have hope of a good future. Until I met him, I don't think I ever appreciated what an easy life I've had. Look at how much more we have than we really need, Mimi. How much would Granddad have had to sacrifice to treat all his employees with more dignity?'

'So, he's turned you against Jarred now? Against your own family, Yardley?'

'I'm not turning against anyone. I'm trying to be realistic. I loved Granddad. Nothing can ever change that. He struggled to do what was best for us, but you don't run a business with your heart. Not if you're good at it, as he was. What I know about things that went on at the plant I've learned from talking to the old-timers.'

Quaking, Mimi gaped at her. 'You're the last hope left for this family. You always understood what it meant to be a Kittridge. You understand the importance of pride and tradition.'

'The Kittridges have a flair for business, true. But we're not artists. Even Granddad knew how to sculpt and enjoyed it, but he didn't have the instinct to create anything special or memorable. That's why he hired artists instead of trying to sell his own designs. He knew his weren't good enough. And that's why he wanted to train Simon and bring him to work for us. Because he knew the company needed a rare talent with a modern eye, to revive our stodgy image. His giving Simon that mold was symbolic of the new beginning he saw in Simon. And that's why I believe Simon is telling the truth. I never knew my great-grandfather, but I don't believe any Kittridge was ever

305

capable of creating that design. If it weren't for Simon's ancestors, we'd be peddling lumber or computer software.'

'My, but he does have you brainwashed.'

'Anyone who knows Simon well enough, becomes familiar with his work, can see how gifted he is.'

'Your grandfather gave him the chance to come to work for us.'

'Don't you see why Simon couldn't do that? It would have been the same old thing. His genius buried beneath our name again.'

Mimi chuckled. 'A genius, Yardley? Come on.'

'Building his own company from scratch, starting his own line of figurines? I call that genius.'

'And this is why you choose to give yourself to that man?'

Yardley reeled at the blunt vehemence in Mimi's words. Reminding herself that she was a grown woman now with the right to be intimate with whomever she pleased, regardless of whether this pleased her grandmother, she refused to deny or minimize her relationship with Simon. Mimi was just going to have to get used to it.

'I love him.'

Mimi's expression withered. 'Don't you see, getting you is just part of his plan? He wants to control Kittridge Collectibles and wipe it out of existence. Look at you, Yardley, intelligent, young, beautiful. You have such a bright future ahead of you. You could have any man in this town. The thought of your letting Simon use you makes my skin crawl. Yes, I admit he's bright. I'm sure he's telling you all the right things. Yardley, dear, I don't want to see you get hurt once he's finished with you. And my God, everybody in town is talking about the two of you attending the dance together, then disappearing before it ended. Simon Blye isn't worth it. A man who cares protects you. He doesn't undermine your business while he's crawling into bed with you.'

'Nonsense. Even if I married him, I'd still control Kittridge Collectibles.'

'*Marry* him? Oh, my God.' Mimi whitened to the color of tissue, shrieking as she doubled over and clutched her side.

Yardley hovered over her. 'Mimi! What's wrong?'

'My side!'

She wobbled so, Yardley had to catch her to keep her from toppling over.

The guest room door flew open. 'What's going on?' Serena demanded.

307

'I'm fine,' Mimi insisted, blinking up at them through tears in her eyes. 'Just help me get into bed, and I'll be fine.'

'Call her doctor, Serena. Just hit five on the auto dial.'

Serena rushed barefoot down the hall to Mimi's bedroom. She was back a few minutes later. 'I got the answering service. He should call back any minute.'

Yardley looked at her grandmother. 'I'm not waiting. I'm taking her to the emergency room. Help me get her down the stairs.'

Serena obliged. By the time they reached the bottom, the phone rang, and the doctor promised to meet them in the emergency room.

'I'll have to wake Casey,' said Serena.

'Let him sleep, Serena. I can manage alone once we get her to the car.'

'All this fuss,' Mimi protested. 'Just let me go to bed.'

'No way,' Yardley asserted.

After a frantic drive to the emergency room of Kittridge's tiny hospital, Yardley was whisked away from her grandmother's side while she filled out insurance forms. When she was finished, she asked where her grandmother had been taken.

'The doctor's with her right now,' the nurse behind the desk told her. 'I'll try to find out what's happening.'

'Just show me where she is. I'm not leaving her back there alone.'

The nurse gave her a long-suffering look, then silently complied.

Simon went home, struck by the vast silence of the house he'd so carefully had built. Just weeks ago he'd believed he cherished peace, quiet, and solitude. Now all he could think of was bringing Yardley here to stay.

He'd never seriously thought much about having children. Now, he wondered whether theirs would have dark hair or spun gold like their mother. The prospect of impregnating her fascinated him, and he was up to the challenge of giving her what she wanted. In fact, he was looking forward to it.

He thumbed idly through the stack of mail the new part-time maid had brought in. He'd found a woman in a neighboring town who had single-handedly started a cleaning service, and he knew she couldn't afford to have security breaches connected to her.

Unpacking took only a few minutes.

Fending off a yawn, he showered and changed

into navy blue sweats, then he built a fire and poured himself a drink. He paced briefly in front of the fire, glancing at the clock.

He'd known Mimi would do something to keep Yardley from coming. Hell, Mimi would do anything to keep Yardley from coming.

He decided to give her another half-hour, then call the house.

With the unsettled feeling that something was wrong in the house, he walked downstairs to the basement and opened the pantry. Beneath the bottom shelf sat a long metal box. Crouching, he worked the combination to undo the lock. He swung back the lid.

Jesus! Staring down, he swept back his hair with one hand. The box was empty. Jarred's mold – gone.

Simon scratched his head. 'Well, I'll be damned. She got it after all.'

He knew the intruder was long gone. But the eerie, lingering imprint of an enemy's presence remained.

For the next hour, he searched his house, every nook and cranny. He wasn't surprised to find that the mold was the only thing missing.

Yardley had the heater going full blast as she drove back toward the house.

'I hate being such a burden to you, dear,' Mimi said from the passenger seat.

'You're not a burden, Mimi.'

'Jarred used to take care of everything. I've been so lost without him. And so afraid my time is next.'

'I know it's frightening, Mimi. But the doctor says you have nothing more than a stomach virus, and not a fatal one. Right now, we what we both need is some rest. It's very late.'

'You think I'm an old fool.'

'No. Remember when Mom died and I spent so much time here with you and Granddad? You both acted like I belonged here and it was okay that Dad left me for weeks on end. I felt as if the two of you wanted me even if he didn't.'

'Your father always wanted you. He was grieving, and unsure of how to bring up a young lady. Why, I'd always wanted a daughter, Yardley. Your mother and I were close, and I think having you with us eased some of my pain at losing a daughter-in-law and a friend.'

'Dad started traveling so much. Sometimes I felt he was relieved when Mom died.'

'It's not easy to watch someone you love suffer. I knew your grandfather's helplessness was worse than death to him. I knew there was no hope he'd get better. He had only one peace ahead of him, and yet when it came I wasn't prepared. And I will forever question whose suffering I was more anxious to end, his or mine.'

Yardley reached across the car seat and squeezed Mimi's hand.

'Too bad Dad and Francesca live way out in Arizona. Maybe if they'd stayed close by, you and Francesca could have gotten to know each other better.'

'Well, as much as I would have enjoyed that, no one could ever take your mother's place, dear. And getting as far away from Kittridge as possible was the main attraction for your father.'

'Would you have fallen in love with Granddad if he'd been poor?' Yardley asked.

'Well, dear, thank God he wasn't poor, so I never had to make that decision.'

Yardley gave her a sidelong glance.

Then she turned the car into the driveway and spotted Simon's truck parked out front. She looked at the clock on the dash and saw it was after two in the morning. What was he doing here?

Her heart lifted. She'd tried to call him from the hospital and gotten his answering machine, and his failure to answer the phone puzzled her.

Simon was exactly what she needed right

now. More than sleep. Whatever had brought him here, she was glad of it.

In his black leather jacket tossed over a sweatsuit, he was sitting in the porch rocker, occupying the seat her make-believe scarecrow had been poised in a few weeks earlier.

She jumped out of the car so quickly, she nearly forgot Mimi. She made a beeline toward him.

'Simon? What on earth are you doing out here?'

He rubbed his jaw. 'Serena told me what happened. I didn't want to go to the hospital because I thought my presence might upset Mimi – ' His voice tailed off as Mimi came up the porch stairs. 'Everything all right?'

Yardley wove her hands together. 'Stomach bug gave her some violent cramps,' she explained. 'Where were you? I tried to call several times and got your machine.'

'At least it's nothing serious,' he said. 'I must have not heard the phone. I was in the basement, the attic, you name it.'

'Whatever for?'

He looked over her shoulder at Mimi. 'I'll explain later.'

'I apologize for my rudeness earlier, Mr Blye,' Mimi told him as she approached.

'Forget it, Mrs Kittridge.'

She stood in the center of the porch, not moving to go in. 'It's rather late for visitors.'

'It's okay. Yardley and I are leaving. We won't be disturbing you.' He shifted his glance to Yardley. 'You are coming, aren't you?' he asked.

Yardley beamed at him. 'You still want me to?'

He lowered his brow in exasperation. 'I'm still up. You're still up. And now that your grandmother has an official clean bill of health, you won't have to worry about her.'

'Yes, of course, I'm coming. Let me run upstairs and change.' She glanced down at her party clothes.

'Oh, no, what you have on is perfect.'

Yardley jumped at the loud slam that shook the porch. When she looked around, Mimi had disappeared.

CHAPTER 14

'You must be exhausted,' Simon told Yardley as he pressed a cold bottle of Corona into her hands. 'It's been a very long day.'

He sat beside her on the edge of the still-made bed.'

'For both of us, Simon. You must be tired from your trip. I'm sorry I couldn't get hold of you earlier. Mimi gave me a scare.'

'I know you're devoted to your grandmother. I'm glad, for your sake, that she's all right. You're here now, and that's all that matters to me.'

A thrill rippled through her at hearing him say it. Yardley angled her gaze upward into his dark eyes. She leaned against his side, liking the hard, rugged feel of him against her.

'I've kept you up late,' she apologized. She took a long swig of the beer, set her bottle down

315

on the nightstand, then climbed on to the mattress on her knees and scooted behind him. Raising her hands, she began kneading the muscles at the base of his neck.

Simon flexed his shoulders. 'God, that's bliss.'

'You haven't yet begun to experience bliss, Simon Blye. Off with your sweatshirt,' she instructed, proceeding to help him shed it.

Glancing over his shoulder, he cast her a sporting look. 'If you're hoping for an argument, you're not getting one.'

'Good.' She kissed the back of his bared shoulder, then continued working his muscles. They slackened beneath her palms as the tension drained.

'Are you upset that Mimi was angry when you left?' he asked.

'She'll recover. I can't say she'd approve of my taking off in the wee hours of the morning with any man. She is, after all, my grandmother. She still thinks of me as a teenager.'

'Yet you came with me anyway.'

'Mimi's going to have to respect that I'm an adult now. The last time I stayed in her house, I was still in my teens. Maybe it's not good for her to depend on having me around just now.'

'My impression of Mimi is she's quite capable of taking care of herself.'

'I wish you and she would find some common ground.'

'We have some. You, babe.'

'And Granddad's mold.' She cast an accusing glance at the original peasant girl figurine sitting atop his chest of drawers.

Simon fell silent. He swilled his beer, then set his bottle down beside Yardley's. 'I don't want to discuss the mold tonight.'

'The issue won't go away just because we avoid talking about it.'

'That mold brought us together. What more is there to be said about it?'

'I wish the damn thing would disintegrate. I'm trying to understand what you're doing. But as long as it exists, it's going to stand between us and our families.'

Simon turned and caught her by the waist. 'Come here. I didn't bring you here to talk about some ancient, corroded mold.'

Laughing, Yardley attempted to slink free as he hoisted her on to his lap. Happily surrendering, she looped her arms around his neck. 'I wasn't finished massaging you.'

'Oh, yes, you were,' he insisted. 'Any more of that and I'll nod off. And I'm not ready to go to sleep yet.'

He pulled down the glittery fabric swaddling

one side of her bosom, exposing her breast for his inspection. 'I didn't think there was a bra hiding under there,' he concluded, stroking her nipple with his thumb.

Yardley drew in a sharp breath as hot sensation swirled through her chest. Her nipple stiffened, and the heat trickled into her belly. She squirmed in his arms.

'I seem to be living more dangerously these days,' she conceded.

Simon fondled the soft underside of her breast. 'Really?' he asked. 'Your recklessness makes you hard to resist.'

'I don't want you to resist.'

'No worry there,' he replied, shifting both hands in front of him to part the crisscrossed panels. His eyes widened appreciatively as the glittery fabric fluttered to the floor.

He reached around her to trace the length of her spine. Yardley shivered in his arms.

'You're so incredibly beautiful,' he whispered, as he ran a splayed hand from the base of her throat, between her breasts, to her midriff. For a man so strong he had a light touch.

He cupped her breasts with both hands, kneading them to an aching tenderness. As the exquisite longing pulsed within her, Yardley felt herself slackening for him, her womanhood moistening. Reaching out, she planted her hands against Simon's flat nipples, combing her fingers through the thick hair on his chest. She traced the copper buds with her fingertips.

Simon groaned.

'I need you with me, Yardley,' he said, smiling at her as he stroked her hair and probed into her eyes. 'I adore you as I never have anyone.'

'I'm here, Simon. I won't go unless you send me away.'

'Never.' He bowed over her chest, capturing her nipple in his mouth, tormenting its hard bud with the tip of his tongue, suckling until pleasure melted her thoughts into a dreamy fog. He caressed her flat midriff, sliding his hand down the slope of her tummy and bringing it to rest between her splayed legs. His intimate touch speared fire through her. 'I want to be good to you as no one ever has.'

She raked her fingers through his thick, dark hair, then leaned forward to nip at his chest. 'You are, Simon.' She raised her head and smiled into his eyes, the heat of his hand nearly driving her mad. 'You have the kind of forceful determination that enables you to accomplish anything. I believe in you. No matter how much you try to deny it, you try to do the right thing. I trust you. I couldn't be here if I didn't.'

He raised his head, inspecting the thin chain suspended around her neck. 'I haven't given you much reason to,' he said.

'I can't help how I feel – '

He silenced her with a hand across her lips. He searched her eyes. 'Would you want someone like me?' Slowly, he retracted his finger to let her speak.

'There is no one like you. And I thought I was having you now.'

'Getting anxious? We have all night.'

'There is something I don't understand.'

His expression darkened. 'What's that?'

'Why does it matter so much what society's leaders here think of you? Why do you demand the respect of people you care nothing about?'

'Because I'll need their support when I run for the city council. I want this to be a good place for people to live – everyone, not just the wealthy. This is my home, and I came back for the same reason you did. But I want things to be different this time.'

She beamed. 'You have my vote, darling.'

He rolled her on to the bed, gliding on top of her. 'Enough talking. Your vote is not what I'm after at the moment,' he informed her, unfastening her trousers. 'Could we maybe finish this conversation later?'

He reached out to turn off the lamp while Yardley slipped off her trousers.

Simon awoke the next morning to find himself hugging a pillow instead of holding Yardley, who had vanished as mysteriously as the mold.

Blinking, he raised his head and smoothed his hair back with one hand. The digital clock said nine-thirty, although it felt earlier. Saturday morning. The faintest light came through windows which revealed a leaden wintry sky outside.

Where had she gone? he wondered, padding naked into the bathroom, then locating a pair of pyjama bottoms and pulling them on. His senses sharpened enough to catch the aroma of coffee, and he followed the smell to the kitchen.

Yardley, dwarfed inside a pair of his sweats, sat at the kitchen table, staring out of the window across the cornfields below and cradling a mug of coffee in both hands. She looked up, flashing him an adoring but worried smile.

'Good morning,' he greeted her, his chest constricting as he bent to kiss her. He'd never imagined any human being could be this precious to him, and his need for her made him feel suddenly vulnerable. Simon prided himself on controlling his own destiny. But he knew her heart was beyond his command. She chose to be with him now, but how could he go on alone if her feelings changed? After edging in this close, could he ever live without her? Could he go on, revert back to his former solitary self, or would he crash and burn like a planet out of orbit? Was she seeing more in him than he could measure up to? Did he know how to love anyone enough?

The lingering taste of coffee on her lips triggered his craving for caffeine. 'You're awake early considering how little sleep we got last night.'

'Umm,' she murmured, her lips rising at the corners in sleepy reflection. 'You looked so peaceful, I didn't want to wake you.'

'For you, I'd gladly sacrifice my rest. What's up, Yardley?'

She sighed heavily, raising her eyelids wide and letting her gaze settle on his face. She removed one hand from the mug and draped it across her stomach. 'I woke up feeling kind of off. I couldn't go back to sleep.'

'You should have woken me up. How do you mean, off?'

'We should talk, Simon, about what would happen if I got pregnant.'

Simon strained to look at her harder. He pulled out a chair and sat down diagonally across from her. His initial alarm evaporated into a sense of wonder. 'Are you?' he asked incredulously, flexing his brow.

Yardley propped her elbow on the table, dropping her forehead to her palm. 'The possibility crossed my mind. And after all I've said and thought about Serena's lack of responsibility . . .'

'Yardley, Yardley.' He reached out to cover her hand on her lap with his own. 'You're getting ahead of yourself. We've been careful. You're worried, aren't you, about how I might react if I got you pregnant? That I'd shun my responsibility?'

She looked up with misty eyes. 'Well, what would you do, Simon?'

'Maybe it's a little soon, but regardless of inconvenient circumstances, it would be our child, yours and mine. I think our making a baby together would be nothing short of a miracle.'

Her forehead crinkled. 'You do?'

He smoothed her hair back. 'I'm not sure what kind of miserable excuse for a father I'd make. But if I had a child, I'd try my damnedest to be someone he could look up to. I want to have a family some day.' He grinned. 'And how much luckier could a kid get than to have a mom who wants to bake brownies and be the room mother at school and knows how to run a business as well?'

'You're mocking me.'

'No chance. I'd be proud of any child we had, now or later. And the one thing I would never do to a child is abandon it. Yardley, I've been trying to figure out how to go about asking you to marry me since I got back. Since before I got back.'

'You don't have to make an honest woman of me, Simon. I have the resources to take care of a child on my own. I wasn't trying to elicit a proposal. I wanted to prepare you. In case.'

He raked splayed fingers through his disheveled hair. 'Dammit, Yardley, I want a family. I always have. But I gave up a long time ago ever thinking I'd meet anyone like you, anyone I wanted to settle down with. I consoled myself by convincing myself that wasn't what I wanted. For a long time, I thought I knew exactly what I wanted, but only now that you've come along am I seeing things clearly for the first time. No kid should grow up without two parents who love him and are there for him. I know that better than anybody.'

'I'm not out to trap you, Simon.'

'A woman like you doesn't have to trap anybody, Yardley. You put yourself at risk every time we make love. No protection is foolproof. To set your mind at ease – if this is a false alarm – maybe we need some additional assurance.'

'I should have thought of that sooner. I wasn't prepared for this to happen. The last few days I've been feeling lightheaded, nauseous, and my period's late. Until this morning, it didn't occur to me what specifically could be wrong. I thought it was just stress.'

'Stress?'

'That's what the doctor said caused my fainting spells.'

'I'm sure I've been adding to it. Look, you could have Mimi's stomach bug, and nerves could be making you late. Let's take off for Las Vegas or wherever and get married now, today, before we even know.'

'Elope?' she asked.

'Sure, why not?'

'I can't.'

He frowned. 'Can't marry me?'

'Can't elope. I don't want to get married without my family there. Mimi's already hurt because Serena ran off and married Beau. And what about your Dad, Simon? I've never even met him. Besides, I didn't say I would marry you. This is making me crazy.'

'I've got to have some coffee.'

She slid her mug toward him and he took a swallow. It was lukewarm and bitter.

'Yardley,' he began. 'When I was still a kid, sometimes I blamed my dad for my mom's leaving. I kept thinking if he really loved her, there must have been something he could have done or said to keep her from going. And I blamed myself because sometimes I thought she left because of me. Whether you're having a baby or not, I'm committed to doing whatever it takes to make you happy. Do you understand? I want you to be my wife and have my children, whether the first one is coming this year, next year, or the year after. Just let's try not to spoil him too much.'

'Him?' Yardley asked.

'Well, if it's a girl, she'd better like football.'

Getting up, he poured himself a cup of coffee, then set it down on the counter without tasting it. He went to Yardley, standing behind her chair and working her shoulders, pressing his hips to her back.

'As long as we're together, we can work through anything,' he told her. 'Let's just take things as they come. You know how much I love you, Yardley. Nothing can ever change that. Just stay with me, babe. I can run to the drugstore and get one of those tests, if it'll set your mind at ease.'

She shook her head. 'I'd rather be absolutely sure. I'll make a doctor's appointment Monday.'

'Good.'

'Simon, Serena told us she saw Granddad give you the peasant girl mold.'

'Did she? It was so long ago, I didn't think she'd remember.'

'That's why I'm not getting an injunction to stop you from selling your copies. The mold is rightfully yours. I have no right to ask you not to market the reproductions. But if we're to have any future together, I have to ask.'

He released his hold on her. 'Ask for anything else but that.'

'Is it so much? You have a good line. You don't need the peasant girl to sell it.'

'Retailers are paying attention to my line only because of the attention she's drawing. Yardley, Kittridge Collectibles is an old established firm with set distribution and contacts. One piece would never make or break you. Evergreen Images is new. People are still skeptical about the future worth of our pieces. The public wants something new and different, but they're reluctant to spend their money on it until everyone else is buying it. You're asking me to abandon a project I've worked hard on, one that's about to

pay off beyond my wildest dreams. I can't give
that up, even for you. I'll never scrape by again,
working for someone else and earning too little
to last between paychecks. I have no family
fortune to fall back on. When I was a kid, my
grandfather showed me pictures of the peasant
girl and bragged about what a fine artist his father
was. I couldn't understand back then why he'd
been denied fame and fortune when he'd made
something that was in a magazine. I decided one
day that I would fix whatever had gone wrong.
This isn't just revenge. This is a dream that has
kept me going most of my life. So far, it's done
well for me. I agree, you have no right to ask.'

'I wasn't requesting it for myself. I know why
you believe you must do it.'

He raised an eyebrow. 'Mimi? She seems to
have taken the situation into her own hands.'

She wrinkled her nose. 'What do you mean?'

'The mold is missing, Yardley.'

'How long have you known that?'

'Since last night.'

'And you didn't say anything about it?'

'I didn't want you to think I was accusing you
of taking it.'

'I didn't, Simon.'

'I think we both know who's responsible. I
doubt you would have had it in you to take it

328

even if you had gotten into my house that night I caught you on the fence.'

'I'm sorry, Simon. I tried to convince her it was wrong. She's got to return it to you.'

'No, she probably destroyed it immediately. Don't even tell her I've missed it.'

'But your orders . . . Your new customers . . .'

'The original mold is worthless. Over a year ago, I cast it and spent months retouching the detail, then I made a new mold from the new sculpture. That's what we're using to produce the new figurines, and we have finished pieces in stock already. I was keeping it only as a curiosity, an antique.'

'I can't believe it.'

'Well, Yardley, you've always known she was out to take it away from me. You were willing to help her.'

'Only because I believed you had stolen it from us. Don't you see, even if she didn't before; Mimi knows now it wasn't stolen? She doesn't care who she hurts to get what she wants, even me. She knows how much I care for you.'

'She must be desperate for something.'

'My grandfather left Mimi well provided for.'

'I wasn't thinking in terms of money. She may have started out wanting to teach me a lesson, keep me in my place, as she sees it. Now, she wants to sabotage me so I'll be less attractive to you. She's afraid of losing you, Yardley.'

'How can I even face her, knowing what she's done?'

'You're welcome to stay here. More than welcome.'

'I can't do that either. Simon, you said you would do anything for me short of giving up the peasant girl.'

'I meant that.'

'Then come with me to the house, and let's have it out with Mimi.'

'You're kidding.'

'I'm not, damn it. I don't want to be in the middle between the two of you, feeling like a traitor to two people I love. Listen to her side of the story and make her hear yours, okay? That's all I'm asking. Whatever our future is destined to be, I want the two of you to make peace with each other. Reach some kind of truce. If you're right about Mimi, she's got to know my falling in love with you won't make me turn away from her. Let's at least try to call a truce.'

Simon studied her intently. 'All right,' he agreed.

Her eyes widened. 'Thank you.'

'I want an end to this as much as you do,' he said.

She gave him a sly smile. 'I know you do. We've got to be careful, though. Mimi has pride strong enough to dam a river.'

'I'll go shower.'

He turned, began walking toward the bedroom, then realized she was on his heels.

'And where are you going?' he asked.

'To conserve on hot water?'

Simon grinned. She shrieked as he swept her into his arms and carried her toward the bedroom. She fell against his chest, laughing.

'Minx,' he said. 'Let me show you just how much I like that idea.'

Simon pulled up in front of the Kittridge house and killed the ignition. Dreading going inside, he gave Yardley a sidelong glance.

'Let's get it over with,' she said.

With a nod, he jerked open the door.

Silently, he walked beside Yardley to the porch. The front door was unlocked. She pushed it open and entered. He followed her into the house. The living room and dining room were deserted.

'She must be in the den,' Yardley suggested, cutting through the dining room that smelled faintly of furniture polish.

Mimi, dressed in pale pink lounging pyjamas

and matching fur-trimmed slippers, was on the couch reading a magazine. Half a cigarette smoldered in the ashtray beside her.

'How are you feeling, Mimi?' Yardley asked.

Mimi glanced up at her granddaughter. If she was surprised to see Simon poised behind her, she didn't indicate it.

'Just tired, dear. Have you had breakfast?'

'No.'

'I have some fresh coffee and Danish Beau brought from the bakery. Why don't we go in the kitchen? You'll join us, of course, Mr Blye?'

'Of course,' Simon murmured.

'Where is everybody?' Yardley asked as they followed Mimi into the kitchen.

'Serena and Casey left early with Beau.'

'Left?'

'Serena has some errands to run. She says she's going back to Tennessee with her husband.'

'What happened to change her mind?'

'Yardley, you know Serena far too well to be surprised by that. She moves as the mood grabs her.'

'But I was going to ask her to stay. Beau could have found work here.'

'He's some kind of musician. He got a call and has to go back immediately.'

'I'm sorry they're leaving, but I'm glad she decided to give Beau a chance. I think he'll make her and Casey happy.'

Mimi shook her head as she arranged pastries on a platter. 'It will take more than I can ever figure out to make that girl happy. I offered to give her a beautiful church wedding and she refused! If you ask me, he's expecting her to support him while he pursues some non-existent career.'

'Serena's always been able to make do with just enough to satisfy herself. She lacks pretension. And Beau had never heard of the Kittridges or Kittridge Collectibles when he married her.'

'She has no common sense. Give her six months and she'll be back. Probably with another child. The fact that children need fathers seems to elude her.'

'Casey's father died, Mimi. Serena couldn't have married him.'

Mimi blanched, wiping her fingers on her pyjama top. 'Why does no one tell me these things?'

'I thought Serena would have told you. She came here anxious to talk.'

Mimi shook her head. 'Who can ever talk to her? She's always off somewhere with Beau.'

'She's coming back to say goodbye, isn't she?'

'They'll be back later this evening.'

Mimi set the platter on the table, then began pouring coffee.

'Mimi, Simon and I would like to talk to you.'

Mimi raised her penciled eyebrows suspiciously. 'Obviously. You two have been hovering over me for the past five minutes. Do sit down. Then we'll talk.'

Yardley sat at the table and knit her fingers together.

Simon stepped closer to Mimi. 'I love your granddaughter very much, Mrs Kittridge. Yardley holds you in high regard, and she wants the two of us to get along.'

Mimi leveled her gaze on him. 'So she coerced you into coming here?'

'He volunteered to come, Mimi,' Yardley cut in.

'Mr Blye, you are set on subjecting my family's company to a great amount of ridicule and embarrassment. My husband was good to you, patiently teaching you his craft. Yet you've done nothing but cause one problem after another since you moved back to Kittridge. And you expect me to approve of your seducing my granddaughter?'

Yardley gasped. 'Mimi!'

Mimi rolled her eyes. 'You don't leave with him at two a.m., stay out all night, and expect me not to know what you've been doing. Heavens, I'm not too old to figure out that much. Are you going to come home too with some bastard great-grandchild? I can scarcely hold my head up on the streets of this town as it is.'

Yardley blanched, then bristled. 'I was the one who seduced him.'

This time Mimi gasped, and Simon coughed into his fist. His skin warmed, although the temperature in the kitchen was not uncomfortably hot.

'Simon and I love each other, and I would really appreciate it if we could all three sit down together and discuss the peasant girl. The Kittridges stole the original work from Simon's family a long time ago.'

Mimi bit her lip. 'Really?' she asked. 'I had no idea.' She looked up at Simon apprehensively. 'All right. You've come this far. Let's talk.'

Yardley stood on the sidewalk in front of Giordano's Restaurant, bundled in a white faux fur coat, her hands stuffed into her pockets and her breath spinning frosty clouds in the night air. Her face glowed red from cold and exhilaration.

'The pizza was wonderful, Simon, thank you. But next time, I'm paying.'

'All right.'

'You could at least make some token protest.'

'If you want to pay for a pizza, you can. My male ego's not that fragile.'

She gazed across the nearly deserted downtown area, stores glowing with lights designed to ward off thieves and only an occasional car passing. The smells of onions and garlic and oregano had followed them outside.

'Come on,' he said, heading toward the monument in the center of town. 'Let's walk off our dinner.'

'They'll be putting up the Christmas lights soon,' she remarked.

'I've never particularly liked holidays. People go mad, as if there were a perpetual full moon.'

'Bah, humbug.' She faked a punch at his ribs. 'That fortune-teller at the carnival was dead wrong. I know everything's going to be wonderful for us, Simon. I can feel it. You won over Mimi. She's going to have a researcher authenticate who the actual artist was, and tell the story in an endorsement. It makes perfect sense. After all, your line is so different from ours, we're not really in direct competition. Why not a joint advertising campaign? You see? Once you made the first move, she was willing to work out our differences. She's probably as weary of all this as we are.'

Simon refrained from pointing out that this promise came from the same woman who had robbed his house. Despite Mimi's patronizing smile and accommodating words earlier, he knew she'd sooner dig for nightcrawlers on her hands and knees than see the names 'Kittridge' and 'Blye' together in print. He would believe in this endorsement when it materialized.

If ever . . .

'I hope it works out that way,' he qualified.

'What are you doing for Thanksgiving dinner?' she asked.

'I don't have any special plans,' he admitted. 'It's just another day to me, Yardley. You're not going to suggest . . .'

'Dinner with Mimi? No. We both agreed it would be too hard to go through the motions this year with Granddad's absence so conspicuous. She's already been invited to spend the weekend with some old friends in Connecticut. But my stepmother, Francesca, always cooks the whole traditional shebang. I'd like for you to meet her and my dad. You and Dad should get along fine. He's nothing like

Granddad. And maybe, as Serena's been saying, I should get acquainted with him a little better myself.'

'Hmm, so that would mean spending the whole weekend together in Arizona?'

'Yes.'

'I'd enjoy that. But I'm not sure I can get away.'

'Bring your laptop. I'll find you a telephone and a quiet corner.' She gazed up at the sky.

'Still worried?' he asked.

She shook her head. 'No. I feel torn, actually. I know it's wrong, Simon. It's too soon for both of us, and yet a part of me hopes there is a baby.'

He came behind her and wrapped his arms around her. 'I'll be disappointed too, Yardley. But we don't have to rush. I promise we'll have lots more chances in due time. I just want to know you're all right.'

'Of course I am. I get ahead of myself sometimes, wanting to do everything at once.'

He laughed. 'Take one thing at a time.'

'With you?' she asked. 'Impossible.'

He came around to face her. 'Try this.' He fished a square wrapped package out of his coat pocket and pressed it into her hands.

'What is it?' she asked.

'Open it and see.'

Her hands shook as she tore back the silver wrapping and white ribbon. The plain white box bore a gold and brown seal imprinted with the logo from a Los Angeles antique shop.

'And I thought you came back from California empty-handed,' she chided, her mouth falling open as she raised the lid. 'Simon, how did you ever find this?' She lifted the gold band with two fingers. 'I've never seen anything like it.'

He took it from her. 'A special engagement ring for a unique woman,' he said. 'Marry me, Yardley.'

'Oh, Simon. Ha!' She extended her ring finger to allow him to slip it on.

His expression remained as solemn as a choir boy's.

'You bought this ring while you were in California?'

'Now do you believe I want to marry you, baby or no baby?'

'Oh, God, I love you, Simon. I always will. And I don't mind declaring it in front of all of Kittridge.'

'Be sure, darling. This is for keeps. I'm talking about watching each other's hair turn white. Well, mine anyway.'

A fat tear rolled down her cheek. 'I wouldn't want it any other way. I was lonely and didn't even know it until I met you.'

Simon put an arm around her and lead her back toward the car parked along the curb. 'Never again, babe. Never again.'

CHAPTER 15

On the drive back to her grandmother's house, Yardley studied the ring on her finger. At least she and Simon could share their good news with Serrie and Beau before they left. She wished they weren't leaving.

'Mind if I turn on the radio?' she asked.

'Go ahead.'

When she punched the dial, the broadcast of the local high school football game came on. She hit the scanner. Another station kicked in, playing country and western music. The song sounded oddly familiar.

'I didn't know you listened to country music,' Simon remarked.

She punched the button to lock in the station. 'Don't you recognize it?' she asked excitedly. 'That's the song Beau was singing the other night!'

Simon crinkled his brow. 'I'll be damned. That's not only Beau's song. That's Beau singing it.'

'It can't be.' Yardley left the station on while the song finished.

'*Beau Jennings, number one for week number three on our all country music charts,*' the disc jockey concluded.

She pressed fingertips to her lower lip. 'Am I the only one who feels like an idiot here?'

'I told you I'd seen him before.'

'Maybe now Mimi will work up a little more enthusiasm over their marriage.'

'Don't you think there's probably a reason Serena neglected to mention that Beau's famous?'

'I don't understand why she wouldn't.'

'She didn't want his success to influence her family's opinion of him. She'd planned to leave him. Knowing who he was would have just made Mimi push her harder to go back to him.'

Yardley raised her eyes to him. 'Mimi was raised in high society. She was brought up to feel threatened by common people. I'm not saying it's right. That's just how she was raised.'

'Does she talk much about her youth?'

'Not really. Why?'

'I just wondered. My grandfather – Lord, that man could talk. I think he remembered everything that had ever happened to him. Used to talk about dogs he had and kids he played with and teachers who whipped him in school. Glenn and I hung on to every word.'

'Is your grandfather still alive?'

'No, he died a couple of years before my mom took off.'

'Have you ever tried to find her? Or your brother?'

Simon shrugged. 'Why should I? Be easier for them to find me.'

'Maybe they tried. You were away from Kittridge for a long time.'

'They're both strangers now. Don't start playing talk show host and telling me I need them to make my life complete.'

'I wouldn't presume to tell you that. Your decision is far too personal for anyone to offer advice. Anyway, you're wrong about Serena. She didn't tell us because it doesn't make a difference to her.'

He turned into the drive, heading toward the house. Parking the car, he cut off the ignition and the lights, but made no move to get out. He turned to her. 'Are we going to tell them?' he asked.

She didn't have to ask what. She knew he was no longer referring to Serena. 'Yes, I want to tell Serena before she leaves. This might not have happened if she hadn't invited you to dinner that Sunday.'

'And Mimi?'

Yardley reached out and wrapped her hand around his fingers. 'She'll be tickled at the chance to stage the wedding of the year! I'm so glad the three of us talked this afternoon.'

'She made those promises because she doesn't realize I can still manufacture the figurine without the original mold. She thinks I haven't discovered it's missing yet.'

Yardley paled. 'Are you sure someone else didn't take it?'

'Someone else with connections to get through my security system into my house? Who, Yardley? Who else would have wanted the damn thing?'

She fell silent.

'I'm not going to say anything. I'm not out to ruin the night for any of us. But about this wedding-of-the-year stuff . . .'

'I've dreamed about a gigantic wedding since I was a little girl. If I'm getting married I want the whole world to know. Even if we end up rushing it a bit. Would you mind a lot, Simon? No slinking off to Las Vegas.'

She opened the car door. Simon got out and rounded the car to meet her. 'Bright stars tonight. Got to be a good sign,' he said.

She linked her arm with his. 'Got to be,' she agreed.

'Whatever you want, Yardley. You've done something your grandfather couldn't. You've discovered my weakness.'

'Oh, really? And what's that?'

'You.'

Yardley beamed up at him. His face was so fine, so intense, so devastatingly handsome. She could look at it forever. At this moment, she was happier than she could remember ever having been before. Surely Mimi would recognize and respect that, and this tug-of-war over the peasant girl could be laid to rest forever.

'Yardley!'

Looking up, she saw Serena standing under the porch light. A gentle tug prodded her heart. Her baby sister's leaving would have marred her happiness if not for the consolation of knowing she and Casey were beginning a new life with Beau. Yardley was beginning to understand why Serena didn't want to settle here in

Kittridge. She and Serena were two very different people, each drawn to places of their own.

Even as she resolved to bravely and cheerfully send Serena on her way, as she raced to the porch to say goodbye, her eyes were filling with tears. She hated goodbyes.

By Monday morning Simon was starting to wonder whether he'd been wrong about Mimi. She'd taken the news of his and Yardley's engagement with gracious acceptance, hugging Yardley, and then hugging him.

'Welcome to our family,' she'd said, while Yardley looked on beaming.

Could he have been so wrong? If he was, who had broken into his house and stolen the mold? Did he have an unidentified enemy?

'I've made your travel arrangements for Atlanta,' Kay reminded him as he passed her office that morning. 'The itinerary is on your desk.'

'Thanks,' he said absently. Settled in his office with a fresh cup of coffee, he sat in the leather upholstered chair behind his desk and thumbed through the folder. He was scheduled to leave in the morning and be back Wednesday evening. Only one night away from Kittridge and Yardley. He felt anxious about leaving her and wasn't sure why. Life went on, even when you were in love.

He tossed the folder on the glass-topped desk, then set his coffee down. Leaning back and stretching out his legs, he crossed them and propped his feet on the desktop, because he could.

A commotion in the hall startled him into an upright position. A streak of maroon wool shot through his office door, followed closely by his secretary. 'Mrs Kittridge, you can't come barging in here like this.'

'Go back to your filing,' Mimi Kittridge snapped over her shoulder. 'I have urgent business with Mr Blye.' She leveled a vulture-like gaze on Simon. He rose, towering over her.

Samantha, normally so composed and efficient that Simon had Kay grooming her for a sales position, stood in the doorway twisting the fingers of both hands together and looking distressed.

'It's all right, Sam,' he said. 'I'll handle this. Would you mind shutting the door?'

Sam looked relieved to do so.

Mimi flashed him a smug smile.

'Sit down, Mimi,' he offered, gesturing toward the chairs opposite his desk.

She situated herself in the center chair, straightening her skirt.

'I don't see any point in dancing around making polite conversation, Simon. You've had your sights set on Yardley since the first day Jarred let you on to our property. You deceived him, flattered him into teaching you skills you chose to use against him. But as long as I'm breathing, you will not continue taking advantage of my granddaughter. And you're certainly not going to marry her.'

'Yardley is a grown woman, a consenting adult. Has it occurred to you we might actually care for one another?'

Mimi laughed into the air. 'Yardley is extremely vulnerable right now. She worshipped Jarred and is still recovering from another bad choice she made back in Boston. You're an expert at getting what you want, and you're preying on my granddaughter. I won't stand for it. Do you think I don't know how far your credit is extended? You're not exactly standing on level ground. Yardley's money would make a stable back-up.'

'Yardley's money is hers and will remain so. I'd never dream of using Kittridge money. What do you want, Mimi?'

'I'm willing to bargain, Simon. I have something you want.'

'Ahh. The mold. Who did you send for it this time? Casey?'

Her features tautened. 'Say what you like. The fact remains that I have it.'

'And that I don't need it. Go ahead and destroy it, Mimi, as you probably already have. I asked Yardley to marry me, and I have no intention of backing down. So you'll just have to live with it.'

'I'll make your life a living hell. And you know I can as long as you stay in Kittridge.'

Simon raised one eyebrow. 'But you won't.'

'I may look like a frail old woman, but I assure you I'm quite capable of dealing with the likes of you.'

'I'm not doubting what you're capable of. But I'll tell you what you're going to do, Mimi. You're going to smile and help Yardley plan the traditional wedding she's had her heart set on, and you're going to support whatever decision she makes about her life. And you and I are going to pretend to like each other, because that's what Yardley wants.'

'Who do you think you are, giving me orders?'

'And if you ever barge in here again and upset my employees, I'll have the security guard throw you out.'

349

Her complexion darkened to purple. 'How dare you? You're common trash, and your fancy clothes and car and house will never disguise that.' She rose from the chair.

'As they did for you, Mimi?'

Her eyes, locked on his gaze, widened. She dropped back into the chair, shoulders sagging.

She raised her chin. 'What do you mean?'

'Come on. You know exactly what I mean. That you never had a wealthy family back in Boston? That you grew up in a crowded apartment with your aunt and uncle and four cousins after your parents abandoned you? Your uncle was a butcher. Jarred must have guessed the truth and loved you too much to care. But what would Yardley think? What would your own son think? And all your snobby friends? I had you investigated after Yardley tried to break in that night. She wouldn't admit it, out of her blind loyalty to you, but I knew you'd put her up to it.'

Mimi glowered at him as though confronting Satan. 'This isn't the last of this,' she threatened.

'Good day, Mimi. I have work to do. And don't worry about the mold. Yardley can explain to you why I don't need it. You really should have learned more about your husband's business before you tried to run it.'

She marched regally from the room.

Simon's gut wrenched as he watched her go. He hadn't wanted to pull his trump card. She'd left him no choice. Mimi's past was a secret he would have preferred not to share. He knew this wasn't the way Yardley hoped he and her grandmother would reach a truce.

And what a fragile peace at that. Exposing Mimi's humble past and ongoing deception to Yardley was not something he ever wanted to do.

On Tuesday afternoon, Yardley walked briskly through the upper level of the Kittridge Collectibles plant, exchanging greetings with her employees as she passed them. She wore a tweed trouser suit with a velveteen collar, and brown pumps, her hair coiled atop her head and clipped with a carved wooden barrette.

She glanced down at Simon's ring on her finger, warming at the thought of him and smiling slightly. He'd be gone only one night, and already she missed him. Tomorrow night, she planned to welcome him with a homecoming celebration he wouldn't soon forget.

Her news after her doctor's appointment would have to keep until then too. She wanted to deliver it in person.

In the airy studio upstairs, she watched as Derek Waters, a moldmaker, poured liquid plaster of Paris over a clay sculpture of a woman in a rocking chair. The intricate carving was so detailed it showed the stitches in her knitting, the lace trim on her dress, the cat curled at her feet.

Silently, she watched the craftsman at work. This process never failed to fascinate her. The patience, the steady hands. Perfection the standard. She'd always enjoyed being up here. The familiar sounds and smells reminded her of tagging along with her granddad as a little girl.

Thanks to the use of acrylics, a mold made today would last forever without suffering loss of detail as the peasant girl had.

She cast Derek an appreciative smile, then went on her way. No one liked the boss looking over his shoulder. Just as she was reaching the stairs, she glanced down and saw Lisa on her way up.

'Didn't you hear the page?' her secretary asked. 'There's a reporter here from the local paper. Says he's doing a story on the peasant girl.'

'Oh, lord,' Yardley said, pressing a palm to her forehead. She was going to have to stall him, give herself time to figure out what to say.

She reached out for the steel railing, closing her hand as she took the first step down. By some odd miscalculation, her hand missed the railing and fisted around air.

Overcome with the awful sensation of losing her balance, she felt herself tumbling, bouncing down the old wooden steps. She heard someone scream. Lisa. Or maybe herself.

Suddenly, everything was still and silent and painful. If not for the pain, she wouldn't have known for sure whether she was alive.

Simon stayed at the gift shop until it closed at nine. The trip had been worth the effort. Customers had streamed around him all day, asking about his line. His line. Actually, the peasant girl had drawn little interest. He began to wonder if he had needed it as badly as he'd initially thought.

The gift shop owner invited him to dinner, so since he had nothing else to do, he accepted. It was near midnight when he got back to his hotel to find the light blinking on his phone. Calling the desk, he expected to find messages from Kay, not from Serena. She'd left a number with a Tennessee area code and noted it was urgent he return her call.

When he dialed the number, he got Beau. 'Serena flew back to Kittridge this afternoon,'

Beau said. 'Where've you been? We've been trying to get hold of you all day. Yardley's had an accident.'

Simon felt the life drain out of him. 'What kind of accident. How bad?'

'Take it easy. She fell down some stairs at work. She's not hurt real bad, okay? You just need to get back to Kittridge as soon as you can. I'm tied up here all week, but I've got a flight out Sunday.'

'Why is Serena staying so long if Yardley's all right?'

'I gotta go. Serena will explain everything. You could try calling her at the house, but they're probably all still at the hospital.'

Beau hung up before Simon could extract any more information.

He knew Beau was keeping something from him. Oh, dear God. If Yardley was pregnant, she might have lost the baby. A sense of loss barreled over him. He braced himself. As long as Yardley was all right, they could get through anything.

Hurriedly, he packed his things, calling the airport, calling a taxi. All he could think of was getting back to her.

Yardley walked slowly through the graveyard, her hands tucked inside the pockets of her windbreaker, her tennis shoes leaving prints in the frosted grass. Despite the brilliant sunlight of early morning, the air packed a cold, cruel bite.

But she barely felt it as she walked. Simultaneously, she wanted to feel nothing and everything. Her muscles were sore and bruised from her tumble down the stairs yesterday, but the pain was minimal compared to the hurt in her heart. How strange to know she was ill when she didn't feel sick.

The silence in the graveyard mocked her. The red sky overhead boasted an obscene beauty. Today, the world should be only gray. Stopping, she stood staring down at her grandfather's tombstone.

'Yardley?'

Her heart sank as she turned to see Simon standing behind her, dark whisker shadow lining his jaw, his eyes wide and puffy from lack of sleep. The sight of him, the alarm on his face, stabbed her like a dagger. Seeing him, his handsome features contorted with worry, hurt more than any of it. She steeled herself to everything she felt for him, resisting her impulse to rush into his arms.

'I've been looking everywhere for you.'

'How did you know?' she asked, remaining several feet from him.

'Serena called and left a message about the accident. Are you all right?'

Yardley took her hand from her pocket and pressed a palm to her forehead. 'For the moment, I am.'

'What happened?'

'I lost my balance and fell down some stairs at work.'

He stepped toward her. 'Thank God you weren't seriously injured.'

Yardley laughed bitterly. 'Guess it was my lucky day.'

'I know there's more.'

'Yes, there's more.'

'A baby, darling?'

With a sad smile, she shook her head. 'No. There never was a baby, Simon. Which in the circumstances is probably for the best.' She took a deep breath. 'I've got to go back to the hospital this morning for tests. I may have a brain tumor.'

Simon gaped at her incredulously. 'I'll go with you.'

She stepped back from him. 'Thank you, Simon. You're kind to offer, but I'd prefer that you didn't. I have so much to deal with right now.'

'Yardley, no. I have to do something. You shouldn't go alone.'

'There's nothing you can do. Look at you, you must have been up all night as it is. Call me later, okay?'

'Yardley . . .'

'Simon, I can't cope right now with worrying over how you feel about this. I know it's selfish, but I have to work this through on my own. I have too much to think about. We'll talk later, okay?'

'All right.' His concession rippled across the landscape.

Yardley's heart sank as she watched him retreat. She needed so badly to touch him, it was all she could do to keep from running after him. But she didn't move. She loved him far too much to make him watch her die.

CHAPTER 16

Halfway to his house, the numbing shock wore off. Simon pounded his fist on the steering wheel, sending the car skidding across the pavement and nearly into the culvert.

Coming to his senses, he found himself sitting on the shoulder of the highway, realization dawning that he'd nearly killed himself. Thank God, this early there hadn't been another car in his path.

For the first time in his adult life he had no idea what to do. On the flight home, he'd braced himself for the possibility that Yardley had miscarried a baby in her fall. He'd been prepared to cope with grief and disappointment. As long as she was all right, he could deal with anything else.

Now, he felt helpless. He knew he shouldn't have let her send him away. He longed to offer some reassurance, some form of comfort against an enemy far too brutal and invasive to imagine. Instead, he'd done as she asked and left her alone.

Surely these tests she was to have would reveal some mistake. A brain tumor? Cancer? Not Yardley. She was so beautiful, so full of life, so loving.

Coming home, for the first time he noticed how lonely and secluded his house looked, set off on the hilltop all alone. As he'd always felt until Yardley came along.

The emptiness he'd felt when his mom left echoed inside him. He remembered that snowy morning, his dad wearing a woeful hangdog expression yet refusing to cry. And he remembered how he'd imitated his father, refusing to cry because he was becoming a man, yet still a little boy inside.

And he would not weaken now, because he simply refused to lose Yardley. No matter how sick she might be, there had to be a cure.

His feet weighed heavy as he climbed the stairs to his front door. Unlocking it and stepping inside, he felt the eerie quietness of a vacant house.

For the first time he could remember, he was in no hurry to get to his office. Instead, he took a shower so hot the water nearly scalded his skin, a cloud of steam engulfing him. He didn't bother to shave, but dressed casually in jeans and an old black corduroy shirt. He put on running shoes but didn't go running. He brewed strong coffee and tried to remember what other morning rituals he could fill his time with.

He needed to sleep, but he knew he would not be able to.

The ringing phone startled him.

'Hi. So you are back.'

'Yes, Kay, I just arrived. Don't expect me in until later.'

A brief silence followed. 'Everything's under control, Simon. I heard about Yardley's accident. Is she all right?'

'She's fine.'

No, she's not.

A longer silence. 'Just call if there's anything I can do for you or her, Simon.'

He raked a hand through his hair. Damn, the whole town must know Yardley was ill.

'Thanks.'

Needing to concentrate on something, anything, he logged on to his computer, searching the Internet for information on brain tumors. The avalanche of listings astonished him. For hours he read. Bum luck. Anyone could get one.

Even kids. Lots of kids did. No prevention. Even a benign tumor in the brain could be life-threatening.

He was looking for hope and not finding any.

By the time he shut off the computer, his eyes were burning. From knowing nothing, he could now almost guess what tests Yardley might be having. But he would never know exactly how she felt inside, hard as he tried to imagine how he might feel. He didn't have to experience her pain, and his imagination refused to carry him that far.

Pacing through the house, he decided he should try to get some rest before going into the office. When he stepped into his room, the first thing he saw was the peasant girl figurine, the tiny dark eyes mocking him, accusing him.

Yardley had asked him for only one thing. The one thing he regarded as too much to give her. Now, he saw how little it mattered. All the money, all the power in the world couldn't spare her this. He'd had too much pride to give it up for her. Had he needed that last stronghold because her last name was Kittridge and he was afraid to love her too much, to trust her completely?

Simon walked to the chest of drawers and wrapped his hand around the smooth, cool porcelain. He lifted the figurine and took a last, long look at it. The dark eyes reflected all the bitterness boiling in his heart all these long years, fueling him along the way like coal in a furnace. And robbing him of his ability to love. To love as fearlessly as he'd always lived. To love as openly as Yardley did.

Raising the statuette behind his head, he pitched it to the wall, watching it explode and shatter into fragments like sparks from a sky-rocket.

Without stopping to clean up the mess, he grabbed his jacket from the closet and went where he should have been all along: to the hospital.

Yardley drove slowly downtown and parked her car at the curb. She felt very tired. But despite Mimi's and Serena's protests, she wasn't ready to go home just yet. They'd been flocking around her all day, as if they could protect her from this thing inside her. As if anyone could.

She had so many things to do. Dustin Holden at the office had been running the business when Granddad was ill. Although he seemed to resent her and they didn't get along well, he was best qualified to take over for her and he was loyal to the company. Moreover, he was one of the few executives outside the family who got along with Mimi. She would leave him in charge.

Opening the car door, she walked towards the brightly lit deli. Her mouth felt dry, and she needed something to drink.

No one was waiting in line, and as she ordered a cola with extra ice she spotted Jack drinking coffee at a corner table. He was reading a newspaper and hadn't noticed her.

The high school student behind the counter handed her a paper cup with a lid and her change. 'Thank you,' she told him.

The bell over the door clanged, and Yardley turned to see Craig Cunningham, Sophie's boyfriend, freeze in front of the door.

She greeted him automatically. 'Hi, Craig.'

'Yardley. I didn't expect you'd be here. I mean, I thought you were in the hospital.' When she met his eyes, she saw not the friendly gaze she expected, but the dark, evasive eyes of the carnival fortune-teller.

Her heart froze. The paper cup slipped from her hand; spilling pop and ice in a dark puddle across the floor.

The stricken clerk rounded the counter. 'Are you okay, Ms Kittridge?' he asked.

She looked down at the mess she'd made. 'I'm sorry,' she muttered. 'I'll help you clean it up.'

'Why don't you go on home, Yardley?' Recognizing Jack's voice, she found him standing beside her. But he was staring at the floor, not meeting her gaze either. Did the whole damn town know?

Jack shifted uncomfortably, staring at the floor. Finally, he raised eyes heavy with pity.

She wished he hadn't looked at her. This was the man she'd once thought of as stable and dependable? She would rather die quickly than glimpse such profound sadness in Simon's eyes.

Couldn't she even do something as normal as buying a soft drink?

The clerk set another cup in her hand. She fumbled for her purse.

'I'll get it,' Jack said. She realized he just wanted her to leave and stop making everyone uncomfortable.

'Thanks,' she said, not looking at any of them as she rushed out of the store.

Serena answered the doorbell.

'Simon,' she blurted, pulling him inside with a hug. He knew then the news was bad. Her eyes were puffy. She'd been crying.

'Where's Yardley, Serrie?' he asked. 'I went to the hospital, but I couldn't find her there.'

'She took off after we left the hospital. Said she wanted to stop and get something to drink. She should be here in a minute.'

'Should she be driving?'

'Probably not, but we couldn't stop her. You look like hell.'

'Thanks. How are you holding up?'

'I'm okay. Come on in the den.'

He hesitated.

'Coast is clear. Mimi stayed back at the hospital to discuss where Yardley might receive the best treatment. The doctors here want to do surgery to find out whether it's malignant.' She hooked her hands in the pockets of her jeans. 'One thing about Mimi, she won't spare any effort for Yardley.' She clasped a hand to her forehead, pushing back a stray lock of hair and shaking her head. 'Oh, God, I can't believe this is happening.'

Simon took a folded computer printout from his jacket pocket and pressed it into her hand.

'What's this?' Serena asked.

'Some of the more specialized clinics. I printed it out off the Web this afternoon. I don't know what to do either.'

Serena's eyes misted. 'Pray,' she suggested softly. 'If you do.'

'I can't. Not now.'

She nodded. 'Simon, I don't know what Yardley needs. She's walking around like a zombie, hardly speaking to anyone. Like she's sinking inside herself. I admit I had some doubts about you when the two of you started getting serious, and I apologize for that. I can see how much you love her. Let your anger go. It won't change anything.'

Simon realized he'd been mad at someone or something most of his life.

'Please stay until she comes, Simon. I know seeing you here will make a difference. Don't be put off by Mimi. She's devastated. I don't think she has the strength to be mean to you today.'

Simon smiled half-heartedly.

Serena tilted her head. 'I hear a car now. That must be Yardley. Hope she had a nice drive, because I'm taking away her keys before she hurts herself.'

The front door opened. Mimi walked in, her grooming immaculate as always, her expression wilted and pale. She'd aged, even since Simon had argued with her in his office.

As she stepped inside the foyer, Serena opened her arms and folded her weary grandmother into them, attempting to comfort the old woman.

Mimi pushed her granddaughter away. 'I'm sorry. I can't . . .'

Serena gaped at her in horror and humiliation. 'Can't stand to be around me? Can't stand the thought of my being well when Yardley is sick? She blinked rapidly as her eyes filled with tears. 'I always knew you hated me, Mimi. But I've never known why and until now, I didn't know how much. Excuse me, Simon.' Her voice faded to a strangled whisper as she turned and ran up the stairs. Tears were streaming down her face.

Mimi turned to Simon, looking vaguely perturbed.

'See what you've done to my family,' she accused.

Simon felt an unexpected pang of sympathy for her. He knew he should hate her. He hated what she'd just done to Serena and was embarrassed to have witnessed it. A grandmother who could love one granddaughter and not the other. *A mother who could love one son and abandon the other.*

'That was cruel even for you, Mimi. Lash out at me, for God's sake, I'm used to it. What do you have against Serena?'

Mimi scowled as though he'd slapped her. 'She's irresponsible, rebellious, indolent . . .'

'Maybe a lot like you once were?'

Her mouth puckered indignantly. 'Serena isn't your concern. If you're waiting for Yardley, you might as well go. She doesn't want to see you.'

'She'll have to tell me that herself.'

Mimi smiled wanly. 'Until today I'd thought marrying you could be the worst thing to happen to Yardley.'

Simon looked down at Mimi. 'I'm through fighting with you. A truck will be here in the morning to deliver the peasant girl figurines and the production materials. Dispose of them however you want. I'm abandoning the project. It doesn't matter any more.'

To his astonishment, Mimi glanced at the staircase, her lips tightening as though she had begun to comprehend what she'd done. Suddenly, she sobbed. She crumpled into a ball, weeping.

Simon would have been better prepared to cope had she drawn a gun on him. Catching her by the shoulders, he guided her into the nearest chair, at a loss to comfort a woman he regarded as scheming, conniving, and incredibly selfish.

'Look, Mimi, there will never be any warm feelings between us, but being in the middle has been tearing Yardley apart. I understand now what I've been doing to her.'

'I'm surprised, Mr Blye, to see you back here at all. You do love her, don't you? I thought you were after revenge.'

'All I care about is helping Yardley get past this.'

Mimi shook her head. 'You have no idea how serious this is. A brain tumor killed Yardley's grandfather, Simon. Maybe I deserve this, but she doesn't.'

He heard a car pulling up outside. Yardley.

'She's here,' Mimi said.

Simon went to the front door, stepping outside before Yardley reached the porch. He wanted to see her alone, away from her grandmother.

In the fading light, her face looked gray and tired. In one hand, she held a paper cup with a straw stuck through the lid.

When she saw him coming out of the house, she halted.

'I have some kind of lesion, Simon,' she said stiffly. 'I'm arranging to go to the university hospital as soon as possible. The doctors there will decide on a course of treatment. They've been doing a new type of laser surgery I may be a candidate for. I don't know how long I'll be gone.'

He stepped forward. 'Don't sound so resigned, Yardley.'

She laughed. 'Resigned? Simon, I want to run

369

away so fast and so far . . . but there's nowhere to go. Just nowhere to go.'

He reached for her shoulders, but she sidestepped him, dodging his embrace. Astonished, he glared at her.

'I didn't do this to you,' he said.

'This changes everything, Simon. I can't possibly make any plans right now.'

'The wedding? We'll wait as long as it takes.'

She pulled the ring off her finger and handed it to him.

'Here. I can't ask you to endure this. I can't hold you to promises you made believing circumstances were different. Simon, you have such a wonderful future ahead of you. I want you to go on with it, not be saddled worrying over me. Just, please, understand.'

'Understand? Never in a million years, babe. I was wrong about you. I didn't think you were the kind of woman who could turn her feelings off when they became inconvenient.'

He brushed past her as he stormed to his car and gunned the motor. Without looking back, he drove into the night.

Yardley was upstairs in her room throwing clothes into a suitcase when Serena came in without knocking.

'I don't know what to take,' Yardley snapped, flinging a pair of slippers across the room.

'Why don't you sit down for a minute? I'll help you get your things together.'

'I'll do it myself. I can, you know. I can still move around.'

'Yardley, sit down. If you're trying to make me feel sorry for you, I'm too mad to muster any sympathy right now.'

Reeling as if she'd been struck, Yardley complied, perching on the edge of the mattress. 'Why are you angry?' she asked.

'All my life I've been compared to this older sister who was a paragon of virtue and ambition. If you only knew how I cringe at hearing, 'Why can't you be more like Yardley?' Not just from Granddad and Mimi, but from Mom and Dad too.'

'Francesca said that?' Yardley asked incredulously.

'More than once. No one's ever had a lot of patience with me except you. You understood how different the two of us were. You accepted me as I am.'

'I wasn't all that tolerant, especially about the circumstances of Casey's birth. I thought you were foolish, until I nearly ended up in the same situation.' She wrung her hands. 'Now, I'd give anything to have it be that simple. A healthy new life growing inside me instead of an enemy invader.'

'Why did you send Simon away?'

Yardley turned to stare at the wall. 'I love him too much to put him through this. Serena, you know how it was with Granddad.'

Serena raised an eyebrow. 'And maybe it will be for you. But stop jumping to conclusions until you know whether you even have the same kind of tumor he did. I believe everything comes in its own time. All I can offer is intuition and maybe I only feel it because I want to so much, but I can't believe you're going to die. And just suppose you are, Yardley. Don't you think Simon is entitled to decide what he's willing to endure? You were the one who wanted Simon to need you. Do you think all that stops just because you're sick? If you had known about this weeks ago, felt this way, think of all you would have missed with him. I'll never completely recover the pain of losing Casey's dad. But if I could go back, I wouldn't have withheld loving him just because we didn't have a lot of time.'

'Don't make me do this, Serrie. I thought I could be there for him, give him a family. Now I don't know that I'll be around to guarantee him anything. Even if I live, I could be paralyzed or handicapped. Simon deserves a whole, perfect woman. I couldn't stand being less for him. I'm not taking him to hell with me.'

'Only porcelain figurines are flawless. Human beings come with their failings. A grandfather too bullheaded not to make enemies. A father who can't understand his eldest daughter's fascination with a life he broke free of. Simon's turning the peasant girl figurines over to Mimi. Did you know that? He's willing to give up everything for you, and you refuse to admit you need him? Somehow, you have more Kittridge blood in you than I do. If Simon got sick, would you abandon him?'

'Of course not.'

'Well, maybe he *needs* to take care of you. I know that scares you, Yardley. You've never been one to lean on anybody. Love him enough to lean on him now. Let him comfort you.' Serena rose to leave. 'I have to finish packing myself. I'll be at the hotel in town. I can't stay here with Mimi right now.'

'Serrie, wait. Can you take me over to his house? I'm not really supposed to be driving.'

'I'll get my coat.'

Simon was out behind the garage splitting firewood when he heard the buzz from inside

373

the garage. In no mood to be bothered, he nearly didn't answer the intercom.

'Damn,' he muttered, finally racing around to the garage to pick it up. 'Yeah.'

'It's Serena, Simon.'

'Come on in.'

After opening the gate, he stepped out into the driveway. A dirty red compact chugged up the driveway. The door opened and the sight of a cascade of platinum blonde hair warmed him to his soul.

The minute the door was closed, the little car sped off into the night.

Yardley looked back with mild annoyance. 'She wasn't supposed to do that,' she explained. She was dressed in faded blue jeans, a flannel shirt and unzipped ski jacket, and dirty white sneakers. In her old clothes, she reminded him of the bungling burglar who'd gotten hung on his fence and still managed to steal his heart anyway.

'Never mind,' he coaxed, taking her by the wrist. She kept her hands stuck in her coat pockets but didn't pull away from him. 'I'll take you home when you want to leave. Come on inside. It's freezing out here. I'll make coffee. We can go around the back.'

He ushered her around the pool to the door, then inside.

'Let me take your coat,' he insisted.

She stood facing him, her wide eyes glazed with a dull sorrow and resignation he ached to extinguish.

'Forget the coffee. I can't stay long,' she said.

He took her coat and hung it on a hook by the door.

She stood watching him, looking oddly distracted. He knew she needed something from him, but he wasn't sure what. Hope? Solace? Company?

Suddenly, his anger rose. He remembered how relaxed and happy they'd been together last time she was here. And now this stupid tumor was killing everything between them. And then he knew he was angry not at God, not even at the tumor, but at himself. He was afraid to try to touch her, afraid she'd back away if he pulled her into his arms as he longed to.

'Come on in the living room,' he urged.

She followed him, but did not sit down.

Simon studied her. 'Excuse me a second.'

Wondering what he was going to do now that she was here, he popped a CD in the stereo. An old rock song shattered the silted silence. He turned back to Yardley, clasping both her hands between his.

'Ice cubes,' he noted, rubbing them with his palms.

'Why are you playing that old music?'

'Dance with me, Yardley.'

'Dancing's about the last thing I feel like doing right now.'

'You love to dance. Remember the country club?' He drew her into his arms, slow-dancing even though the music was fast. She swayed slightly, small and precious in his arms. He never wanted to let go.

But the song ended.

Yardley raised her head to him. 'The country club was a lifetime ago, like a dream.'

'Dreams go on. So you told me.' Reaching up, he touched his thumb to the delicate hollow of her throat and rubbed the soft skin there. She didn't pull away, but he felt her trembling.

'You shouldn't touch me,' she warned.

He stared into her wary gaze. 'I want to feel you, to be deep inside you as much as ever, babe. Nothing's ever going to change that.'

Her eyes fluttered shut. 'No, Simon. You mustn't. I have nothing left to give you. I only came here to make you understand how I feel. Please don't be angry at me.'

His hands moved to the front of her shirt. She

376

stood still as a sentry. He pushed the top button free.

'I'm mad as hell.'

His fingers dropped to the second button. Her slender hand rose to clasp his broader one. He froze, staring at the fingers gently wrapped over his. Yardley's tenuous glance followed his own, then rose to meet his.

His voice was rich and husky. 'Don't shut me out. I'm going to make love to you. Now.'

'I can't, Simon.' The anguished plea tore from her throat.

Simon prodded her with a half-smile. 'Oh, you can, darling. I know you can. You're not different now, Yardley. You're the same woman who loves carnivals and silly Hallowe'en decorations and babies. And making love.'

Haltingly, she dropped her hand away. Simon resumed working the buttons, all the way down, pushing aside the thin fabric to reveal her lacy little white bra. Pulling her close enough to feel the tips of her breasts against his hard chest, he looped his arms around her to unhook it from the back. Once it fell free, he eased the blouse off her shoulders then disengaged the bra.

She stood straight before him, her creamy breasts bared. Although the room wasn't cold, goosebumps dotted her skin.

Bowing his head, Simon cupped one breast in his steady hand, lifting it to him as he took her nipple in his mouth. His nose pressed to cool skin smelling of spring flowers, he began suckling her. Her body stiffened, but he did not stop. She did not move away.

Like a man possessed with insatiable hunger, he teased the rosy bud with his teeth, alternately nipping and sipping, filling his mouth with her sweetness, savoring the taste on his tongue. Her hand dropped to his head, fingers weaving into his hair. With mounting jubilation, he felt her tense muscles slackening, her nipple hardening.

He had lost too much to let her go. If he let her slip away without a fight, his own life meant nothing.

Finally he released her, burying his head between her breasts. When he looked up, he saw blue eyes lightened with fear and tinted with passion.

'Are you cold?' he asked.

She nodded. 'I can't seem to get warm.'

'Come upstairs with me?'

'If that's what you want.'

He swept her up into his strong arms. 'The bedroom's much warmer.'

Carrying her up to his bed, he pulled the quilt down with one hand, then he set her atop the sheets. He draped the quilt over her shoulders like a cape.

Then he began taking her shoes off.

'Simon, it's not fair . . .'

'Life's not fair.'

'We can't just go on and pretend nothing's changed.'

He tossed her sneaker to the floor. 'One last time, then. You can give me that, can't you? So I'll have something to remember you by after you run off and leave me.'

'I'm not leaving you because I want to. God, Simon, do you think loving you has ever been convenient for me?'

He pulled the white cotton sock off her foot, and, moving her foot on to his lap, massaged her sole with his hand. 'I want to touch every part of you,' he told her, bringing her foot up and kissing her little toe. A sob escaped her throat, and she tried to wriggle free, but he held fast to her. He kissed the ball of her foot.

'If you can tell me you don't love me now, I'll stop, Yardley. But if you say it, watch that bottom lip of yours. It's a dead giveaway.'

Pulling pillows forward, he eased her back against them, relieving her of her other shoe and then her slacks and panties. He gazed down appreciatively at her naked body while he stripped himself bare.

She clamped her eyes shut. 'Don't you understand? I don't want to love you. It hurts too much.'

He crawled onto the bed, stretching out beside her. 'Nothing could ever make me stop wanting you, Yardley,' he said, stroking her flat belly. 'Open your eyes.' As she did, passion settled over her face.

He shook his head. 'Why are you in such a damn hurry to die?'

His hand slipped lower, and her muscles contracted under his hands.

Tears pooled in her eyes, and her lashes fluttered rapidly. 'I don't want to die.'

He meshed his fingers into the downy hair between her legs.

'There are many ways to die. When you shut out joy. When you devote your life to revenge.' He slid two fingers inside her. 'This is what matters, Yardley, you and I together, what we feel for each other. What we get from life is the moments and feelings we take from it. I was dead inside for a long time before you came hopping over my fence. Do you think I wanted to care about you? Do you think I wanted to think about you all the time? Do you think I want to be going crazy inside for fear of losing you forever? You awoke something in me I didn't even know was there, you forced me to feel emotions I thought were weaknesses. And I'm not letting you tune out on me, darling. Love won't keep us alive, but it's all we have to hold on to really.'

He smoothed her hair. 'Don't make me stop, Yardley. I can't make love to you if you don't want me to. I'm begging you.'

Her tortured eyes searched his. Finally, she spoke in a voice scarcely audible. 'Don't beg, Simon. You don't have to, ever.' Tears were streaming down her face as he mounted her, parting her legs with his own and claiming her with his mouth.

With a surprised and mournful wail, she bucked beneath him. Undaunted, Simon slipped his splayed palms beneath her. Then he traced her womanhood with his fingertips, probing as he relentlessly drank her in.

Her spasms came in a wrenching bout. She sobbed as the pleasure won out and she succumbed to it and to him. After waiting until she was still, he laid his cheek across her belly, her muscles relaxing beneath him gradually like the stiffness wearing out of a new pillow.

When he moved up to look at her, he wasn't surprised to see she was weeping. What caught him unaware were the hot bitter tears filling his own eyes.

'Go on and cry,' he urged gently, stroking her hair and damp brow as he glided inside her. He kissed the tip of her nose, the bridge of it, the base of her temple, squelching down his own tears as her flesh tightened around him. 'Oh, sweetheart. Do you feel me? I'm with you, inside you. Cry or scream or curse me if you must. Just don't lock me out. Can't you see you're breaking my heart? I love you, Yardley, and whether we have six months or sixty years, I want us to be together.'

Yardley arched herself to him and met his eyes. 'I'm so afraid, Simon.' Her voice was raspy. 'I can't bear the thought of this being the last time . . . Don't you understand, each time, I'll have to wonder if it is?'

Simon kissed her into silence, his own tears stinging his face. 'I can't bear thinking of that either, darling. Don't think it. Just think of us together now. You will fight. And I'll be right here with you no matter what. Besides, you still owe me a golf lesson.'

She was laughing and crying at once. As his tears flowed and mingled with hers, he moved within her, hoping to somehow transfer the power of his body, to renew her hope that no matter what, life was worth living. Just as she had done for him.

EPILOGUE

Six months later

'You're awfully quiet,' Simon noted as he navigated the Jag along the winding country roads outside Kittridge. 'Not having second thoughts, are you?'

Yardley turned and studied her husband's handsome profile. Still uncomfortable wearing short hair for the first time in her life, she absently raised a hand to the back of her neck. She smiled.

'About you, Simon? Never. Bringing our honeymoon to an end makes me sad, though. I loved Corsica.'

'But we're almost home now. This is the real beginning.'

She gazed out the car window at the sprawling countryside, sunlit and kissed by air sweet as lilacs. Kittridge would always be home to her. Coming back never failed to evoke a bittersweet nostalgia.

Simon turned the car into an unfamiliar drive.
'Where are you going?' she asked.

'Home.'

A white-frame colonial nestled amid towering shade trees loomed on the horizon. Bright tulips and daffodils peppered the yard around it.

'This isn't where you live, Simon,' she pointed out.

He eased the car to a stop. 'It's where *we* live. I thought you might prefer this. Fits more with the type of house fit for a family.'

Yardley fought the tears stinging her eye. 'Oh, Simon, is that too much to hope for? I'm so afraid right now to want too much.'

He got out of the car. 'Come and look at the place, Yardley.' He rounded the car and opened her door, taking her hand as she got out. 'We'll take everything one day at a time. And I have big plans for today, Mrs Blye.' He shot her a wink.

Yardley grinned through misty eyes. The warm sunshine on her bare arms had never felt this good before, the sky had never looked bluer or clearer. Remission was a beautiful, if transient, word.

'I like this place already,' she remarked as they approached the porch. 'It feels like home.'

Simon turned to stare at her. 'You're right. I felt comfortable about the place immediately.'

'How soon can we move in?'

'We are moved in, darling. Mimi arranged it while we were gone.'

'Mimi did? I'll have to call and thank her.'

'Well, no. I don't think you'll have to.' He fished in his pocket. 'Hmm, let's see, I have a key somewhere.'

'You have it right in your hand and you know it. Quit leaving me in suspense, Simon.'

He pulled the key out of his pocket and unlocked the door. He let it swing open.

A huge bouquet of fresh-cut spring flowers sat on the table in the entryway.

Yardley paused at the threshold, looking in. 'We've come a long way from my breaking into your house as a burglar to coming home as your bride.' She breathed deeply. 'I can almost smell dinner cooking.'

'And this time I intend for you to be fully conscious when I carry you inside.'

'Ah, Simon, would you mind terribly if I broke tradition and walked in under my own power?'

He stepped back. 'Be my guest.'

But Yardley stopped to kiss him before proceeding through the open doorway. She was in no hurry; her time with Simon was too precious to rush through. She intended to savor every minute of their life together.

She turned to walk into the living room, grinning as Mimi came scurrying around the corner. She placed a bottle of champagne in Simon's hands.

'Welcome home, both of you,' she said, pausing to give them each a hug. 'Marriage must agree with you, Yardley. You're glowing.'

Yardley cast Simon an adoring glance. She couldn't believe how content Mimi seemed with herself now that she'd confessed the truth about her background.

'We didn't mean to intrude. Serena and I just finished cooking dinner for you.'

'Serena's here?' Yardley asked, peering around the corner into the kitchen.

Serena came out, flanked by Beau and Casey. 'I'm so glad you're back, Yardley. I have this wonderful idea for a new figurine. A modern-day version of the peasant girl.'

'Really?' Simon asked.

Yardley groaned. 'We're not doing another peasant girl. You're taking this partnership too seriously, Serrie,' she complained.

From behind, Beau hugged Serena around the waist. 'She's putting you on, Yardley.

Serrie's going to be far too busy with the baby coming to be meddling in the business.'

Yardley blinked. 'A baby. How wonderful!'

Simon, beside her, squeezed her hand.

Laughing happily, she hugged her sister, then Beau.

'Now that you and Simon are settled, Serena and Beau have invited me go spend a few days with them in Nashville,' Mimi announced. 'You'll be all right here, won't you, Yardley?'

'Simon and I will be fine.' Glancing at her husband beside her, she knew she could face anything.

Tomorrow came with no guarantees. It never would. Never had. All she could do was live and love so completely that each day that passed would become the most treasured of keepsakes, to hold in her heart forever.

THE EXCITING NEW NAME IN WOMEN'S FICTION!

PLEASE HELP ME TO HELP YOU!

Dear *Scarlet* Reader,

Good news – thanks to your excellent response we are able to hold another super Prize Draw, which means that **you could win 6 months' worth of free *Scarlets*!** Just return your completed questionnaire to us **before 31 January 1998** and you will automatically be entered in the draw that takes place on that day. If you are lucky enough to be one of the first two names out of the hat we will send you four new *Scarlet* romances, every month for six months.

So don't delay – return your form straight away!*

Looking forward to hearing from you,

Sally Cooper

Editor-in-Chief, *Scarlet*

*Prize draw offer available only in the UK, USA or Canada. Draw is not open to employees of Robinson Publishing, or their agents, families or households. Winners will be informed by post, and details of winners can be obtained after 31 January 1998, by sending a stamped addressed envelope to address given at end of questionnaire.

Note: further offers which might be of interest may be sent to you by other, carefully selected, companies. If you do not want to receive them, please write to Robinson Publishing Ltd, 7 Kensington Church Court, London W8 4SP, UK.

QUESTIONNAIRE

Please tick the appropriate boxes to indicate your answers

1 Where did you get this Scarlet title?
Bought in supermarket ☐
Bought at my local bookstore ☐ Bought at chain bookstore ☐
Bought at book exchange or used bookstore ☐
Borrowed from a friend ☐
Other (please indicate) _____

2 Did you enjoy reading it?
A lot ☐   A little ☐   Not at all ☐

3 What did you particularly like about this book?
Believable characters ☐   Easy to read ☐
Good value for money ☐   Enjoyable locations ☐
Interesting story ☐   Modern setting ☐
Other _____

4 What did you particularly dislike about this book?
_____

5 Would you buy another Scarlet book?
Yes ☐   No ☐

6 What other kinds of book do you enjoy reading?
Horror ☐   Puzzle books ☐   Historical fiction ☐
General fiction ☐   Crime/Detective ☐   Cookery ☐
Other (please indicate) _____

7 Which magazines do you enjoy reading?
   1. _____
   2. _____
   3. _____

And now a little about you –
8 How old are you?
   Under 25 ☐   25–34 ☐   35–44 ☐
   45–54 ☐   55–64 ☐   over 65 ☐

cont.

9 What is your marital status?

Single ☐ Married/living with partner ☐

Widowed ☐ Separated/divorced ☐

10 What is your current occupation?

Employed full-time ☐ Employed part-time ☐

Student ☐ Housewife full-time ☐

Unemployed ☐ Retired ☐

11 Do you have children? If so, how many and how old are they?

_____

_____

12 What is your annual household income?

under $15,000	☐	or	£10,000	☐
$15–25,000	☐	or	£10–20,000	☐
$25–35,000	☐	or	£20–30,000	☐
$35–50,000	☐	or	£30–40,000	☐
over $50,000	☐	or	£40,000	☐

Miss/Mrs/Ms _____

Address _____

_____

_____

Thank you for completing this questionnaire. Now tear it out – put it in an envelope and send it, before 31 January 1998, to:

Sally Cooper, Editor-in-Chief

USA/Can. address
SCARLET c/o London Bridge
85 River Rock Drive
Suite 202
Buffalo
NY 14207
USA

UK address/No stamp required
SCARLET
FREEPOST LON 3335
LONDON W8 4BR
Please use block capitals for address

KEEPS/10/97

Scarlet titles coming next month:

MIXED DOUBLES Kathryn Bellamy
Ace Delaney – the bad boy from **Game, Set and Match** –
is back! On the surface, Ace and Alexa Kane have nothing in
common, but somehow fate keeps throwing them together.
Has Ace finally met his match?

DARED TO DREAM Tammy McCallum
Lauren Ferguson never imagined that her obsession with
Nicholas Kenward's medieval portrait would lead her into
adventures beyond her dreams . . . Yet suddenly she's
spiralling through time into Nicholas's arms.

MISCONCEPTION Margaret Pargeter
Margaret Pargeter's back . . . and she's writing for *Scarlet*!
Guilty and confused, Miranda knows better than to protest
at Brett Deakin's high-handedness. If she ignores him,
surely he'll get the message? But he doesn't – he proposes
that Miranda becomes 'Brett's bride'!

THE LOVE CHILD Angela Drake
Alessandra loves Raphael, but her obsession is destroying
their impetuous marriage. Saul and Tara love each other,
but worry about Alessandra is driving them apart. Then
there's Georgiana who's determined to punish Saul *and* the
women he loves . . .

Did You Know?

There are over 120 _NEW_ romance novels published each month in the US & Canada?

♥ **Romantic Times Magazine** is **THE ONLY SOURCE** that tells you what they are and where to find them–even if you live abroad!

♥ **Each issue** reviews **ALL** 120 titles, saving you time and money at the bookstores!

♥ **Lists mail-order** book stores who service international customers!

ROMANTIC TIMES MAGAZINE
~ *Established 1981* ~

Order a <u>SAMPLE COPY</u> Now!

FOR UNITED STATES & CANADA ORDERS:
$2.00 United States & Canada (U.S FUNDS ONLY)
CALL 1-800-989-8816*

* 800 NUMBER FOR US CREDIT CARD ORDERS ONLY
♥ **BY MAIL:** Send <u>US funds Only</u>. Make check payable to:
Romantic Times Magazine, 55 Bergen Street, Brooklyn, NY 11201 USA
♥ **TEL.:** 718-237-1097 ♥ **FAX:** 718-624-4231

VISA • M/C • AMEX • DISCOVER ACCEPTED FOR US, CANADA & UK ORDERS!

FOR UNITED KINGDOM ORDERS: (Credit Card Orders Accepted!)
£2.00 Sterling–Check made payable to Robinson Publishing Ltd.
♥ **BY MAIL:** Check to above **DRAWN ON A UK BANK** to: Robinson Publishing Ltd., 7 Kensington Church Court, London W8 4SP England

♥ **E-MAIL CREDIT CARD ORDERS:** RTmag1@aol.com
♥ **VISIT OUR WEB SITE:** http://www.rt-online.com